THE LAND BETWEEN

by

CATHRYN HANKLA

BASKERVILLE PUBLISHERS

Copyright 2003 by Cathryn Hankla

Baskerville Publishers, Inc.
2711 Park Hill Drive
Fort Worth, Texas 76109

All rights reserved, including the right to reproduce this book or portions thereof in any form whatsoever without permission in writing from the publisher.

Library of Congress Cataloging-in-Publication Data

Hankla, Cathryn, 1958-
The land between / by Cathryn Hankla.
     p. cm.
ISBN 1-880909-64-2 (alk. paper)
1. Self-realization--Fiction. I. Title.
 PS3558.A4689 L36 2003
 813'.54--dc21
                                    2002011824

Manufactured in the United States of America
First Printing, 2003

Acknowledgements

I am grateful to Hollins University, the Virginia Foundation for Independent Colleges, and Fundación Valparaiso for support during the long journey of this book. A circle of friends has also sustained me, and without their enthusiasm, criticism, practical help and comfort the book would never have been completed. I especially thank my mother, who read the first draft and kept asking when the book was going to be finished.

by Cathryn Hankla

Last Exposures (poems) (LSU Press, 2004)
Poems for the Pardoned (LSU Press, 2002)
Emerald City Blues (poems) (Tryon Publishing Co.,
             2002)
Texas School Book Depository (prose poems) (LSU
             Press, 2000)
Negative History (poems) (LSU Press, 1997)
Afterimages (poems) (LSU Press, 1991)
A Blue Moon in Poorwater (novel) (Ticknor & Fields,
      1988; reprinted by Univ. Press of Virginia, 1998)
Learning the Mother Tongue (Stories) (Univ. of Missouri
             Press, 1987)
Phenomena (poems) (Univ. of Missouri Press, 1983)

THE LAND BETWEEN

*"All nations of the ancient world knew the theory
that life was a mystical thread
spun by the Virgin, measured and sustained
by the Mother, and cut by the Crone.
The Goddess Aphrodite took trinitarian form
As the Great Moira, said to be older than time."*

—Barbara G. Walker,
The Women's Encyclopedia of Myths and Secrets

The Hole

The Murder Hole was supposedly near the property Moira and Paul rented, but they hardly knew a soul who had seen it, except for one: the old man who patched their roof. He said he might've been there once—which meant he had definitely been there—when he was a boy. It had been so long ago now that he wasn't even sure where the hole was exactly. "That blasted hole—it's unlucky" was his only comment. Then he'd turned back to whistling and mixing tar.

Neither Moira nor Paul had heard of anything good or bad that had come out of the hole, but they heard story after story about things that had fallen in. "I guess the danged hole swallowed it," the neighbors exclaimed, in one breath excusing themselves of responsibility and invoking uncommon powers. Hapless hunters and hikers, hoboes and unwary domestic animals, silver spoons, farm implements, telephones disconnected for want of payment, eyeglasses (about a hundred pairs of these from children who "lost" their glasses), pocketknives, pearl necklaces, socks, hats, gloves, missing shoes and mother-in-laws, wardrobes and sideboards, even a marriage partner or two had lost footing, slipping down into the hole's open mouth. Just about anything a person could miss or bid good riddance was said to have fallen into the hole. Even with The Murder Hole clearly labeled on topological maps, it remained more legend than fact.

An industrial engineer named Randy Seigle wrote to Paul

about his party of amateur spelunkers who were trying to map the hole's interior and its surround. Seigle's letter was pretty vague, but it was clear he had cavern fever. With Dixie Caverns right down the road, Luray and numerous others on private land up and down the Shenandoah Valley, Seigle's hunch seemed plausible. He asked permission to search their woods for another entrance, "a possible tunnel to unexplored space." Paul had informed Randy Seigle that the hole was not located on his property, according to any map he had ever seen, but he and his friends were welcome to park their vehicles without further arrangements, as long as they did not block the drive.

ONE WINTER'S NIGHT

AN ICY SPHERE briefly replicating the full moon, Moira's breath hung in the air. It was one of those sparkling winter nights that promised falling stars. She slipped out the back door to grab a few more logs, not wanting to wake her husband and hoping Heathcliff wouldn't bark. She hoped the dog had not awakened Ian when leaping from the foot of his bed where he slept every night. The sky shone with winter constellations. Orion raised his bow over a setting Venus. The frigid air burned into her lungs with her quick breaths. She grabbed what she needed and turned back to the door. Heathcliff stood watching her through the screen, wagging his tail, only pretending to guard the house. Moira spoke to him in a low tone, coming back inside. "It's okay, Boy." The top of his head was spiked with fur tuffs sticking up at wild angles. Heath had "bed head." It made her smile with affection for the scrawny mixed hound that had come wagging up to their house one afternoon. She headed to the wood stove with Heath at her heels.

Stoking the wood stove was not her favorite chore, and she often had to call Paul to help her. "Someday we're going to own a house with central heat and air," Paul pronounced every summer when the upstairs ceiling fans couldn't keep pace and each winter when the whole family nursed dry coughs from breathing dust. The romance of wood heat had become especially inconvenient when Ian had begun crawling. They had to practically build a fence around the stove to protect him from his own curiosity. More than once she had heard that shaggy dog story about how saving money by chopping firewood led to needing to buy an expensive pickup truck, which led inevitably to wrecking it, and on to the hospital for expensive treatment, and so on and so forth, until the amount invested far surpassed any amount that could be saved by humbly heating with wood. The story was funny because there was definitely some truth in it, and yet there was something Moira liked about the whole process. She preferred wood's measure of reality: real wood transformed into real fire, producing real heat. She liked the elemental alchemy.

Moira unloaded the red oak logs from the canvas carrier onto the hearth and performed the required operations before attempting to open the stove door. Once in a while the stove failed to catch, or the chimney failed to draw, or the fire smoldered as they slept, silently filling the downstairs with plumes, so that they woke to a blaring smoke detector and she had to race Ian outside. This time she must have remembered the sequence correctly because smoke did not pour into the room when she slowly swung open the door, poked around the ash-coated coals until they flared into flame, and arranged two new logs, carefully allowing for adequate air flow. She twisted the lever to secure the door again, removed the childproof handle, and rapidly adjusted the appropriate slots. Moira and Paul slept with the stove handle in the drawer of their bedside table the way some people might secure a gun.

Moira eased back beneath the covers. Paul had been fighting a cold all week and needed his sleep. On nights like these when one person was too tired or sick to lend body heat to the other, she was especially glad of the down comforter she had insisted upon. She luxuriated in its warmth, its soft cocoon. Positioned on her back, she tried to fluff her pillow without shaking the bed too much. She lay watching the shape of the mountain through the matchstick shade. Moonlight brought the nearby mountain forward until it seemed to be part of the room. Moira closed her eyes and still saw the double-humped shape of its summit, a jagged outcropping named for its first owner, MacLeod, to which locals referred as "Old Bonehead" or "The Skull." She thought she would drift into sleep as soon as her feet warmed.

But in the next moment she heard Ian calling out, "Mommy, Mommy." Moira roused herself and went to him. She could see by the glowing tyrannosaurus nightlight that Ian was sitting up, clutching his stuffed rhinoceros.

"I'm here," she said. She sat next to him and comforted him with a hug.

"I got scared."

"I'm here now." She pulled the covers up snugly to his neck and rubbed his back a few strokes. Ian tucked his blond head down on his pillow, nestling in his covers. She could hear his breathing deepen almost instantly. She would never stop marveling at Ian's mercurial mood shifts—one minute he could be crying his heart out and the next laughing.

Moira put herself back to bed and fell asleep. Jolting up some time later, Moira checked the clock. 4:00 AM. She didn't know what had wakened her. She sat still, braced against the brass headboard, and listened for a sound. Snap of a branch, wind whistling down off the ridge behind the house, windows rattling, a pop in the stove, Heathcliff's toenails on the wooden floor, Paul's phlegmatic breathing—these were sounds she knew. As Moira counted them and listened, the familiar creaks and rustles of the house calmed her. She listened for any shifting from Ian's room; she heard nothing. She laid her head back on the pillow. In less than a second she heard it again, something out of place. She sat upright but lost the sound again. Her heart's rhythm sped up, and she felt a fluttering, a hiccup in her chest. She pressed her hand against her heart. Why wasn't Paul waking up? The lump of husband beside her didn't budge. Paul's breaths were labored because of his cold, but he slept on, undisturbed.

As her eyes adjusted to the dimness, Moira scanned the contents of the moonlit room. The rocking chair by the window was strewn with an odd mixture of their clothes—bras and jeans, a ripped T-shirt, lumps of texture that meant other items hid beneath these few distinguishable ones. An edge of bathrobe was caught in the closet door, his or hers, she could not tell; the tropical fish mobile over the bed fluidly inched around until the angel fish was swimming over her head. Nothing to fear.

Moira began to experiment with the intermittent sound by laying her head back down. Each time she put her head on the pillow she heard the sound, and when she raised it she heard nothing. What was she really hearing? After a few minutes of this she began to identify music through static, a jumble of lyrics. Moira listened a few minutes more. She knew it was country music, something mournful about divorce and picking through the bones of memory. She had never known the teenaged boys who lived in the house down the hill to play anything but heavy metal. And she'd never heard their music except in the summer when the windows in both houses were open.

When the country song ended, so did the static, and Moira heard a melodic radio voice repeating call letters. "WYND Chicago. Windy radio," the announcer smoothly intoned. It stunned her so that she could barely focus on another word, even with the voice so clear in her ear. She lived in Southwest Virginia, tucked between a ridge and a mountain. Chicago was so little on her mind that she knew it wasn't likely that she had misunderstood the call letters or made them up. She got out of bed and found a blanket. She curled up on the downstairs couch, eluding the sound, which only seemed to reach her when she laid her head on her pillow. Even so, her body was shaking.

Once she had drawn the blanket around herself she no longer received the radio station, but she was still shivering, and not from the outward chill. She reached down beside her and found Heath's head to comfort them both. At last she fell asleep sitting up.

The Energy Business

Paul liked to say his business brought him into contact with "the two P's: yuppies and hippies." The first were suburbanites who could afford solar blankets for their swimming pools and, at the other end of the spectrum, back-to-nature types, even survivalists, who stockpiled guns, ammo, and canned food and dug fallout shelters on their property, which was generally inaccessible without four-wheel drive. When Paul was planning to try an expansion into wind energy, he wrote to a company with the reputation of knowing wind inside and out, hoping to distribute their products in Virginia. The owner, Martin Cicatio, replied with a phone call, offering a management position, with an option for partnership in two years. Even without the partnership, Paul's salary would be four times what he was netting in commissions. Paul lobbied Moira hard for the move. The alternative energy business was slow in a state noted for coal mining on one end and Colonial Williamsburg—where lost arts like glass blowing and paper marbling were preserved—on the other.

In short order Paul liquidated his business and by late September had started work in California.

Moving

It made Moira nervous to watch the two women sent by the moving company wrapping her best china and fitting it into boxes like so many pieces of a puzzle. They handled her most fragile possessions without hesitation, tucking and rolling them into bubble wrap with a few quick motions. She needed some air, a walk; she excused herself and headed down the driveway to the country road.

She would miss these soft, ancient hills, even the ugly Virginia pines that dotted them. She tried to notice everything, to ingest her familiar surroundings and imprint them on her memory. How many times had she walked this same stretch of pavement, thinking only of her own worries, not seeing anything around her? She tried hard to empty her mind and just be aware, to open her eyes, to quiet all of her mental leaping. The white house on the hill glowed with fresh paint, taking on the casts of the colorful trees around it, the sky, the ground below, reflecting them brilliantly, like a quick flash of white truth in deep silence, the poof of a deer tail just vanishing. Heavy, blue-black berries of the sagging pokeweed hung in clusters on red-veined stalks: Indian ink. She had shown Ian how to crush the berries and write with the indigo mess using a pen whittled from a soft stick. She had shown him how to peel a sycamore twig and shred it into a natural toothbrush, pretend he was an Indian boy brushing his teeth. Anything to get Ian to brush his teeth.

Moira stopped by a large turtle that had been crushed by traffic. Its divided shell left a tracery of space like the uneven sections of land left between roads dotted on a map. Red lines staggered across its old rutted dome. No head. Its head had disappeared inside for good. With the turtle's remains at her feet, Moira looked out over a fifteen-acre tract of bright yellow, blooming ragweed. The gold shot through Moira, more than just into her eye, and while she focused and unfocused, taking in nothing but that shock of yellow, thousands of monarch butterflies fluttered up from those ragweed flowers, billowing high into the air. In one moment, the turtle lay dead at her feet and the butterflies took her breath away with their startling sash of orange and black silk unfurling in the sky. She forgot where she was, she was so lost in that moment. Maybe it was her old self that she was leaving behind, as she emptied her anxieties into that image, those thousands of butterflies lifting off as one body, one stunning mind, into the air above the field.

MOIRA helped the women pack. Nothing seemed so important to her anymore. These were only objects, nothing alive.

"This is lovely, what do you call it?" asked Sarah, the larger and more outgoing of the pair.

"A Ming jar," Moira told her. "Hand-painted. A wedding gift."

Sarah turned the hummingbird-patterned china between her hands before holding it aloft. "Hazel, have you ever seen one of these Ming jars?"

Hazel glanced toward the jar without interest and continued her packing. "I guess I've got to have seen about every shape of china thing there is. You'd be surprised how many people got real expensive things in houses smaller than this."

"It has been cozy," Moira said, looking around the blank walls of their living room. It hit her hard that she was leaving her home, and for what? She was afraid she'd wind up in a Hitchcock movie, which was about all she knew of California, that and earthquake footage on the nightly news. She felt her overdue tears rise in her eyes and did not stop them as they spilled down her face.

"Oh dear," Sarah said, "I'm sorry, what have we said?"

Moira motioned that she was all right, wiped her eyes. Someone was knocking on the door.

"Let me get it." Sarah waved Moira off and went to answer the door.

Moira stepped into the bathroom and dabbed water on her hot face with Ian's endangered species sea turtle cloth, the only thing left on the rack.

"Look, Mommy, look." Ian raced into the bathroom, waving a crayon picture.

"Let me see," she said and bent down to him. He clutched a red biplane torn from a coloring book. Beside the picture he had drawn his own blue bird. "That's so good!" She kissed him, sweeping him into a hug while he squirmed. Ian was recently five and did not appreciate being held for long. She followed him out into the living room to thank the Kenners for babysitting. Their new tenants would be their daughter and son-in-law, and as kind as they had been to Paul and Moira, they were thrilled that their own grandchildren would now be living close by.

Tomorrow the packers would return to disassemble the bedrooms and load the truck with everything, including the car. Moira would have Ian up and out early; she did not want him to see his stuffed animal collection tumbling into boxes and have him worrying day after day about whether or not they had enough air to breathe in there during their cross-country ride. Moira had tried to keep Ian's attention focused on his first airplane trip and not on the move itself. They'd been looking at pictures of 747's, and older planes like B-52's, Hellcats, Avengers, B-17's—Memphis Belle in particular—Da Vinci's models, Icarus' wax wings, even Ben Franklin's kites, anything that flew or had wanted to fly.

Ian was restless that night and had a hard time falling asleep. "Mommy, where did all the wings come from?" he asked.

"Different people design them, remember? Like the Wright brothers designed their plane." Moira said.

"I mean before that," Ian had said. "Who 'signed the birds?"

Of all the winged things Ian had seen, space shuttle included, he still loved birds best.

Just as Moira was falling into bed, bone weary, the phone rang.

"Is everything set?" Paul asked.

"I think so. Jessy is picking us up in the morning."

"Good. You and Ian are going to love it here."

"What about the smog?" Moira asked.

"You know there's worse air in the Southern Appalachians. Acid rain—"

"I built a last fire tonight," Moira broke in. "The first fire of the season. The stove caught like a dream."

"At least we won't have to envy our neighbors' wood piles out here. I'm going over to Martin and Cindy's for dinner."

"That's nice. Do they have any children?"

"Well, no. Actually, I think Martin's still married to someone else. But you'll like Cindy. She's really friendly. I can't wait to see you, Hon."

The next sound Moira heard was her clock radio chiming headlines. She threw her robe on against the chill and went to the kitchen to make herself a cup of coffee, calling "Wake up" into Ian's room as she passed. She'd forgotten that the whole kitchen was packed, but it didn't deter her. The helpful box labels allowed her to locate the coffee-maker and a mug. Luckily she'd left the coffee in the refrigerator for the new tenants. She sipped her coffee black and gazed distractedly out the window toward burnt orange leaves that were still clinging, trying to bring herself fully awake. She had imagined she would feel bereft on moving day, but she had to admit that with boxes surrounding her and Paul already gone the rented house didn't feel like hers anymore. In a few hours another couple would be moving in. She didn't feel sad, just blank, and muscle tired.

But she would miss fall, the changing tints of leaves and the winnowing to bare limbs again. Poplars, locusts, scrappy pines and hemlocks, sycamores, and several oak varieties, a mix of volunteer trees bordered the gravel drive. Better for shade than color, oaks could not rival the flaring red of sugar maples, whose numbers were scarce here, or even the vibrancy of vines, like Virginia creeper, that already glowed a deep scarlet. In the midst of these reds, poplar leaves tending ocher and umber, her eye fell on two mud-encrusted jeeps parked at odd angles, blocking the turnaround point in the drive.

It took her several seconds to remember Paul's open invitation to Randy Seigle, whom Moira had never met. She remembered that he had parked his party of spelunkers there before over the summer, but the jeeps had crept silently up the drive before dawn and managed to leave without Moira's notice. Randy Seigle had left thank you notes on the front porch each time.

"Ian, are you up?"

"Yeah."

"I'm going outside for a minute."

She walked to the coat closet in the foyer, flung open the door, and reached inside before she saw that, except for a few stray hangers, the closet stood completely empty. She had only left out the big cotton sweater she planned to wear on the plane. As for the shoes she had habitually left by the door, she had put them away back in the spring when they became a sad reminder of Heathcliff's disappearance—shot, stolen, or lured by a scent. It happened to a lot of dogs out here. She pulled the sweater over her robe and headed outside to check the jeeps for keys.

A light frost had thatched the grass with white nests. Fog had yet to burn off the creek. The Farmer's Almanac said this would be a bad winter, and Moira could feel it coming. Sharp and cold through her socks, the gravel and acorns of the driveway hobbled her. The more acorns, the colder the winter. She reached for the door of the first jeep and found it locked. Both sides. Same with the other jeep. An inspiration prompted her to turn back and try the rear latches—but no luck. On to plan B. During her gingerly trip across the gravel, she turned her head toward a stirring sound, but it was only a busy squirrel spiraling up a tree, face chubby with acorns.

Moira rushed Ian into the bathroom and exercised all of her patience to let him dress himself while he asked her a hundred new questions about the airplane: "How high will we go?...Will the wind hold us up?...Can I touch a cloud?...Will the plane hurt the birds?... When we land will I feel different?"

He sat on her bed sipping orange from his super heroes cup while she threw on her own clothes.

"Ian, we have to find the cavers."

"This juice tastes funny."

"We'll get some better juice at breakfast, in a little while." Moira didn't want to take Ian into the woods with her, but the arrangements were all made and she could not impose again on the Kenners. They would be showing up to supervise the movers soon enough.

"When I grow up I'm going to marry you," Ian said, without warning.

"I'm your mother," Moira said. They had been through this before, many times over the past year. "I'll always be your mother, and I'm already married."

"Oh, I know *that*," Ian said, as though the fact bore no relationship to his announcement.

Moira and Ian were nearly out the door when she remembered the wood stove. She knew it needed refueling.

"Wait right here, " she told Ian and ran upstairs to retrieve the handle that would open the door. She threw a fresh log on the coals, closed the door and hesitated for a second before she let the handle drop to the hearth where the new tenants would find it easily. She did not wait to see if the log caught.

Moira and Ian started up the old logging road behind the house. The disused road looked more like a trail, rutted, overgrown, and even mossy in places, but it was still the easiest path to the top of the ridge. From there, if she had not run into Seigle's party along the way, she might be able to spot them without having to walk all the way to the ridge crest. These days, Ian weighed fifty pounds, and he was sure to tire if they were out too long. Not much time anyway, she thought, and a glance at her watch confirmed it. The movers were scheduled to arrive within the hour.

Without thinking, she tugged Ian's arm a bit too hard.

He winced and pulled away.

"I'm sorry." Moira lightened her grip and slowed to her son's pace. Her heart began racing as they plodded uphill. Through the noise of their own passage over sticks and leaves, Moira listened for signs of Seigle's party. No sounds penetrated the shuffling of Ian's feet and her own breathing—its volume steadily increasing with her heart rate. She felt out of shape for this forced early morning march. Ian's hand felt warm in her grip, but the rosy color of his face, the pink tip of his nose, and his silence soon revealed fatigue.

They stopped. "Listen, Ian, and see if you hear anything."

For a few seconds nothing impressed them but silence,

and then they heard squirrels scaling the brittle limbs or scampering near tree trunks, and wings fluttering. And Moira felt some living thing's eyes on them. She had felt this sensation before out of doors, and usually, if she looked hard enough she could find a creature, sometimes a praying mantis, a chipmunk, a deer, or even a snake staring at her, attentive, guarding against her invasion. Something was watching them now, but before Moira could locate the creature, Ian said something that she did not quite hear, because at the same moment she thought she heard a man's voice. More vibration than words, the sound tugged at her consciousness.

"Hush," she told Ian. "Listen." Moira tilted her head and held her breath. After exhaling, finally, and drawing a quick breath she heard the voice again. "Near the sourwood tree—" she thought it said. There was a sourwood tree that marked one corner of their property, orange flagging around its trunk like a seam. Moira encouraged Ian up the path.

Though she hadn't walked up this road in a while, still she remembered a clearing and a large rock located just below the crest of the ridge. The rock could not be much farther. Ian tugged Moira backward, hanging on her arm so that she almost had to drag him. Gravity and Ian's weight worked in concert against her muscles. Her urgency increased, balanced against their step by step struggle. She knew that Ian was going to protest vocally at any second, and she would have to carry him the rest of the way. Moira was not sure she could. The big granite rock popped into view as though it had been suddenly unveiled. Lichen that looked like crimped paper, but stiffer to touch, formed target patterns. Paul had told her that lichen was one sign of a healthy forest; like salamanders, it was very pollution-sensitive.

"Sit down and rest," Moira told Ian and waited for him

to settle on the ground at the base of the boulder, too tired to complain.

Rough, uneven sides made the rock easy to climb, and at the top a shallow bowl offered a lookout perch. Moira scaled the rock easily and stood to survey the area below and above her. Even with leaf fall under way she could not see very far, and despite her mission her eye began to seek out color. Heavy, drooping Ailanthus fruits, pomegranate red, hung lushly. When they dropped they would leave sparse sprays of spindly limbs. Moira had always liked the tree, but despite its name the Tree of Heaven or Ailanthus was really only a fast-growing weed, and as soon as its spectacular bunches of seeds dried it would look like a weed again. To the left and slightly down from the Ailanthus she spied an odd color—blue. And the blue began to move.

"Hey!" Moira called. "Hello!" She waved her arms in the air, keeping her eye on the royal blue blur.

"Mommy," Ian called up to her. He started scrambling to climb the rock.

"Stay there, Ian, I think I see someone. Hel-lo!"

Moira yelled again, stretching out the second syllable and waving her arms. She caught herself, pitched her shoulders forward and her hips backward, to shift her center of gravity before she toppled. She waved again, this time with only one arm, and called out, "Help!" She thought that would get his attention. A dull pain spiraled through the muscles of her back, snaked up her spine, and jabbed her beneath the shoulder of her raised, waving arm. Too much packing, she knew. Another sort of ache pulsed at her lower back, but she kept shouting and waving until the blue blur halted and called back, "Hello—" There were more words, but Moira could not make them out. When the blue blur turned and headed toward her, slowly scaling the ridge, she stopped waving but kept occasionally coaxing, "Here, up here," although it was already clear that the man was sure of her position.

When they could see each other's faces, he said, "Are you all right?"

"Oh yes," Moira answered and climbed down from her perch on the rock.

The man's deep auburn beard made it difficult for Moira to read his expression. He stopped at the foot of the rock and checked Ian over with a kind but penetrating gaze.

"We're both fine," Moira said, jumping down to the ground. "I'm Moira Robbins, this is Ian…We live right down there, and—"

"Oh, I hope you don't mind the jeeps in your drive this morning. I'm Randy Seigle." He extended his arm and Moira placed her hand in his warm, firm grip.

"Any other day it would be fine, but you see we're moving today."

"And you've had to chase all over the woods. I'm sorry." Seigle pushed his glasses up on his nose.

"If I hadn't heard you calling someone I don't know how I would have found you," Moira said.

"You heard this?" Incredulous, Seigle pulled a walkie-talkie from his jacket pocket. "You must have spectacular hearing. I'll just call Jeff again. He's on the other side of the ridge with another guy. We can move the jeeps right away."

Then two other men, one grizzled with soft eyes and the other all sinew and youth, strode out of the trees. Seigle introduced them as "Cap and Buck. My associates."

Moira, Ian, and Seigle headed down the logging road. Cap and Buck straggled along behind them, leaving a gap that gradually widened into fifty yards. Their collective footfalls over leaf litter were all the sound they made at first, until Ian and Seigle began speaking at once.

"Mommy, I'm tired," Ian was saying, interrupting Seigle, who was trying to ask, "Where are you moving?"

Moira stopped pulling Ian along and started to lift him

onto her hip. Her face revealed the pain she felt in her back.

"I'll take him." In an instant, Seigle lifted Ian from Moira's arms and settled him atop his wide shoulders.

"How far do you think I can see?" Ian beamed down from his new height.

"Hold on tight, Ian," Moira instructed. Ian grabbed around Seigle's throat in a choke hold. "Not that tightly!"

Seigle responded by taking both of Ian's hands to steady him.

"I see Africa," Ian said. "I can see the elephants."

Seigle bounded down the slope with Ian, while Moira tried to match his strides.

"We're going to California, outside of LA," she said. "On a plane," Ian added. "I'm going to start school!"

"That's great," Seigle said.

"Mommy, I'm cold."

Seigle stopped for a moment and pulled a red knitted scarf from his jacket pocket. As if this were a magic trick, Moira expected to see birds rising from it. Instead, he wrapped it around Ian's neck. The bright wool draped over his shoulders, down his chest and back. Moira caught Seigle's eye to thank him, and they went on with their conversation. "My husband's with a new company."

"Solar?" Seigle asked.

"Primarily wind, I think."

"I wish more people were thinking like your husband."

Ian was bouncing up and down in Seigle's rhythm.

"Have you found what you're looking for?" Moira asked.

"Not yet. We're about halfway through the survey. I still think there's another way in."

"What are you looking for?" Ian asked.

"Another big hole in the ground," Seigle said.

"Oh, that," Ian said, as if he knew all about it.

In several minutes of fast paced chugging they popped

out of the woods. The Kenner's pick-up was parked in the driveway.

"Looks like a party." Seigle shortened his strides to a stop.

"At least we've beaten the moving van. Come on inside," Moira invited.

"I'll just go ahead and move mine while I wait for Jeff." Seigle carefully lifted Ian down to the ground before loping down to his jeep.

They found the front door standing open, and Moira's nose told her the story.

"We came on in," Mr. Kenner said. "The stove was smoking—not too bad, though."

"We aired it out. Good thing we come on a bit early." Moira could read the concern in Mrs. Kenner's expression. "I hope the stove don't always do like this," Mrs. Kenner said.

"I didn't wait for the log to catch," Moira confessed. "It's my fault."

"We found him," Ian said.

Mrs. Kenner raised her eyebrows in puzzlement.

"Roger, handy as he is, won't have no trouble, no trouble a-tall," Mr. Kenner said kindly, appeasing his wife and Moira at once, while bragging about his son-in-law.

Randy Seigle stuck his head through the door. "Jeff is here now. We'll just be going."

"These are my neighbors, the Kenners. They own the property. This is Randy Seigle, he's looking for a cave. Maybe you wouldn't mind if he parked in the driveway from time to time?"

"I'd be very grateful if we could. It would only be a few times a month, less often maybe," Seigle said.

Mr. Kenner shook Seigle's hand, "Pleased to meet you. That would be up to my son-in-law Roger who's moving in here. You'll have to ask him. Sorry I can't help you."

Mrs. Kenner, who never missed a chance to canvas for her oldest daughter, blurted, "You married?"

Ian piped up. "My mommy's married."

Everyone laughed, saving Seigle from embarrassment.

Ian had the floor and made his pronouncement, "I bet you'll find that Murder Hole."

Mrs. Kenner's face drew up, "Don't say that word, child."

"The real question is, where does it lead," Seigle said.

Mr. Kenner, tried to stare Seigle still. "I wager it ain't worth the trouble."

Seigle turned, addressing only Moira, "I hope your move goes well." Then he ducked out the door.

Leaps

IAN DOZED in the back seat while Moira and Jessy tried to keep their conversation light as they drove to breakfast, something they did often, but today both women understood that they were embarked on a new chapter. Moira did not know how to say goodbye to Jessy. Their friendship went back to college orientation week when Moira had walked uninvited into Jessy's open dorm room, lured by classic Rolling Stones. Pop music was all the rage then, and Moira found it bland. Jessy was squawking right along with Mick, watching her red mouth in the mirror. Moira stepped into the room and joined in with the chorus of "I Can't Get No Satisfaction." From the moment they met they were established as terrible singers and friends for life. They had lived near each other ever since. Jessy was a reporter for the same newspaper that Moira had quit working for when Ian was born. She had thought she'd return to proofreading and layout when Ian started school, but now she was leaving.

"So what's Randy Seigle look like?" Jessy asked, in her characteristic way of getting to the bottom of things, especially when it came to men. She flicked ashes out the window. Moira shot her a disapproving look, and Jessy added, "Yeah, I'm stunting my growth again, all right, already."

"He has a dark red beard," Moira replied. "And piercing eyes."

"What color?"

"I—blue, or gray, I think."

"You'd make a great reporter, sheesh."

"You know, Mrs. Kenner asked him if he were married."

"That's terrible. The nerve." Jessy whipped around a curve and slowed suddenly to avoid a logging truck that filled the road. "Everyone out here drives like maniacs. So what did he say?"

"He didn't answer."

"With a best friend like you no wonder I'm the most eligible spinster."

"You have a lot of friends who aren't married."

"Yeah, did you catch my series on single mothers?" Jessy checked the rearview mirror.

"Seigle is very tall," Moira said. "Broad-shouldered, but lanky, you know."

"A retriever." Jessy's system of categorization of the male species consisted of filing them according to the canine they most resembled.

"No, more of a setter."

Jessy glowered. Her code proclaimed the setter the world's most idiotic dog. "Oh, please. He is not. You're lying."

"He's really more of an Irish wolfhound. But there's something else mixed in, something intense, maybe exotic."

"Bichon frise?" Jessy asked with irony.

"No, nothing frou-frou or cute. Seigle's a ground tracker, not the type with his nose in the air."

"Glad to hear it. Now if I can keep Mrs. Sherlock Kenner on his case. You're obviously not going to be any help."

Familiar landmarks tumbled past the car: the falling-down barn, the new house being built beside it, the burros, the horses, the creek winding through the valley. Everything she saw only meant that she was leaving. They sped along, turning off the narrow country road onto the main highway. Moira checked Ian, and he was peacefully sleeping. He didn't share her anxiety and that was good, even if it made her feel more alone. Jessy picked up speed. No thoughts in particular went through Moira's mind, or there were no words for what she was thinking or feeling, except *lost*. Her home was back there and strangers were moving her furniture, loading it into a truck.

Jessy kept looking at the road ahead, but she might as well have been reading Moira's mind. "This is awful, but you're going to be fine," she said.

Jessy's tone of voice made Moira want to wail, completely lose it, but she did not want to upset Ian. Moira focused straight ahead without really seeing anything.

"It'll be okay," she said.

"It really really will," Jessy reassured her, then tossed her cigarette out the open window.

They topped the mountain and accelerated down the other side, negotiating the curves a bit too quickly. Moira trusted Jessy to slow down, and Jessy touched her brakes before the next hairpin. Then, just there, on the roadside, Moira saw the young buck pause, hesitate for an instant before bounding. Jessy did not even see it. They passed the animal safely. Both the deer and they were safe because of a moment's delay, a slight pumping of the brakes. Moira flipped back through the morning, a morning of delays, to the one telling moment that had kept the deer from shattering the windshield with its hooves, neck, and mossy antlers. Was it the moment of loading Ian into Jessy's car, when she had stooped to re-tie his shoe? Or the moment Randy Seigle paused to lift Ian to his shoulders, or when he pulled that red scarf from his pocket? Was the one important moment when the Kenners decided to arrive early, opened the door of her house, and fanned the smoke back up the chimney before it could pour from the windows and doors like water from a spout? How long had Moira spent listening, alert for sounds in the woods that would tell her that another human being walked there jingling keys? What about the long moment in which she shut her eyes lazily before rising, so she could savor her last waking in her own room, own house, own bed? Had one such moment kept them from colliding with the buck, or had his instincts alone saved him?

She shuddered in her not knowing and did not speak. The deer, alerted to its own internal rhythm, had stiffened at the edge of the road, pausing before it bounded up the embankment, into the path of Jessy's car. "He who hesitates is lost," Moira's mother had liked to remark. But not this time. What was that other saying she often repeated? "The race is not to the swift." Glassy-eyed hesitation had saved them. The deer's liquid black eyes, black water that would shatter with a dive, had been held in the grip of the mountain, waiting until the moment said, "Go ahead, leap."

"Keep watching the skies," Jessy said.

They had already checked their bags through to LAX. Moira turned toward Jessy for the inevitable moment of separation. "You always say that, but what does it mean?"

When she was a junior in college, Moira had lost her mother to cancer. By then, Jessy was a constant in her life, creating a continuity as strong as silk fibers that ran through that vital loss and past it, into the construction of new connections with Paul, and then Ian. Jessy was the first thread.

"I don't know, but do it anyway." Jessy dipped a hand into her voluminous bag and presented Ian with a compact video game for the trip. "I think you'll need this."

"*Alien Explorers*, awesome!" Ian snapped up the game.

"I don't have anything for you, I'm afraid." Jessy turned to Moira.

Their sudden hug brought Jessy's shoulder bag jiggling down to the crook of her arm; it landed between them. Through Jessy's arms Moira felt both tension and warmth. A feeling of darkness, of loss, enveloped Moira when they pulled apart—in a matter of hours they would live three time zones away.

"Well, see ya later," Jessy said, and quickly turned.

"After while, crocodile," Ian echoed, as Jessy had taught him.

Moira could still feel Jessy's arms around her, as she and Ian rode the escalator up to the metal detector and the gates. With tears pressing behind her eyes, Moira looked back, but Jessy had swung through the revolving doors and all she could see was one of her legs striding away.

When Moira passed under the metal detector's arbor, she set off the buzzer and had to retrace her steps.

"Don't worry lady," the attendant said. Did he think her tears were over this?

From her pockets Moira pulled assorted quarters and dimes. She dropped her bracelet, watch, and ring onto the plastic tray presented to her, while Ian stood on the other side of the barrier, clutching his new game and balancing his weight from foot to foot, an exercise he had recently begun practicing in odd moments, as if he were poised on an invisible threshold. His tips forward and backward were none too subtle at times, but often Moira found him difficult to read. She would encourage confidence when Ian needed cuddling—or baby him when he needed to break free. She couldn't seem to get it right.

At the green light Moira stepped forward and set off the alarm again. The attendant asked her to step behind the conveyor for a body check.

"I'll be right there," she called to Ian. "Wait for me, honey." He was absorbed in his game.

The attendant on the other end said she was watching him, "Don't worry."

The baton swiped up and down her legs, over her torso, and beneath each arm.

"All clear," the checker said.

Unsettled, Moira walked through the arch, collected her jewelry, and grabbed Ian's hand. He pulled away.

A few minutes later Moira and Ian boarded and settled into seats near the wing, with Ian by the window where he could monitor the view. They would have a short layover in Chicago, their only stop. Moira fished a pillow from the overhead compartment and sat back down to adjust Ian's seatbelt. Ian had insisted upon wearing Seigle's bright scarf.

"Aren't you hot?"

"No," he said but let her take the red wool from around his neck. She folded the scarf into a neat package and slipped it inside her carry-on bag, taking out her copy of *Jane Eyre*, one of her favorite books, and a favorite of Jessy's, too. They had argued for years about Rochester's call across the moors to Jane, whether it was really telepathy or something else. Moira maintained that the seemingly supernatural moments in *Jane Eyre* were really only aspects of love. Jessy liked to remind Moira, when she went starry-eyed, that Rochester had had to lose his sight and a hand before becoming worthy of his beloved sprite Jane.

Moira held the book in readiness on her lap. The most difficult books were easier to read than people. She pondered Randy Seigle. What kept him so focused on his explorations? It was a hobby, but obviously something more. You don't spend hours and days tromping around unless something drives you to do it. He could probably measure the last year of his life in trips into the woods, in the miles he had put on his hiking boots. She wondered if she would ever find something outside of her family that moved her as much.

They were crossing time zones to another point in space. Spaces of time. For Ian, telling time was confusing, but time was also simple. Time consisted of before he was born and after. But mostly of the present. Moira envied him that.

"Mommy, we're moving," Ian said, his voice both

thrilled and nervous.

Moira reached for his hand. The plane taxied into take-off position, and after a pause, sped down the runway.

"Ian, see if you can feel the exact moment we lift off."

This was a trick of focus that helped Moira and she hoped it would work for her son. Holding his mother's hand seemed to comfort or distract him enough, and he peered out the window at the wing, noting each adjustment of flaps.

"Awesome," he exclaimed, as Moira felt the plane lift. Her eyes were closed.

This moving across the country felt less real than a leap of imagination to join Jane and Rochester at Thornfield Hall, or Jane's leap of faith to follow the voice that called her back to England. Moira opened her book and tried to sink into it.

SOON AFTER TAKEOFF from Chicago's O'Hare, Ian settled in with his new video game. An old hand at airplane travel by his second leg of the trip, he had stopped gazing incessantly out the window. Moira watched as Ian patiently explained the game, "You see, Mommy, these aliens bump into each other's antenna and their heads explode!"

"That's clever," Moira said, and continued to watch as Ian decimated several aliens. Their antennae stretched while they moved down the screen in a staggered free-fall. The trick was to turn them toward each other as they fell, and then—"Bam," Ian said—they blipped off the screen and two more began falling. As the score added up, the creatures grew smaller and harder to control.

"How'd you get so good at this so fast?" Moira asked.

"Timmy has one," Ian said.

Moira wondered if Ian had said goodbye to Timmy. She focused on the game, cheering aloud whenever a pair of aliens locked antennae like antlers and subsequently vanished.

A flight attendant, wearing a worried expression and a Marine buzz-cut, scurried down the aisle checking each passenger. When he spied Ian's video game he promptly reached over Moira without a word of warning or an "excuse me," snatched it up, hit the off switch, and tossed it back.

"Don't use that in-flight," he said.

Ian looked to Moira for an explanation.

"I've never heard that before," Moira said. The jerk, she thought.

In less than five minutes, the same brusque attendant cruised down the aisle again and stopped at their row.

"The captain has asked that no radio phones, CD players, laptop computers, or video games," he emphasized, "be operated during the flight."

"You turned it off," Moira said.

"Are you sure?" His face was serious.

"Absolutely," Moira said. "Is there a problem?"

"The captain will alert the passengers of any problems. Enjoy your flight." He sailed off toward the cockpit.

At some point near the end of their journey, the plane popped out over green, tree-spackled hills. The trees grew dense as the hills rose into the San Gabriel mountains. At the summits, nothing grew; the mountaintops appeared to be scraped raw. Dense clouds clung below the peaks. Perhaps it was Moira's first glimpse of smog. The plane's shadow grew larger as it dipped closer to the thick cloud cover.

"Are we going to bump the clouds?" Ian asked.

"We're going to sail through them again."

"These look more solider."

The plane met its darker shadow and popped through the clouds to the sprawling city below. Moira read a rooftop sign, "Home of the Faith Dome," wondering what was beneath. Just a church, or some strange California sect?

Just before they landed, twenty minutes late, the pilot finally came on to announce that because of interference with the plane's navigation and communications systems, they had strayed a few miles off course during flight.

"We're about ten minutes outside of LA now, in line for landing," the pilot continued, "and it's another beautiful Southern California day—a clear 80 degrees on the ground. An attendant will speak to you next, with information about connecting flights. Again, sorry for any inconvenience our brief delay may cause you. We hope you've enjoyed your flight with us today. Thank you for flying Lynx Air. We get you there."

Seigle's Quest

RANDY SEIGLE sat at his roughhewn oak table alone, topographical maps of southwest Virginia spread beneath his staple bottle of John Jameson & Sons. The square-cut crystal glass felt right at home in his hand as he pored over the elevations and sipped. He tracked the dotted line representing the Appalachian trail and then followed the watershed along which it ran with one wide thumb, before his attention shifted across the valley to the opposite ridge, and he had to turn back a page in the map book he favored. His informal survey of the wooded acreage that included the Robbins' property was almost complete, but his hunch had yet to pan out. In his gut, though, he still believed there had to be a back door and a wet cavern stretching between that opening and The Murder Hole. The earth scent almost beckoned him. He felt kinship with the creatures of that cool darkness, with blind, colorless fish, troglobites whose sensitive vibration receptors allowed them to hunt. But his last trip out there, same as the several before, had been a waste; he knew that just as well.

4 AM, foggy, first frost. Seigle had met his partner Jeff Stacey in the lot behind the convenience store so they could drive in tandem to the Robbins' property. Seigle won the coin toss, so they took the twisting back route, twenty-five miles instead of more than fifty around by the interstate. Either way it was about an hour over from Blacksburg. Seigle led the modified caravan, carrying Cap and Buck Simmons,

a student Jeff had probably recruited from the bar with promises of beer. L.T. rode with Jeff. And by the looks of L.T., slumped in Jeff's passenger seat, he was packing his usual hangover. For mid-week it appeared excessive. Seigle wondered what he'd do for an encore come Saturday night. Hate to see that one try to sit up Sunday morning.

They arrived and parked by 5 AM. Spilled out in two directions, in unbalanced parties of two and three. Seigle took the odd lot, Cap and Buck, roughly northwest. Jeff and L.T. lumbered off due east by the compass. Except for flushing a white-tailed buck with a gnarled rack like the branches of a live oak, they turned up nothing. By its girth Seigle judged that grandfather buck to have been dodging bullets for a dozen years or more. A ragged white scar shone along its haunch, bolting down its hind leg. Buck Simmons had put his imaginary gun up to his eye and said, "Bang, bang" when it leapt, showing no respect. Seigle was reminded of just how much he preferred his solitary ramblings to this ill-organized crew.

Seigle preferred to tramp alone and lose himself, scouting every inch of earth until whatever was in him that needed exercising was well worked. He'd been doing this a long time—five years—long enough to wear out several pairs of good boots. The scar tissue that had been forming in the meantime, repairing the little injuries around his heart, was becoming more impenetrable than the original muscle. Seigle had had a slight heart attack, and part of his therapy had been to walk. The walks lengthened and lengthened until they were something of a life in themselves. He had begun by walking for his health and now hiked for a purpose, yet he still did not know where his walks were taking him. The metal stents in his narrowed arteries that allowed him all of this renovation were mostly forgotten. A hunch sustained him.

The party he'd taken out there—with the exception of

Jeff Stacey—didn't care whether they found anything or not. For them, it was a lark. Seigle didn't even know how much Jeff had told them—just enough, probably, to get them to call in sick or use their day off, as Seigle had. It seemed to him now that he and his group had criss-crossed more than seventy-five steep acres of woods, that his objective, his obsession, was not misplaced, but that it had developed a mind of its own. It lured him on, tested, even played with him. A ranger at Dragon's Tooth told him that a through-hiker on the trail had stayed with a gritty old hermit-farmer who said he'd poked around The Murder Hole when he was a boy. That old farmer seemed to know something about the hole no one else did. The hiker had never even found the hole, but he told the ranger where the old man lived and Seigle remembered.

For what it's worth, Seigle would like to find that old guy and talk to him, and now he had a reason. Jeff thought they should keep their traps shut, not go blabbing too much, in case they did find what they were looking for and would need to run a fast land deal around the locals. If Jeff could keep his mouth shut then, that would be the first time. Full of schemes and bad credit, Jeff was the kind of guy who talked too much when he drank and had the bad habit of assuming others weren't as smart as he was when actually they were smarter. But it had been Jeff who showed him what a hole was, Jeff had been the first to take him down, giving Seigle a taste for caving that had become a hobby and a craving. Every aspect had fascinated him then and still did. The cool, dank air in his lungs, the feel of the ropes in his hands. That first time he'd had no gloves and burned his hands good going down, pulling his own weight. It made him focus, forget about his suspect ticker and a few other things he'd rather leave behind. The cure for rumination and every fear was to find a way to live in the moment. Caving did that for him.

On their last trip out, Jeff was pissed about having to move the jeeps, but Seigle tried to placate him afterwards with breakfast at the "Retreat and Eat." Seigle almost packed in a box turtle on the way but managed to miss it. "The turtles are on the move," he told Buck beside him in the other bucket seat. "Carrying the world on their backs." Buck shot him a stupid grin, but didn't ask any questions. "Hindu legend," Seigle added.

"Don't forget Injun," Cap chimed in from the back jump seat. "Sunshine draws them to the road. Same with snakes. In spring they go courting, using the roads. In fall they squeeze a little more heat out before they go down for the winter."

Seigle checked the rearview to see if Jeff would follow his swerve. He did not.

"Damn Stacey," Cap muttered.

"You got that right." Seigle gripped the wheel and set his jaw.

The first time Seigle had seen inside a cracked turtle it wasn't quite dead but bleeding profusely, a bright red that surprised the hell out of him. What had he expected? After all, the insides of all things resembled each other, even the earth's core was red, molten fire. Seigle hated to see turtles cracked, a sure death sentence. He thought it was a world cracked, and a serious offense against nature to intentionally kill a living thing. Jeff was an ass. He seemed to get a rush out of torturing things.

While they sat at table waiting for their sausage gravy and biscuits, the standard fare at the R & E, they mapped their next foray, with ballpoints etched a circle around an area of about a square mile just over the Robbins' property line.

"We'll need to look up the owner and get permission," Seigle said.

"Naw, we don't need any permission," Jeff said. "I know

the guy, friend of mine."

"What's his name?" Seigle asked.

"I forget," said Jeff. "You got beggar's lice all over your beard, you bastard."

After chasing his hangover with red eyes—a redneck concoction of tomato juice and Schlitz—L.T. said they should "Go down." Jeff was ready. Cap begged off, said he'd hitch back home, but they took Buck, already green from trying to keep up with the professional guzzlers, over to Wier's cave, where they'd been down any number of times. Seigle went along, sensing the need for some measure of sobriety.

Wier's cave opened beneath an old oak tree, the roots of which had split and buckled, and plunged down again, leaving a large enough hole for a man to walk upright in. The mouth area was framed by rocks and frequented by high school hoods and lovers, judging from the assortment of crushed cans and half-buried condoms. After that short upright walk in, though, the fun started, and the human debris generally ended abruptly as one approached the narrow, vertical shaft that dropped thirty feet into what they had dubbed the lobby, a seven- by ten-foot room.

"There you go. By the book," Jeff said, as Seigle lowered his survival pack on a guide rope, per regulation.

"Safety precaution," Seigle told Buck. The pack contained the emergency supplies Seigle never went down without: first-aid kit, space blanket, energy bars, water, tools to repair the carbide lamps, flashlight, and compass, notepad and pencil, waterproof matches and candles. Seigle was using an LED headlamp—the latest thing and very reliable—but Jeff stuck with the gear that had been passed down from a coal-mining relative in Buchanan County, and favored a carbide headlamp and lantern he lit with drops of water. The water activated acetylene gas that ignited with a hiss into a striking blue flame.

Seigle gave a tug on the rope that dangled into the shaft.

"We might use the automatic ascender coming back up," he said to Buck. Seigle's legs felt heavy.

"We won't need that, just shimmy," Jeff wiggled his hips and laughed. He liked to muscle his way whenever possible, free climbing or braced between his feet and his back in tight tunnels such as this. Jeff claimed the gadgets slowed him down too much. At least he was wearing a hardhat. He offered his coveralls and hat to Buck, who cannily refused them, and thereby earned an ounce of Jeff's respect. A lot of good it would do him, thought Seigle, when a rock knocked him cold. He kept Buck back as Jeff and then L.T. chimneyed down. When it came Buck's turn Seigle clipped him on the line and showed him how to rappel in case he got tired of inching. Buck bumped to the bottom with beginner's style (none). Seigle hooked himself onto the rope and chimneyed after him, pressing his spine to one wall and walking his legs down opposite, hands pressed alongside his back to contact the wall. The rough rock grazed his back even through his coveralls, and he knew Buck would be sore tomorrow. He'd have to learn to trust his own limits, though, if he were going to join this party. Seigle wasn't his daddy.

Buck Simmons was the only one left in the lobby. He was waiting in the area of faint light below the shaft when Seigle touched down. Seigle's headlamp revealed Buck's drenched face. He was breathing hard for a young college kid, almost panting.

"You're making us old guys look good," Seigle said.

Buck answered with a thin smile. Seigle shot him a thumbs-up, and Buck returned it.

Beyond the lobby were two horizontal shafts that led in different directions. The more inviting passageway could admit a crouching man, but about ten feet in, the wall clamped down and the rest of it could only be negotiated by crawling through a trickle of cold water.

Buck started for that bigger opening, but Seigle redirected him into the smaller one. "Follow me," he said. They squeezed through and propelled themselves along by wriggling for only about five feet until they could almost stand erect again beneath the drapery deposits that grew along the slanted ceiling. L.T and Jeff were waiting when Seigle popped out. The three of them stood there shooting the shit for a minute, waiting for Buck. Then Seigle called into the passageway, but there was no response. "He must have turned back."

"Turned tail, you mean," Jeff said. "That's why I wanted to bring the squirt down here. Bucky don't look like no caver to me."

Jeff had called it correctly. Buck Simmons had panicked quick and inched himself backward toward that shaft of light in the lobby. He'd ascended that rope quicker than Alice ever tumbled down her rabbit hole. Buck was waiting for the rest of them up above, in the open air.

When they'd all climbed out, Buck eyed them sheepishly. "I couldn't breathe," he said. "I've got asthma."

Seigle nodded. Call it asthma, or whatever you will. He'd seen it happen before, attacks of claustrophobia. Seigle loved the smell of earth clawing into his throat and lungs, had forgotten the sensation of choking it had first produced in him, the anxiety of being loaded down with gravity from stagnant air. He liked the heaviness, sometimes he dreamed he was there, breathing that air, its musk of roots and worms. He liked to feel as if he were a root, some kind of buried nutrient, a vegetable or a mineral, iron ore that would be unearthed in time. Maybe he was a seam of quartz rippling through limestone. He thought it might suit him more to be a turnip or a potato. He might be a radish man. Or maybe he was a parsnip, something ghostly pale and uncommon.

Buck's flannel shirt hung in rags in the back where he had scraped along that rutted wall. That's what the coveralls were for. Seigle reached into his pack. He handed Buck his extra flannel shirt. "Put it on. Or you'll catch your death."

"Yeah," Jeff said with a smirk. "Don't chill out."

L.T. sniggered.

Seigle turned to Jeff. "You're a piece of work."

"And you're our own little Mother Teresa. Why don't you make sure Bucky gets back to campus." Jeff turned toward his jeep and L.T. tagged along.

"Mother—" L.T. muttered before breaking into a laugh."

"Shut your trap," Jeff spat at his buddy. They got in the jeep and drove off.

VANITIES

MOIRA sat before the vanity, smoothing on eye shadow with a cotton swab. She could not remember the last time she had worn makeup, but it had been fun to shop for the new cosmetics. Her free gift had been a Dead Sea mud facial.

"Are you coming?" Paul was waiting on the landing.

"It's impossible to be late to a party," Moira said.

Paul walked back into the room. "But we're the guests of honor." He strode behind Moira, touched her shoulders, and bent his lean body down to look into the mirror from her angle. His dark, unruly hair fell over his left eye. Moira dubbed it his "Elvis effect." Moira thought his hair was nearly as sexy as his tilted smile.

"Why don't you check on Ian." Moira examined her makeup, turning her head from side to side.

"He's playing that game Jessy gave him, and Broder's glued to the tube."

"Do you think he can handle the job?"

"Broder is fifteen."

"I know," Moira said.

"They'll be fine. He has Martin's number. Are you stalling or what?"

Her hand sorting through the various shades in her new box, Moira selected her lipstick. Deep red. It was strong for a blond, the clerk had said, but she could handle it because of her dark complexion.

"How do you do that?" Paul was mesmerized by each

stroke of the tiny paint brush over her lips.

"Would you stop hovering? You're bugging me." Moira blotted her lips. She had forgotten the lip liner. Flipping her fine, straight hair out of her face, she stood up, then tugged her dress into place. She tucked an errant bra strap beneath the black silk sheath. For a moment she scooped up her hair and studied the effect. Maybe she should have invested in a French twist for the occasion. Too late. She stepped into her pumps and followed Paul downstairs.

Leaning over Ian, she kissed the top of his head. The aliens on the little screen were tumbling through space, touching antennae and exploding.

"Wow," Ian exclaimed without looking up.

"Be good, you two," Moira said.

Broder momentarily straightened his slumped posture on the couch. His bright red hair reached his shoulders. His baggy clothes might fit him in about ten years.

"Broder saw a UFO," Ian said.

Moira stopped in her tracks. "Really." It was a comment not a question.

"It was in a field, Mom." She glanced at Broder who made no comment one way or the other.

Paul grabbed her hand. "We're out of here." He ushered her through the utility room and into the attached garage.

"Don't you think Broder is a little strange?"

"He's a teenager. His father's brilliant—you'll meet him tonight." Paul opened his wife's door for her.

"Distract me with chivalry." Moira settled into her seat.

Paul hit the remote to open the garage door. The day they arrived from the airport, Paul had handed the remote to Ian and let him push the button, but when the car rolled forward the door started down again. "This is not a toy, Ian," Paul snapped. But Ian insisted he hadn't done anything. "I could have wrecked the car. Give it to me." Paul had tried pushing the button with no result and finally held the transmitter beneath his chin, using his body as a passive antenna. It worked the way holding the old rabbit ears helped TV reception. The door reversed itself and started back up.

Tonight the door opened without a hitch.

"New batteries," Paul said.

They drove out of their cul-de-sac in their new sedan. Paul had traded up. Each garage they passed jutted forward, unnaturally trained toward the street. The concept of having neighbors had changed from meaning the other folks who lived on the same road, whose houses Moira couldn't see from her own, to meaning these strangers whose houses rubbed up against her own. In Virginia, Moira had felt close to her neighbors just because she waved to them in passing and they returned the gesture. Now she was close, too close, and yet much farther removed from the community. The development felt like a maze to her. One late afternoon when Moira had needed a break from unpacking, she and Ian ventured away from their end of the street, walking past dozens of recessed front doors painted in shades of Fiesta wear. The subtleties of taste displayed by the landscaping didn't add much distinction to any of the houses. Moira had grabbed Ian's hand just at the moment when he'd spied a stray white landscaping rock and bent to pick it up. He'd pulled away and scooped up the little treasure. "Look!" He displayed the bright rock on his open palm. It glistened, catching sunlight.

"Do you like it here, Ian?" Moira asked him.

"Yeah, it's great," he had said and thrown the rock with all of his might.

A kid called to him from a front yard a few doors down. "Hey, want to play frisbee?"

Ian started off toward the kid with Moira calling after him, "Do you know your way home?"

Ian had stopped. "Mom, it's just down that way." He pointed.

Moira had let him go and found her way back with the help of his directions.

THE PARTY spilled out patio doors onto several tiered decks that extended from Martin Cicatio's mountain villa. Leaning against a torch-lined railing, Moira took a deep breath to fortify herself. She had left Paul inside attempting to describe to Cindy, who had been born and raised near these arid, brown mountains, the exact shade of the Blue Ridge. "Smoky gray-blue or even indigo, in different seasons, in different lights," he had said while Cindy gasped, remarking that she had not realized that the Blue Ridge was truly blue.

The outside air had begun to revive Moira when a man flowed by, gracefully stretching his arms in bizarre positions. He stepped toward her without acknowledging her presence in the least and expelled a breath like a belch as he held his shoulders level, his head erect. Without explanation, he turned and blazed a new path, eventually finding a place to lie down on the deck. His inhalations were as audible as his exhalations. Moira tried not to stare.

Cindy appeared beside Moira. "You okay?" Cindy asked. Dark short hair framed her round face.

"I'm not used to the wine."

"Martin is generous with refills." Cindy smiled.

Moira leaned closer to Cindy, catching a whiff of spicy fragrance. "What's that man doing over there?" Like a dancer moving around the floor, the deep breather rotated again as he floated to a far corner of the deck.

"Oh that's just Nick. He's doing his Alexander exercises." Moira waited, but no further explanation was offered. "So, Paul tells me you work with Martin," Moira said.

"We're an unqualified office-romance cliché. But I want you to know that I've been with the business five years.

And I wasn't sleeping with Martin before he split with Carla, no matter what you hear." Cindy looked Moira in the eye.

Moira was taken aback. "Oh, I haven't heard anything," she managed.

"I guess I'm on edge. Martin's been trying to persuade me to quit work. I don't know what I'm going to do with myself if I do." Cindy shook her head as she spoke.

Before Moira could offer any words of sympathy, or any words at all, Martin appeared as if on cue. Wine sloshed over the rim of his glass, onto his pointed, snakeskin boots. "Here she is," he said, indicating Moira to the wiry man behind him. In complete contrast to Martin's dark, world-weary face, the man with him was blond with a light brown beard. Airedale, thought Moira. In a party of glowing tans, the man's pale face marked him as a dog without a bone.

"Andrew Polaski," he extended his hand.

"You're Broder's father. Thanks for sending him over tonight."

"You're welcome," said Andrew, shaking her hand.

"Andrew's our resident brain." Martin took a deep draft from his glass.

Nodding to Andrew, and with a light squeeze on Moira's arm, Cindy exited past Martin without comment. He hadn't wasted any breath to acknowledge her.

"We're lucky to have Andrew on board. Between him and your husband we've got all the bases covered. Now if you'll excuse me." The diamond on Martin's right ring finger flickered as his eyes darted toward his next conversational grouping.

Andrew stood awkwardly. Moira didn't know what to say, either. Cindy was now standing just inside the door, in the middle of a clump of loudly laughing people.

"So who's that bald man hanging on Cindy's every word?" Moira asked Andrew.

"A producer. I think he's one of Martin's old friends."

Andrew's tone did not give away anything to extend the meaning of what he said.

"Are there a lot of movie people here?" Moira scanned the living room as well as she could from her place on the deck.

"Quite a few I suppose. Some actors. Some directors."

"I don't recognize anyone," Moira said.

"Not even Dane Battreaux?" Andrew took Moira's shoulder and turned her a few degrees. "In the corner, by the bar."

Sure enough. There was one of the most handsome men she had ever seen, stuffing shrimp into his mouth and chewing wildly, washing it down with whatever he was drinking.

"He must like shrimp," Moira said and laughed with Andrew.

But she had to admit that Dane Battreaux was even better looking in person than he was on screen, if a lot shorter. She had never noticed before the way his head appeared to balloon from his shirt collar, out of proportion with his body. Highland Terrier? Perhaps, but she needed Jessy's help with this one. Moira turned toward Andrew, who was most definitely an Airedale. "So what do you do in the company?" Moira asked.

"Long-range research and planning for the new energy project," he said succinctly.

"What project would that be?"

"We're in an early phase with it."

Andrew's conversational skills were clearly maxed. She got the feeling there was only so much she had the right to know, and it didn't sit well. "What did you do before?"

"I was working for the government. For the Goldstone Station." Andrew glanced at Moira's half-empty glass and snatched it from her hand. "I'll get you a refill."

"Oh, okay, thank you," Moira muttered as he hurried

away.

Moira decided to get some of that shrimp for herself and started inside. Cindy tagged her as she stepped into the living room.

"I want you to meet someone, Moira. This is Dane Battreaux."

And there he was in her face. He snatched her hand to his lips as if it were a tasty morsel. After seeing his enthusiasm for shrimp, Moira was afraid he might bite her accidentally, but he merely slobbered over her knuckles and mumbled an acid greeting, "Welcome to the third circle." Moira noted his spectacularly wide rear as he suddenly turned and loped away.

"What an ass," Cindy said. But Moira wasn't sure she had made the connection. "Let's repair to the hot tub, why don't we?"

"I'm sorry," Moira said. "But I didn't bring a suit."

"Oh, you can use one of mine—or not, if it pleases you." Cindy grabbed Moira's hand and would not let it go until they had wandered through the house to a changing room downstairs. The spa was on a lower level deck, just through a sliding door. "Meet you outside." Cindy handed Moira a suit and left her to change.

Dutifully, Moira struggled into the glittery hot pink tank suit. It stretched, like one of those impossibly snug rubber bands, the kind noted for securing broccoli stems. The straps cut into her shoulders when she tugged down the seat; the thong reamed her crotch unmercifully when she tried to get more breast coverage. The eight-year age gap between her and Cindy was showing in the mirror. Moira wrapped a towel around her waist and sucked in her stomach. "Here we go," she told herself.

As she neared the hot tub her eyes were slow to adjust to the dim lighting. Still, she could readily see that the men and women who occupied the tub were bare-chested. She spotted Cindy waiting on a bench with another woman.

"Looks like our time is up," one of the men said from the tub.

"Oh, we can wait," Cindy said. She introduced Moira to Trisha, whose mane of red hair seemed to flare, shining when she moved her head into the path of the floodlights.

"But I'm puckering," one of the women whined from the hot tub. "Could you hand me my towel?" But before Cindy could find it and hand it over, the woman rose in full Venus mode, without the modesty of the flowing locks. Then Venus snatched the towel and proceeded to dry her bobbed hair first.

Then the two men pulled themselves out, waggling their parts to their towels. Moira had never known a man who wasn't easy in his skin and never a woman who was, without qualification, until this woman standing before her, who seemed perfectly content to dry her hair dressed in nothing but tan lines.

"A little heavy on the chlorine," one of the men remarked.

Nod, nod from the other man. "I hear it causes cancer."

"Really?" said the remaining woman, who then scrambled out of the water.

The four of them trailed back into the house talking about the health threat of halogen lights.

Moira followed Cindy and Trisha into the churning water and found a comfortable spot with a jet pummeling her lower back. She shut her eyes. Just as she began to relax she heard Cindy mutter, "Oh, no."

Just then a woman's voice inquired, "May I join you?"

The large woman was already lowering herself into the water, sloshing it over the other bathers in chaotic waves. The three women moved around to make room for a fourth.

"By all means," Cindy said.

"I'm Sufi," the intruder said, widening her gaze in

Moira's direction.

When Moira introduced herself she was treated to a dissertation. "You have been known by many names." Sufi began, nodding knowingly. "Aphrodite, Mari, Hymen—"

Trisha laughed, but Sufi continued, unfazed, "Venus, and Androphonos destroyer of men among them. Older than time itself, you are, and Queen—"

"Oh I didn't know anyone else could be queen," Trisha broke in again, and Cindy laughed heartily.

"Moira, Queen of the sea, ruler of birth, death, love, time, and fate. You have also been worshipped as the Virgin Mary."

"Thank you," said Moira and laughed. "I think."

Lesson all finished, Sufi turned to Cindy and asked, "Are you Shawn?"

"No, I'm not." Cindy did not volunteer her name.

The four women shut their eyes and let the water work its magic for a while. When Moira opened hers she saw Sufi floating toward her, eyes closed. Moira shifted toward Cindy. Sufi appeared to be sleeping—sleeping and floating. Cindy raised a finger to her lip and directed Moira to follow her out of the tub. Trisha came along, too. They got as far as their towels when Sufi roused and began to speak in a low, husky tone.

"It is imperative that the vibrations find loving ears and that capable hands perform the work of the other world. Each day you must eat an apple for purification."

Cindy was rolling her eyes and walking toward the sliding doors.

"Can we just leave her like that?" Moira asked.

"She's fine. She's a faker," Trisha said.

Sufi continued, "The work of the realm without end goes on in your heart. Make an offering of sage as you descend a staircase. And never hold back a wind..."

"Can you believe she's still stuck on that channeling

routine? Sufi's the grand dame of drama. And she acted like we'd never met. She knows who I am. Shawn is an evil character on *Night Follows Day*, by the way."

"Sufi used to play Kiki, the mother of transvestite twins on *Night Follows Day*. Carla was on the show briefly," Trisha clarified.

"Martin's ex-," Cindy said.

"Oh," Moira said.

"What I want to know," Cindy said, smoothing back her hair from her eyes, "is why, given all of the things they could tell us, these spirits are, like, obsessed with bowels and apples."

Trisha laughed loudly.

"I mean it," Cindy said.

"What is supposed to be speaking through her?" Moira asked.

"A thousand-year-old Chinaman named Li Wu," Trisha answered.

Moira laughed.

"After you've been out here a while it stops being funny," Cindy said. "Sufi's always behind the curve and short on funds."

Moira was still a little unsure of the situation. "Could she drown?"

"Absolutely not," Trisha said. "She's rather buoyant!"

"Let's get changed. We have some welcoming gifts upstairs to present to you and Paul." Cindy led the way.

THE LARGE PINKISH SHELL had been hollowed from its center to the rim without a break, to form an unbroken circle bracelet. Moira examined her gift from Martin and Cindy, as Paul walked into the bedroom, back from having driven Broder home. "Martin told me your bracelet is authentic, antique."

"It's lovely," Moira said.

"California tribes used them to trade with the Anasazis who lived farther inland. So you like it?"

"I do. It's unusual. We should have them to dinner soon." Moira dropped the bracelet onto the bureau. "It was nice of them."

"I stashed that cognac in the bar. Good stuff. So what did you think of Martin?"

"Oh, I didn't get much of a chance to talk to him."

Paul moved toward Moira, bent and kissed the back of her neck. "Are you tired?"

"Not really," she answered. Paul tucked himself behind her and began rubbing slow circles over her shoulders.

"That feels nice." Moira leaned back into him and felt his interest intensify.

They lay down together and Moira brushed the length of her torso, beginning with her breasts, over his lean stomach and chest for the first time since the move.

"Do you like it here?" Paul asked.

"So far," Moira said. "This part is going well, I'd say."

They made love more than once.

"The wine doesn't seem to have affected you. That was great for someone your age," she kidded him.

"Yeah, not bad for an old guy thirty-five." Paul patted his firm stomach.

Moira almost forgot to ask, but as they were nestled together, falling asleep, she remembered. "What's the Goldstone Station? Andrew said he had worked there."

"He did? I didn't know that. It's a listening station for SETI, the search for extra-terrestrial life. They've had cutbacks." Paul said, pulling her to him. "The public doesn't care about space anymore. It's passé, like everything from the sixties."

"Not everything," Moira said. "Kiss me."

Sipapu

Seigle went, on his next day off, to try to find the farmer or hermit or whatever he was, who supposedly knew the interior of the hole like the back of his hand. He also appeared to own the land they wanted to survey next if the ranger was right about where he lived.

Parked on the dirt shoulder, as far off the road as he could without straddling the ditch, Seigle stepped from the jeep and his foot landed on a skinned snake. Its spine was exposed. Half of the flesh curled to the side as if it were simply the old skin being shed. But the dense muscle fabric and black skin, peeled from the ribs and vertebrae, looked more like a flat inner tube than the filmy translucency of a shed skin. Many times he had come nose to nose with complete sheaths, no tear anywhere save for a pair of round eyeholes. Those perfect skins looked like clear masks. He had seen sheddings so recent that they shimmered, still damp. The ripped-up snake had only fooled him for a second, only for a second had he mistaken its corpse for life. Relating the unfamiliar to the familiar must account for nearly all of man's mistakes, Seigle thought. But there was no way around it—it was the way we learned. That being the case, he wondered how any human could ever gain knowledge that was truly original, confront facts that the mind could not assimilate by relationship to stored data. Was it possible for a mind to ever free itself of the burden of the familiar long enough to recognize the new? He thought this was probably what set apart the brilliant from the ordinary, an ability to venture into the unknown free from the known.

Seigle worked his way through the overgrowth of weeds and tangled wild grapevines, spooking a wild turkey as big as a car door and a trail of chicks into the air. He stepped up on the porch and knocked on the farmer's door. Rocking gently back and forth on his heels for a time on the rickety porch, he waited, knocked again, waited, but had no luck. After a time he ambled back to his jeep, wondering if he were being watched. At any rate he wouldn't meet the old farmer today. He decided to substitute an easy three-mile hike on the Appalachian Trail to the top of The Skull. The head of the trail he had in mind started up MacLeod mountain only a short drive away.

CLEAN WHITE BLAZES kept him on target as he wound up the well-trod path. He could feel the sweat trickling down the small of his back and from beneath his armpits as he pushed the last few hundred yards to the summit. His head cleared even as his glasses fogged from the exertion.

Perched on The Skull's granite boulders at about 3,200 feet, he could see the ridge back, running like a dragon's spine, speckled with fire-colored foliage, off to his right, wavering north. When he'd first started hiking and gotten hooked, he had thought he would undertake a hike of the whole A.T., from Stone Mountain in Georgia up to Maine with nothing but the company of a walking stick. As he sent his eye traveling along the watershed, he remembered having flown in a small plane; his vantage was about the same then as now on the valley floor below. Poised on an enormous jutting outcropping, he leaned a little too far and was stopped by the dipping sensation of gravity that hit his stomach. If he were a painter he would try to capture the layering of slate blue over this atmosphere that had no hue, which clung over the distant range of mountains. He would try to find a color for the air he breathed.

His gaze went halfway out again, into the valley space, and stopped; it limped back without a focus on any particular thing in the landscape below. Nothing but a maze of foliage, mottled in its dying season. A few dozen snags, and a patch that lightning had definitely struck its match to, consuming an acre or two before burning out. There was a sliver of daytime moon above him. Soon the first planet would be sending visible light through cold, black space. Stars were sky people, according to Indian legend, who had migrated from the earth, becoming stars when they died. Seigle knew he was of the earth, not of the star tribe. He felt neither old nor wise enough. The valley rose up to meet his searching gaze. A ribbon of water glistened below the knob where he sat. A few strips of grazing land and alfalfa divided the steep ridges from each other. Clouds floated above, casting roving shadows on the contours of the fields below. Seigle searched those shadows for a different darkness that wasn't illusion but depth: a darkness that revealed an open mouth. Where, he wondered, in that cleft of forest, beneath the miles of ground he had already covered, did the crust turn thin and mock him, a cavern hidden beneath the callused soles of his feet?

Some western tribes used round rooms for worship, kivas, which contained a sipapu or small hole in the bottom. The sipapu was a symbolic birth channel, to and from the spirit world of the ancestors below. Ancestors above and ancestors below. Between, lay the land of the living. But there was always a current moving between the worlds, a passageway. This is what he sought: a way through. A connect. That cavern isn't hiding, Seigle thought, I am. But he didn't know if he were adept, ready to wriggle from his old skin.

Two metal stents eased the blood flow around his heart. He had been lucky, his doctors said, lucky that he hadn't needed bypass surgery. Sometimes he thought he could feel them, the metal devices scaffolding his clogged vessels. He thought he could see his own death in the mirror when he looked into his eyes above his bearded face. Death or fear of living. He took a deep breath and exhaled slowly. A snake's internal organs are strung in a line down its length, but snakes under boa size have only one developed lung. Descended from lizards, snakes have adapted with limblessness for traversing dense vegetation. Although they cannot hear airborne sound waves, they can sense very well, picking up low-frequency vibrations in the bones of their skulls as they slink over the ground. He must amputate his grasping thoughts so that he too could hear in shadow, see through bone. Hold the earth to his ear.

Goddamn hole. He wasn't done yet. He would search it out, enter its riddle, heft its heart in his hands before he was through.

The Wheel

WITH SO MUCH TIME to herself, Moira felt strangely light and ungrounded. In their new family routine, Paul dropped Ian at school, and Moira then looked ahead to the whole morning and afternoon, until it was time to pick him up. Last week Ian's class had visited the Coso Range canyons, and the ranger had taught them how to make their own petroglyphs. Ian brought home a flat hunk of rock with an unidentifiable animal scratched into the surface. He had also traced and cut out his own version of a medicine wheel, coloring in the four directions.

"Black is for the west." Ian had waved the wheel beneath her nose. "The sun sets in the west."

Moira picked up the phone to call Jessy. The email she had received made her miss Jessy's voice; she wanted to see how the latest project was progressing. But a glance at the clock, the time difference, stopped her. Jessy would be sleeping, or at least Moira hoped so. Jessy had said she was trying to set up an interview with Randy Seigle for a feature about his Spelunking Club. "Local interest," she called it. Jessy was definitely interested. She had also said it was spitting snow. Snow. Moira loved it. The wind had whipped flecks of icy snow around their house back in Virginia, rattling the rustic window screens, sometimes sucking them into the air and plopping them down on the ground. She remembered snow that billowed like sea spray around them, as if the lone house on the hill were a rock formation on the shore. At this moment, however, an ever-present swath of sunlight was burning through her sliding door from the porch. Seventy-five degrees—again. For days her eye had been dulled by volcanic rock and buff-colored hills as she searched for the golden foliage of fall that she had left behind. The direction that tugged and pulled was red, east, the rising sun. Every ragged, windblown leaf back there that twirled itself to the ground was a lost flame, like part of her magic left behind. Like persistent drops of water in a crevice of limestone, thoughts of home were wearing on her sound bedrock.

Just this morning she had asked Ian, as he fiddled with his medicine wheel at the breakfast table, "Do you like it better in the black or red direction?"

"I like it now," he said definitively. "*Tuttle* Island, that's where we live. All of the directions are good ones."

There was a clump of sage that she could see from the back porch, silver against the desert. She would learn it turned yellow with blooms, the color of the south, as yellow as the fields of goldenrod she had left behind. But for now she felt that being in the desert was to be outside of time, where wind and sun eroded earth too gradually for human beings to understand, with changes too subtle, and too few colors she could name. While weather carves a single sandstone monolith into an eerie totem, dinosaurs give way to microwaves....All she really knew was that through this harsh and pared down landscape she could almost see the evidence, almost believe what physicists like her husband claimed, that matter, when examined closely, looked like empty space. For the more she looked the less she saw.

Most days a polluted haze obscured the new mountains surrounding her, so that she could not get to know them. She looked out into the scrub-studded land behind their house, at the edges of the development, starved for variations that her senses were not yet attuned to see. She wondered what water fed the blackened and twisted palms, wondered how this world continued without the comfort of shade, the relief of a snow day to renew the plants at their roots. Moira brewed herself another cup of coffee. Martin had assigned Paul to drum up new accounts for an expanded wind farm. Paul's people skills were too valuable, Martin said, for Paul to stay tied to his desk. His nights were getting later and later. But he had assured Moira that he would be on a different assignment within six months. That's what Martin promised.

The house was falling into place quickly, perhaps too quickly. As soon as Moira had her family and herself settled in she would have to think about her next step. She still needed some drapes. She had never consulted a professional decorator before, but she thought she'd try Trisha, the decorator whom she'd met at the party. After getting the number from Cindy, who was at the office and too busy to chat, she called and left a message for Trisha.

Her stomach was beginning to sour from too much caffeine; Moira popped a bagel into the toaster and switched on the television. A commercial for a soap opera began with swelling Muzak as a hulking man shrilled, "Helen, you've got to stop fixating on Earl's death. You're alive. We're alive. You have our daughter to think about." Helen falls sullenly into a chair wearing only a slip. Woodwinds trill as the camera zooms in, to a tight close-up of Helen's tragic expression. "He was my only brother. I should have died too." Voiceover croons the hour of the upcoming program, as the theme music roars more loudly than a bad pork chop. Moira winced. Who watches this crap? When the phone rang, she muted the television as she answered.

"It's Trisha. Nice to hear from you. You called about window treatments?"

Window treatments not drapes, Moira noted. "Yes, thanks for calling me back so quickly."

They arranged for an appointment that afternoon, because Trisha had had a cancellation.

The fruit basket brimmed over with mangoes and kiwi. Moira gathered one of each, peeled and sliced them into a bowl and added yogurt. She poured the coffee down the drain and started water for a cup of herbal tea, soothing chamomile blended with peppermint to settle her stomach. The colorful fruit in her bowl looked vaguely convalescent. To complete her pampering, she decided she would take a soak in the tub. Or maybe a mid-morning nap would clear her mind, and when she got up she could just start this day over again. Not that there was anything particularly wrong with it—it was merely a lump of a day, unformed and empty of purpose. As such, it felt heavy and awkward around her neck. Some underlying gravity of sadness was working its way into the mix. She did not think often of her mother, but as she laid her head back down on the pillow her mother's face floated in and out of her mind. And it was the image of her mother's face during the time of what she had referred to as her "condition," skin drawn paper thin in places, eyes set in deep wrinkles. At fifty-two her mother had been relatively young when she died from lung cancer, but the yearlong battle withered her. And there was nowhere to point for a cause, as her mother had never held a cigarette to her lips.

Moira's father had drifted out of the picture when she was too small to hold a memory of him. What she had kept was a black and white photograph of herself as a toddler, sitting high on her father's shoulder. Holding her in place with a firm hand against her stomach and chest, he beamed at the camera. The sun shone through his wispy blond hair and hers, turning an angle of light into double halos. When her mother died she had hoped, futilely, she knew, that he might appear at the funeral, but of course he had not. She had no idea where the beaming man was now and little understanding of why he had apparently stopped smiling and left them. With his parents, her grandparents on that side, long dead and no aunts or uncles that she knew of, there was not much to go on. For all she knew her father was also dead, but she did not think so. No reason in it, just a hunch. Paul's parents were wonderful grandparents to Ian, but it saddened Moira that they were all Ian would ever know. One set was missing. Hers.

Casting the sadness from her mind, Moira concentrated on systematically tensing and releasing each part of her body, moving up from her feet. The coffee had probably made a nap impossible, but at least she could relax. Last night she had awakened from an odd dream and then lain awake. She had finally gotten up, walked onto the balcony off their bedroom. Recalling the dream, her eyes had focused on the sky until she could see stars through the haze. For hours it seemed she had gazed toward the Milky Way as though into a deep cavern, knowing that ten percent of those stars filtering through the lights of civilization were suns like hers, with planets, perhaps, like earth.

Her dream had been a kind of register of her homesickness. She had roamed in a copse of trees, their stodgy trunks as large as giant sequoias. Paul had told Ian just the evening before that they would visit the big trees very soon. But in Moira's dream the tree trunks of old growth were also the legs of ancient turtles that plodded through time. Curved mosaic backs of turtles caught the sunlight, providing sheltering shade for the earth below. Moira had tenderly touched each of the trunks, the gnarled legs, and felt the cool relief of dense shade beneath the backs of these giants. The sheets felt cool against her skin, and she pressed her eyes closed. Phosphene patterns swirled, changing from spirals to checks to triangles, like a liquid version of a kaleidoscope. Riding in cars as a child and faced with learning the meaning of boredom, Moira had discovered these whorls beneath her eyelids, amazed that she could still see with her eyes closed. The patterns comforted her.

She must have fallen asleep because something startled her awake. A sound like shoes scuffing through fallen leaves, but lower pitched. Something electrical, perhaps, but what? Moira shifted position and the sound shut itself off. She relaxed again and felt ready to rejoin her nap when an unexpected wave of low static engulfed her. Then she heard a loud click, followed by a whirring that gradually subsided, blending back into humming static. It jolted her again, the click escalating, increasing in volume, until she could hear that the swirl of sound was made up of voices. They lapped at her ears, blurred in overlapping layers of tonality, like water wearing away a sea barrier wall. The voices formed a buzz of human noise that swarmed around her. Moira rose from the bed and hurried from the room without thought to where she was going. She just had to flee.

As she reached the landing, having made her way halfway down the stairs, she collapsed with her head in her hands; she covered her ears. Her skin was flushed and clammy, and now the clamoring voices seemed to be coming from inside her own head. No distinct words, only an alphabet soup of sound. And then mercifully there were other identifiable noises that burrowed through, taking on reality, the doorbell and a barking dog.

Moira rose on wobbly knees and made her way to the front door. She opened it to find Trisha balancing a heavy fabric sample book in one hand and her suitcase-sized handbag in the other. Five feet behind her a black and white dog was dancing down the sidewalk, bowing and then saluting, rising up, yapping at the door as if he could not decide whether to be submissive or on the offense. Trisha's permed hair seemed to stand on end and her eyebrows rose. "What's up with your dog?" she inquired above the barking.

As Moira tried to answer she saw the scene before her

shrink in a series of tightening frames. The last thing to vanish was the black and white cur's last bow toward the door. Then someone muted both sound and picture. Moira slipped down to the threshold. In the darkness she searched for a door to enter. Or did the door lead out?

A sensation, like the touch of chili peppers to her lips, roused her. She opened her eyes to see Trisha staring down at her wearing a startled expression.

"How do you feel?' she asked.

Moira's head was pounding. She found it difficult to reply.

"You lost it." Trisha threw back her gauzy scarf and dropped something into her giant purse. "I sprayed a little pepper mace toward that dog and it seems to have brought you around. Let's get you inside." Trisha helped Moira to her feet. "Your skin feels clammy."

Filling Moira's copper kettle to make tea, Trisha commented, "My grandmother had one of these. I've got an enamel kettle. Never needs polishing. But this is the real thing."

Moira's head was slowly clearing. She tried to respond to Trisha but nothing quite came out. She lowered her head into her hands and sobbed.

Trisha let her cry without interrupting. For which Moira was grateful. The telephone rang, but she let the answering machine pick up. When she was cried out, Trisha handed her a tissue and slid a cup of tea across the breakfast bar. Three ornate silver rings adorned Trisha's fingers. Each setting held a different rough stone.

"I must be tired, worn out from the move. All of the changes." Moira rubbed at her eyes and blew her nose.

"Yes, it's stressful," Trisha said. "When I moved here from Minneapolis, I couldn't get used to the weather—or the lack of it. All of this sameness day after day, and then there's a fire or two, followed by a sprinkle called rain, and then maybe an earthquake."

"It's snowing in Virginia," Moira said. She dropped her teacup to the counter. "I feel a little sick to my stomach." Moira couldn't make the rest of the story come out. The buzzing sensation, the waves of engulfing sound that had panicked her. But Trisha was waiting for more. "I think I'm hearing things," Moira said and forced a laugh.

"You were meditating?"

Moira shook her head.

"It seems like everyone out here is having Kundalini lately."

"What?"

"A zap of spiritual juice from the universe."

"Really? I was just upstairs trying to take a nap."

"Show me the space," Trisha said with authority.

They took the tour and wound up standing together at the foot of the bed. "Well, there are two problems here that I can see," Trisha began. "Your bed is in the wrong place and your headboard is metal. What's beneath?"

"Oh, just some storage boxes."

"I mean what room. Utility?"

"Yes."

"Another problem. I bet your bed is right over the washer and dryer. Interference."

Moira registered her incredulity in a raised eyebrow. The brass headboard worked for her, kundalini notwithstanding. "What are you talking about?" She asked.

"Ancient Chinese principles of balance and color. You've heard of F'eng Shui, haven't you?"

"Oh, of course," Moira said, not really certain of what it meant, only that it was all the rage.

"Everything in nature creates its own cycle, destructive or creative. The five elements follow each other around the wheel. But it doesn't really matter, just trust me on this. Your bed faces the bathroom and is blind-sided by the door.

You can't see who's coming, so internally you stay on edge. Not good."

Moira ploughed through the heavy book of fabric samples while Trisha sketched a new arrangement for the bedroom. When she was satisfied, she passed it to Moira.

"Your back will be toward the door when you sit at the vanity, but that's not a problem. The mirror lets you see what's behind you. I can have a couple of the guys come over and tote the furniture."

"Paul is going to think I've flipped when I tell him we have to move things around—again."

"My point exactly. He expects you to keep adjusting things." Trisha flipped her curls from her eyes. Her hair wasn't really red—the shade was closer to mauve.

"Oh, go ahead and call them."

Trisha got on her phone and by the time she'd finished she had booked the movers, two stunt men who were also lovers, to rearrange the furniture. She left the bedroom diagram with Moira and took the order for window treatments. They were doing drapes and shades in the bedroom and valances for the living room.

Moira wandered back upstairs and stood in the doorway of her bedroom. It still looked fine to her. She liked the brass headboard that Paul had selected. As she surveyed the room she noticed the blinking light on the answering machine. She played the message.

"Hey Moira!" Jessy's voice chirped. "Seigle just called in. I must have left him five messages. But we're meeting tonight. I miss you. I hope everything's all right out there."

Dante's Wood

"We've got the green light from the farmer," Seigle said, filling Jeff in over the phone. "I went out there and it's all set."

"You going Sunday? It's my free day."

"Don't know yet."

"What's the matter, padre, you getting religion?"

"Hell no, just feeling like—I don't know." Seigle rattled on, clueing Jeff in that the newspaper had called him. Jeff seemed almost jealous when Seigle told him that Jessy was interested in their venture. Seigle didn't volunteer that he had already met the reporter at a bar for a drink.

"Jessy Davidson. She'd like to tag along with us some time. What do you think, amigo?"

"*I'm* Tonto," Jeff said.

Then Seigle discovered that Jeff only wanted to know if the woman were worth his time, pretty enough to bother with. For no particular reason Seigle told him she was already taken, married.

"All's fair in love and war," Jeff responded. "But you never said if she was good looking."

Seigle said she had talked fast. That's all he noticed. "We were on the phone, man."

"Even on the phone, I can tell cute from cow." Jeff said. "You're hopeless."

"Yes, and you're no fucking Tonto to me, whatever that means," Seigle replied and cut off the conversation. For some reason he pulled the phone cord out of the wall afterward. He just felt like it. He took the phone on his chest as if it were a baby and fell back onto his bed. Sometimes he'd like to cut loose from Jeff, but they had started this together and Jeff still seemed determined to see it through. The arguments kept the thing alive if nothing else did. Tonto, the fuck.

Dante reserved a special murky pool in hell for flatterers. The pool was filled with human excrement and the flatterers themselves, naked, mucking along. Is that what he had fallen for when the woman reporter had called? He wanted to believe his goal was worth the effort. Jessy had left the ball in his court; he was to call her when she was welcome to join them. Otherwise, no story. Up to him. Well, what wasn't? He felt like he was enduring some permanent personal ice age, perpetually awaiting his thaw. Pretty soon he would wake up one morning, look in the mirror, and discover a face as grizzled and wizened as Turner's, the old farmer he'd talked to earlier in the day. This time he had caught him at home.

Turner had told him he believed Seigle had been closer to what he wanted when he was "over the Robbins' way." Yet he did give Seigle and his team access to his land. Said he knew his own property like the back of his hand—he'd actually said that, turning his weathered hand over to display a tracery of knotted, indigo veins—and it didn't hold "no secrets." That's what Turner said.

When Seigle told him they'd already searched every inch of the Robbins' property, Turner tugged down the brim of his feed store cap and said, "You don't say." Talking to this man was really like a chat in the mirror, helpful only if you already knew the answers to your own questions.

Seigle thanked him for the access and asked, "Do you want us to phone you when we're on our way?"

"I wouldn't have one. Took it out when my wife died.

Just come."

They shook hands. Then Seigle pushed his glasses off his nose, nodded, and loped through the yard, vanishing into the landscape beyond. Edging a field, he came to woods at the back of the property leading up to the ridge. He noticed that the goldenrod was withered, dried like old corn stalks, signaling full-blown fall. The more things died, bringing on frost and cold nights, the more Seigle's eye alighted on any shred of color: miniature daisy-like weeds still blooming purple and yellow, defying the inevitable. Even the purpling stalks of the pokeweed supported a few heavy clusters of deep black berries. Berries clung to folding stems that collapsed beneath their weight.

Every living thing Seigle passed seemed to be holding on, just that. Not quite ready to give itself over to dormancy. Deer hunting season would be upon him in a month's time, chasing him indoors to fires, wood smoke. Seigle wanted to have something before then, something to show for all of his tromping. That's how he had met Jeff. Back when Seigle had started up walking for his bad heart he'd lost track of hunting season, paid it little mind, and just as he'd crested a hill in November he'd heard a voice from above address him, "Hey, Sitting Duck."

Seigle had looked up into the deer stand he'd never noticed before and cringed. Jeff had a dead rabbit by the ears and a rifle in the other hand.

"Is that how you shoot rabbits?" Seigle asked him.

And Jeff had just about fallen out of his tree laughing. "If I shot a rabbit with this, all I'd be holding would be the thought." Dropping the rabbit, Jeff had climbed down then, using the crude steps he'd nailed to the tree, and offered Seigle a beer.

In the middle of the morning, Seigle took the beer, mostly because he knew the rifle wasn't far away. "Thank you," he said.

"I've got all the comforts of home," Jeff said. "Except a woman." Jeff eyed Seigle and waited for a reply. "What do you think, Sitting Duck, could my tree use a woman's touch?"

Seigle shook his head. "I have no idea."

"Drink up," Jeff said. "For tomorrow we die."

Seigle couldn't think of anything to say. He had gulped beer.

Now Seigle wanted to believe that he was more evolved than Jeff, but the one time Seigle had lived with a woman he'd forgotten to talk to her. Not forgotten, really, but he had suffered from a bad idea he'd had. He thought they had a special bond, he and his girlfriend. He thought she had agreed to his idea of good relations, which entailed a man and a woman occupying the same space, sharing meals and sex and leaving each other for work and then returning. He knew now that he hadn't had enough imagination for a good relationship. All he knew was what he had seen, his parents sharing a life and seeming content. Hardworking people, they were called, he supposed. But there must have been a lot more to it, more than he had seen. He knew that by now he was supposed to know what it was, but he'd never run across it.

In his youth, Seigle had been surrounded by siblings, neighbors, friends, classmates, then frat brothers, office mates. Now he was at the top of the heap, the managing engineer with a private office in the plant. And the factory was on the edge of a small university town. He had three siblings spread out from Florida to South Dakota with whom he exchanged Christmas and birthday cards. With so many miles between them they'd agreed five years earlier to stop going through the hassle of sending gifts. It was a relief. He never knew what to get his nieces and nephews. On their birthdays, though, he still sent them some money tucked in the card. Then he received some personal mail, their awkward thank you notes that all began Dear Uncle Randy.

Seigle had walked several miles along the watershed beyond Turner's place, blazing his own taciturn trail, sometimes crossing or following old paths or animal tracks. He stopped in a spot that felt solid yet soft and lay down on a bed of moss crusted with acorns and leaves, to let the filtered sunlight of a last warm day penetrate his flannel shirt to the flesh. After a spell, the backs of his legs, his back, began to feel damp, as he stayed sandwiched between brown earth and healing warmth. His mind cleared. He thought of nothing, moved nothing, didn't twitch a muscle, nor did he open his eyes. The slurring sound of leaves drying on the branches, caught by the breeze, brushed like cymbals, reached but didn't disturb him. Between earth and air, at first it was difficult to keep himself from cataloguing every stirring, every sound. He listened to his own breath, and soon the minutes passed easily. Seigle was practicing being still. He was "being his doing" as the mystics said. Or not doing, just being. Being still. The sunlight was pouring straight into his chest.

And then it came to him easily that the cave he thought he was seeking was where it needed to be. But was he? If he were as well placed then he wouldn't need to look. He would find what he sought without looking.

He wanted to be like the earth itself, more his creature self of sensation with less self-consciousness. Or was it that he needed more consciousness or consciousness of another kind? He wasn't sure. Acorns burned small bruises into his spine, while through a crust of crumbling leaf litter, the rear of his jeans was soaking up the moisture left from the rainstorm of a few nights before. There he lay on the ground with a hard-on pressing tight against his jeans. The knot was persistent. Seigle sat up, blinking. Wind lifted the hair from his scalp and combed out his beard. He thumbed his glasses off his nose and raked his fingers through his beard.

He sat there until he could feel the cold moisture from the ground soak through his shorts, as cold against his butt as the sun had been warm against his chest. His thoughts were leaping then from subject to subject, as he attempted to get his body, that separate part of it that had sprung up on its own, under control.

Finally he had focused on mashed potatoes, something mundane. Gravy drenched mashed potatoes. The knot relaxed. He got up and made his way back to his jeep. He drove straight to the "Retreat and Eat" with those potatoes firmly in mind. Then he had gotten there and ordered French fries. He didn't know why.

Seigle opened his eyes on his bed. Flat on his back, he was lying and still holding the phone over his heart. He thought he should call someone but he didn't know whom. He sat up and tried to plug the phone back into the wall jack, but the plastic had snapped off the plug and he'd have to replace it. Nothing left but to go to the bar. Have a drink and hear a sodden story or two from someone he'd never talk to in daylight. He thought he'd return to the same bar where he had met Jessy the night before. Maybe she would be there.

Messages and Black Holes

Ian sat in the center of the sunken living room, a collection of rocks, sharp sticks, shells, along with a library book spread on newspapers surrounding him. A large sheet of drawing paper, completely colored over with thick, black crayon looked like a hole in the floor. Moira paused, stopped by the illusion. She bent down to the crayon black hole, feeling as if she were tumbling forward, and plucked up the sheet by a waxy edge.

"What's this?" she asked Ian.

"You scratch the black off and what shows through makes a picture. And I painted these rocks dark and now I'm going to scratch pictures on them."

Thinking she should probably ask him to relocate to the kitchen, where the tile could not be hurt by some spilled paint, she sat down next to him and replaced the black sheet on the floor. It look like an opening that you could step through, a tunnel, a passageway to another plane.

"Homework?"

"Not really. I learned this on the fieldtrip. But we only had time to make one rock."

Moira watched as Ian began his picture on a palm-sized, flat rock. Flecks of brown paint sprinkled the newspaper as he patiently etched with the sharp edge of another rock. Ian's minute scratches revealed no hint of the whole image he was holding in his mind. She had no doubt that he did have a design planned from the outset, because at three he had built a whole fort with plastic blocks. Absorbed in his task, he traded his rock chisel for a pointed stick and continued to abrade the paint from the rock. Most of the paint flecks were falling on the newspaper. She decided to leave him where he was.

"I won't bother you, then." Moira rose from the floor and headed into the kitchen to bake a batch of cookies before starting on their supper. When she had scraped the last dozen gingersnaps off the hot cookie sheet, she heard Ian calling her back into the living room.

"Mom, come look."

Ian held out a rock for her inspection. She studied it on her open palm. The two little stick figures stood hand in hand, like paper dolls. Their heads were rectangles and beneath the rectangles their bodies were triangles. One figure carried a bow at the end of a stick arm. The other figure seemed to have an appendage, like a beehive, growing out from its head. Both of the figures bore a pair of antennae.

"There're like your alien explorers," Moira said.

"My teacher said these are ceremony headdresses." Ian handed her another small rock that bore a figure.

"Ceremonial headdresses. Is this a bird, then?"

"No, that's another anthropomorph," Ian carefully pronounced, though the word sounded more like *antoemuff*. "I'm making zoo*muffs* on the black paper."

Moira looked more carefully at the drawing and discerned that the figure's two stilt legs ended in human feet.

"It's a shaman," Ian said. "There's one in our book at school."

"You know what a shaman is?"

"Someone that walks like human beings but can see up higher, I think."

Moira nodded. "That's a good way to think of it." She set the bird/man down. "What animals are you going to draw?"

"*Tuttles.*"

Moira pointed to the beehive shape. "What's this?"

"It's where the ear goes. I saw one in the canyon. We saw babies coming out." Ian pointed to a collection of scratches inside the triangular body of the beehive figure.

Thankful for the rough symbolism, Moira waited to see where Ian took the conversation, what he wanted to know. She took a deep breath and prepared herself for one of those crucible moments in parenting.

"My teacher says nobody knows what the rocks mean, they are so old." Then he pointed to the birthing figure. "It's still inside her stomach," he said.

"Yes it is," Moira said, exhaling. She glanced toward the black drawing sheet and saw that Ian had already begun to pare away some of the crayon to reveal an image in the corner. A pattern of spirals and checks drew her eye. She studied the positive and negative space that formed a small turtle shell. "Why don't you make this bigger, to fill the paper?"

"They're going to swim—all over. Mom, why do *tuttles* go inside shells?" They had seen sea turtles at the beach in South Carolina, gone out with flashlights to find their nests with a team of conservationists bent on keeping the tourists at safe distances from the little bit of wildness still trying to survive on the over-developed shoreline.

"Because they feel safe there."

Ian watched his mother's face intently as he thought it through. "It's dark inside, isn't it?"

"Yes, I think so."

"They can't see, so how can they run away?"

"They're not fast enough to run. Shells are their protection, and they just have to hide until the danger passes."

"That's sad," Ian said. "What if they never come back out? They'd starve. And someone might step on them." It was clear that Ian had been percolating these worries for a while. There was a furrow of concern stretching across his brow.

"Turtles wouldn't be made that way if it didn't work," Moira said. "Some predators can't see very well if their prey doesn't move. It's a good camouflage to just stay still."

Ian took in her explanation and nodded as if to say it was okay with him.

Moira picked up the book Ian had near him and flipped it open.

"My teacher told us a legend about the stars—it's where the old people go when they die. They light up the sky for us."

"That's a beautiful story," Moira said.

"It's in there," Ian said, indicating the book. "I can't read it yet, but it's in there."

"I'll read some of this to you whenever you want," Moira said.

"I told her my dad says stars are gas balls."

"I bet she liked that."

"She told me I had a smart dad."

"You do," Moira said and gave Ian a brief hug. He set back to work on his page of turtles, patiently scraping through the crude crayon surface to reveal a chiaroscuro of turtle shells. Moira found it difficult not to stare at the designs that slowly emerged beneath his small hands. The turtle shells were growing larger as the intricacy of the task Ian had set himself was not quite matched to his precocious but still developing coordination. The patterns that held her attention recalled the phosphenes, the wobbly spirals, checks, and triangles, that had swum beneath her eyelids along with the buzzing of voices she had heard. As she silently watched her son's progress she knew those voices were just beneath the surface of the present moment, and were she to listen for them she felt they would overtake her, burst through the thin film that separated their world from hers.

"I used to be a star before I was in your stomach," Ian said without looking up. His hair shone a shade of blond so light that it was almost white, catching a stray angle of sun that tracked across the room in late afternoon.

"I can believe that is true," Moira said. "You shine for me."

Ian flashed his mom a big smile.

A Legend of the Turtle Tribe:
Leaving and Returning

There was once a race called the Turtle Tribe, an ancient race that lived in caves hewn from rock and were known to carry their few possessions on their backs in compact bundles—although no one ever left home. Yet all day long they still carried their provisions on their backs in rope-wrapped bundles, as if they might be leaving the shelter of their cave on a moment's notice. Until a stranger wandered through and wanted to marry one of the Turtle maidens, no one thought of venturing beyond the caves.

There was a strange way of aging among the elders of the Turtle tribe. The children and youths shone radiantly, their skin and hair like bolts of sunlight, their teeth so white that to cover the mouth when talking was considered a courtesy to the listener, who might otherwise be struck by blind spots in his vision. After a childhood and adolescence of intense beauty, members of the tribe wrinkled overnight and began to move on creaking joints quite suddenly. Unless their lives were shortened by accident, they stayed this way so long, typically living over two hundred years, that it was hard to tell how old any individual was after the age of twenty-five. Male and female, middle-aged or ancient, they all resembled each other. All, except the children and the youths, were stooped and decrepit.

When the visiting stranger saw a young Turtle girl named Pokil bathing at a spring, he fell in love and could not help but try to follow her home. The stranger hid behind a live oak and watched Pokil return to her cave, pulling herself up by way of ingenious hand and foot holds chiseled into the soft rock walls. The stranger started up the wall after Pokil, but before he had reached the top his feet got tangled up, a foothold crumbled, and he found that he could not climb any higher. Slowly, he let himself down step by step. By the time he reached the ground again night had fallen. The stranger slept, resolved to climb all the way to the cave at first light. He had to see the lovely girl, whom he already thought of as his own.

At first light, he began to scale the wall, using the chiseled steps. His feet were large and awkward. This time he reached no higher than he had before, and it took him all afternoon to inch his way down again. Exhausted, he lay on his back and closed his eyes. He felt a drop of water on his dry lips. It was the girl, standing over him with a gourd dipper brimming with water.

Blinking back his tears, the stranger raised his head, and Pokil let him drink. When his thirst was quenched, the man said, "I have been trying to follow you, so that I might ask your father for your hand."

How polite this man is, thought Pokil. But he knows nothing of our Turtle ways, that is clear. "That is not our custom," Pokil told him, while holding her hand politely over her shining teeth. "We do not pair in marriage, but live in bonds of sympathy with all beings."

"Would you consent to love me, then?" asked the ignorant stranger.

"Of course," Pokil answered, thinking that the man now understood.

"Tomorrow, you will travel with me to my home in the Green Trees and help me raise a family." The man observed that his future bride was already packed. She wore a bundle on her back.

Pokil replaced the gourd dipper in her bundle, turned away, and started up the wall.

"Stop!" the stranger cried. "You must stay with me."
"Very well."

Pokil lay with the stranger that night, teaching him some of the songs of the Turtle tribe.

When he woke from his deep slumber, Pokil was gone. All he could see were the steps studding the wall like so many shadows. The stranger camped at the bottom of the stairs for a year without ever again seeing his shining Pokil. Each day he tried to scale the wall, and each day he failed. Finally he journeyed back to his home in the Green Trees, defeated and alone, ignorant that his Turtle bride had given birth to a son with long legs like the trunks of giant trees.

When Pokil's son was six years old he was already too tall to stand upright inside any of the Turtle caves. In a few years, with the blessings of the elders, he set out to find his father. Pokil filled her son's bundle with dried berries, nuts, and meats. The son wandered far from the Turtle caves and slept in the open under canopies of constellations. He saw shooting stars and dreamed of green trees.

After a journey of many years he heard a flute piping notes he remembered from one of the Turtle ballads. He started singing the words he had learned, Under the earth, under the earth, all Turtles remember who gave them birth... He traced the music and found his father living in a giant fir tree high on a mountain. Even though the son carried his provisions on his back like one of the Turtle Tribe, his father recognized him at once. Long slender legs marked the son as part of the Green Tree race. The father had never taken a wife and was overjoyed to meet his son.

"I must see Pokil before I die," said the father. "Take me to your mother."

"I have nearly spent all of my youth to find you, my father," the son said. But without his resting more than two days, they set out together.

When they had returned to the tribal grounds, where

the steps rose to the Turtle caves, the father had little strength left in him. And the son bore the age wrinkles of his mother's tribe around his neck. Like the great rings of an old tree, his skin hung in bands of wrinkles, nearly obscuring his features. That night the two tired old men, father and son, slept at the base of the wall.

In the morning, Pokil was standing over them. The gourd dipper that Pokil held blocked out the bright shape of the morning sun. The stranger opened his eyes and saw an old Turtle with crusted shell and wrinkled head, offering him a drink. Inside the wrinkles were shining eyes looking into his. Cool, spring water touched his lips, reviving him. And then he watched Pokil embrace her only son who had left a child and returned an old Turtle.

Voices and Dreams

Moira sat at the dining table's head, with Paul on her left and Ian on her right so she could help him cut his chicken with her sharper knife. Paul reached across to heap potatoes onto his son's plate.

"I don't want all that," Ian complained.

"Then don't eat them," Paul said.

"I don't want them on my plate." Ian flashed a sudden Viking warning, in ice blue eyes. Then he began staring into his lap.

"Let's not argue over our food," Paul said and stuffed potatoes into his mouth.

Ian spooned up a bite of baked chicken, avoiding the potato mound as if it were something toxic that had invaded his supper plate. With his free hand he wiped his bangs from his eyes.

"Looks like it's time for a haircut," Paul said, although his own unruly locks were partially obscuring one of his eyes as usual.

"Maybe we can fix that after supper," Moira offered. Ordinarily a peaceful child, Ian turned savage when faced with the barber. Only once had Moira taken him, and ever since she had snipped his silky, straight hair herself.

"I think it's time for a real haircut," Paul said. "So, Ian, what do you say?"

Paul was obviously losing his mind. His challenge fired toward Ian while he was chewing. He opened his mouth, displaying a glob of unwanted potato. And suddenly Moira felt sick to her stomach. The nausea caught her unaware, climbing steadily higher until she needed to move fast or be sick at the table. Covering her mouth, she pushed her chair back and ran for the nearest toilet.

It seemed that Paul was right behind her, knocking on the bathroom door. "Honey, can I do anything?"

"Just take care of Ian," she said.

"Are you sure?" Paul opened the door a crack.

She stood over the sink washing out her mouth, splashing water on her face. Her cheeks were flushed but she felt all right. "I'm fine now," she said, reaching for a towel. "I think I'll just go upstairs and lie down for a few minutes."

"Call me if you need anything," Paul said.

IN THE SAME WAY that the flicker of darkness during the action of a blinking eye escapes consciousness, Moira did not realize she had been sleeping until she awoke to a murmur of voices. The evening had darkened around her while she'd napped, and now a stray shaft of streetlight partially illuminated the bedroom. As her eyes adjusted, the sounds distilled into individual voices, into sentences. She thought she would go downstairs and see what was on television. It was blaring so loudly. But when she tried to sit up she felt a stabbing in her right frontal lobe. Almost yelping, she lay back down, momentarily flattened by the pain.

Now the volume of the already strong voices was turned up a notch higher, the words so distinct that she could not escape listening. But although she could hear every word, the sequence progressed by non sequiturs; Paul must be channel surfing. Along with each snippet of sound, sometimes she thought she saw an image.

—A middle-aged man wearing a filthy denim jacket kicked a door open then turned to shout back into the house: "I'm fed up, I'm leaving. This is a nightmare."

— "Drinks on the house! I just won the lottery!" cried a balding man in bright red suspenders.

—Lying in her dark room, the little girl said her prayer aloud. "Now I lay me down to sleep, I pray the Lord my soul to keep. And if I die before I wake, I pray the Lord my soul to take. God bless Mother, George, Papa and Sadie, and Fluff. A-men."

— "Okay Big Shot, what's next?" A man faced a woman.

"Don't come near me, do you hear me?" The couple faded before Moira could see either very clearly.

—Two men in black clothes, driving. "This the house? Jackie said it was a two-story. You got a light on you? Looks dark."

"Yeah. I've got a whole bonfire." He held a gas can aloft. "Want a match?"

—A young man pleaded through a cracked window. "Francie, come on, let's go."

From the darkened bedroom beyond the window, a girl answered, "Are you sure about this?"

"Don't you love me?"

"They'll kill us, Roy."

"They're your parents. They're not going to kill you," Roy reasoned.

"It's you I'm worried about. My dad can get really mad. Like ballistic, postal."

No matter how her head pounded, Moira could take the channel surfing no longer. "Honey," she called. "Could you turn off the TV?"

It seemed almost in the next instant that Paul stood at the foot of their bed. "Ah, you're awake. Better? I was just up here and you were sleeping."

"Could you get me some aspirin?"

"Of course. Mind if I turn on a light?"

"Go ahead." Moira closed her eyes against the bedside lamp.

Paul returned from the bathroom with two pills and a glass of water. Moira gulped down the aspirin. "Ian in bed?"

"Oh, yes. Since eight." Paul stripped off his shirt and pants. "You must have picked up a bug."

"What were you watching down there—so loudly?" Moira tried not to sound too cranky.

Paul rolled into bed beside Moira and wrapped his arms around her. "I was catching up on my accounts."

"Just now, I mean. When I called you," Moira said.

"I haven't had the set on all evening. I've been catching up on work." Paul gave her the customary squeeze and shifted to his side of the bed. "Sleep well," he said.

Even unsettled, Moira was so exhausted that she fell asleep when the aspirin kicked in.

THE DREAM always began in partial darkness, as though through a haze of isinglass.

A man crouches to open a small door. He pushes through. She can only see his back, a dark hump filling dark space. At once his body fills the opening and then vanishes, pops through. She must follow, pursue him. The walls of this place are slick, viscous beneath her touch. Her fingers want to dart away from the slimy surfaces. Her feet want to rise up from the floor where they creep along in stealth. Her hearing opens wide to compensate for what she cannot see. All of the extra senses that she has abandoned or that have dwindled, abandoning her whole race, now reappear and stake their claims on her consciousness.

The protective layers that she has constructed crack and peel like eggshells down to the thin rubbery membrane, the sack that holds the white around the yolk. She wonders if this is what it means to go mad. What will be left at the core? Afraid that she cannot stop this opening that has begun in her, one hand flies to her mouth and covers it, an attempt to shield her from the stench of her own fear. The fear overwhelms her in white waves with the intensity of labor pains. She steels herself, balances against the slick walls until the darkness closes around her like a fist.

The dream ended. And Moira forgot it upon waking. Paul slept peacefully at her side, but Moira woke fully alert, her heart pounding without a reference point for her fear response. Easing gently out of bed, she found her robe and tiptoed toward Ian's room. He was curled on his side, hugging his stuffed rhino. She closed his door, leaving the crack of comforting light he demanded, and padded down to the kitchen.

Without pausing, she picked up the phone and dialed Jessy's number. Janis Joplin's voice greeted her on the answering machine.

"Hey, it's me," Moira began. "Sorry I missed your call earlier...."

Jessy picked up. "Hey, let me just turn this off."

"I'm sorry to wake you," Moira said. It was all she could do not to cry when she heard Jessy's groggy voice.

"That's okay. What time is it? I was working late and I must have dozed off. Oh my god," Jessy said. "Have you looked at the clock? Are you all right?"

"Yeah. I had some sort of stomach virus earlier, but I'm fine. How was your meeting with Seigle?"

"God, the man's gorgeous. But what's with that thing he does, thumbing his glasses off his nose. Like maybe he has sinus problems?"

Moira sat down on the kitchen stool already feeling more relaxed as their laughter easily filled the space between Virginia and California.

"I couldn't get much out of him. You didn't tell me he had the personality of Natty Bumppo. I think I might need to go down with him, I mean caving, first. Do some research, you know. Did you know he works at the munitions plant, industrial engineer?"

"That part I knew."

"So how's your tribe?"

"Ian's great. He loves school. Paul's really busy right now. Traveling a lot."

"And you, how are you?"

Here was her chance. But she couldn't think of any way to say it. "Okay. A little weirded out, maybe. We went to a hot tub party."

"Sounds horrible. Pretty soon you'll be seeing visions of Elvis."

"I might be already," Moira said, her heart knocking hard in her chest.

"You sound all right to me," Jessy soothed. "Give it some time."

"I hope so," Moira said. "This neighborhood looks like a Spielberg set." She heard Jessy laughing. It was the most reassuring sound. "Hey—did it really snow there already?"

"Only a few flakes. And then it turned warm again, you know it never stays the same long here." Jessy's voice trailed off and then she was saying, "I'm sleepy, gotta go now."

With the phone antenna extended over her head, Moira said goodbye. She kept holding on to the receiver as silence returned. She could not let go.

Star Walkers

Trisha popped a lumpy blob of chocolate into her mouth. "Want a turtle?"

Moira reached for a piece of candy, tasting buttery chocolate, caramel, and pecans.

"Chewy, eh?" Trisha managed to say.

Moira wished Trisha would watch the road a bit more closely. She braced herself, one foot set reflexively against an imaginary brake pedal.

"Am I making you nervous?" Trisha asked.

"Oh no." Moira consciously relaxed her shoulders, pulling them down from her ears.

"I'm in the car a lot, driving to appointments. I can do anything in the car. Paint my nails, polish my shoes. I get all of my best ideas for interiors while driving. Last week I read a novel."

"I've never tried books on tape," Moira said.

"Neither have I. I just balance the book over the steering wheel." Trisha veered off into the right lane and approached the on ramp in a bumper to bumper conga line of commuters. "Have you noticed how many old cars are still on the roads out here?" Trisha's orange scarf clashed electrically with her amazing hair.

"No," Moira said, noting that Trisha's Plymouth Volare was no exception.

"No salt on the roads to rust them out." She merged, blasting onto the freeway. "Everything lasts longer here.

Except maybe marriages." Although Trisha laughed, her tone turned glum.

Moira supposed that old cars were a fitting California idea of the antique—something still shining and on wheels, moving fast. A multitude of little monkeys, brown and black, tumbled over Trisha's blouse in a positive/negative pattern. Whimsical. Moira thought that those monkeys would probably not feel at home in Minnesota, where Trisha was from. But Moira had always heard that it was impossible to know a place until you had left it. Perhaps she had misjudged Minnesotans' capacity for whimsy. For a while they rode quietly. As they neared the city, Moira stared as palm trees flipped by the window. The palms seemed forged or fake to her.

"Date palms," Trisha said. "Imported, though, not native. Iran or Australia, I forget."

Moira wanted to see oaks at the end of their turning, dropping their final leaves, ushering in cold weather and snow. Trisha followed Sunset for several blocks, then turned north to intercept Hollywood Boulevard, and pulled up to a parking meter.

"I thought you might be interested in seeing the old walk of the stars."

"I would," Moira said. "What is it, Mann's Chinese Theatre?"

"Exactly. Now the tourists go to City Walk, but you're going to be a native, right?"

"Do natives go here?" Moira asked.

"Of course not." Trisha laughed. "But then, who's a native?"

Moira and Trisha walked between two teenaged Latinos on promenade. They were dressed approximately as Broder had been, in baggy low-slung pants and backward baseball caps. Gang attire was just another suburban style. She wondered how long it would be before Ian demanded some outlandish fashion and had his hair cut conspicuously. Two young Asian men passed them, wearing the same costume of baggy pants and huge shirts. Anything but tattoos for Ian, Moira had already decided. Even an earring would be all right.

Soon the stars appeared beneath their feet: Tito Puente, Judy Garland, Wayne Newton (Wayne Newton?). She walked on, over a more select crowd: Buster Keaton, Kenny Rogers, Marilyn Monroe. Her feet kept walking on stars, past restaurants, postcard shops, photo-opportunities, a wax museum, Ripley's Believe It or Not. At Mann's Chinese Theatre they stopped and wandered over the blocks of concrete bearing celebrity hand and shoe prints. "I love you all," Shirley had written. A mother deposited her little girl in the lap of a red gargoyle for a snapshot. Before she could step back far enough to snap the photo her daughter burst into tears.

Moira bent down and measured her hand against Clark Gable's. He should have left prints of those massive ears, she thought. Seeing Bette Davis's spike heels and small, spidery hand prints left Moira wondering how women of that era ever walked under their own power. Surely they never ran.

Many of the panels were elaborately inscribed to a mysterious and well-loved "Sid," who must have owned the theater. Footsteps swarmed over the panels, and Moira followed the feet up to faces of all ages, dimensions, expressions, and colors. Many of the visitors only looked through cameras, not straight at anything before them. They looked directly at neither Donald Duck nor Roy Rogers nor Elizabeth Taylor's concrete blocks, but only through their lenses. Yet their indirect approach was appropriate here.

Trisha touched Moira's shoulder. "Had enough? How about a screen test?" Trisha pointed to a wilted sign propped in a shop window that promised two-minute screen tests with the cardboard star of your choice. You could even graft your head onto the body of a two-dimensional star and emblazon the whole weird creature on a one-size-fits-all T-shirt.

The two of them walked on. Every block or so they passed a man digging in a hole. Something seemed to have burst. Moira stopped with Mickey Mouse beneath her feet, both feet planted firmly on his star.

"It feels safe here," she said.

"Mickey Mouse is perverted," Trisha said. "Haven't you ever noticed how he leers at Minnie? And that squeaky little voice—"

"Okay, okay," Moira said, stepping off Mickey. But she was not happy about it. The whole street reminded her of that rigged arcade game with the mechanical claw. The trick was to pick up a hundred-dollar bill with the claw from the mess of worthless baubles and manage to drop it into the funnel. But the claw never clamped tightly enough to hold the bill. The scene around her smelled of stinking feet and tasted like pink cotton candy. Her teeth ached from the sugary coating spread over the noise and clutter. Trisha's monkey shirt appeared to have found its zoo.

"Do you like sushi?" Trisha asked.

"Maybe," Moira said, hoping for a well-done hamburger. "I really don't know."

"Well, then, you probably do. Come on, let's go to my favorite sushi bar and then on to the Southwest Museum for some Indian culture."

"Sounds good," Moira said.

ONCE INSIDE the restaurant they stopped before a glass case of whole fish arranged on black platters. Each fish was presented as a perfect specimen on its own terms, no garnish required. Trisha smacked her lips and pointed to a slab of purplish red flesh.

"Tuna," she said.

"I'll be right back." Moira headed for the ladies' room.

She splashed water on her face before the mirror, dried droplets with a scratchy brown paper towel that smelled vaguely of fish. Her stomach flip-flopped wildly as she stared at her flushed face. Then the color drained out, all except for a pale green tint. Her stomach had felt yeasty all week, as though something were trying to bubble up into her throat. She kept looking at her own face, searching for what? She ought to do something with her hair, she thought. It hung in blond strings around her face, just brushing her shoulders. With one hand she pushed her hair high off her forehead. The kind of effect favored in the thirties. Merle Oberon. Not bad. Maybe she would let her hair grow another month or two and try wearing it in a bun. She could have stayed right where she was, simply waiting for her hair to grow two inches, but she forced herself back to the table. Trisha was waiting.

"My friend has never eaten sushi," Trisha told the chef. He was a small man with a round face framed by shiny hair and punctuated with black eyes as flat as disks in a board game.

"I'll prepare something special." He bowed and returned to his work.

In a few minutes Moira was staring down at a plate that looked more like a piece of art or a bouquet, with each bite of food occupying its own shape, color, and position in the palette.

Trisha directed her to try a spring roll, pointing to a white coil of rice ribboned with an orange gel. It sat with two others on a bed of dark green something.

Moira took a small bite and tasted mainly an overwhelming saltiness. The look of this food was far more delicate and fragile than its taste, but she could swallow it. She sipped tea and investigated the various shapes on her plate. One she recognized as the raw tuna Trisha had admired. She didn't think she could eat it, but she raised the glossy fish to her mouth. It did not smell fishy, and all she really tasted was texture, something clear and sharp and quickly swallowed. The jasmine tea followed it well. She felt full after only five little petit fours of raw fish—sushi. The word helped it go down.

"You approve?" Trisha asked. "He's a talented chef."

"Yes," Moira answered and meant it.

LATER, they stood before glass cases of artifacts in the museum, reading each plaque with interest. Moira tried to take in as many facts about the different tribes and their rituals as she could; she was thinking of Ian. She'd like to come back here and bring him. Baskets, pottery, jewelry, dolls, fetishes—each detail stripped from lives far more complex, Moira thought. But even so, these small details revealed clues. Trisha told her that because of a court ruling the museum had been required to make a list of all of its holdings, sending out over a thousand letters of inventory to different tribes. The tribes then had the option of leaving the artifacts with their current curators or of having them returned to the tribe. Curators worried that the tribes might opt to re-bury all signs of their early civilizations. Even reburial of human remains posed a loss to science. Moira imagined a giant hole in the ground, with each layer of time dropped back into the pit and sealed. All the same, she thought the dead would rather be buried than studied.

In the gift shop, she found a Zuni fetish of a crude amber turtle for Ian. She also bought a cheap kachina doll for Trisha, a small thank you for the day in L.A. The roughly carved kachina had black feet, a blunt, turquoise body, and an orange, block head with flat handle ears and a protruding nose shaped like a wine cork. The wooden replica was nothing special compared to the wild, masked faces of ceremonial kachinas Moira had studied through the glass in dimly-lit cases. The real kachinas wore fur-trimmed leather, their faces gathered by seams, sewn into unpredictable expressions. Some were frightening and some sad or joyous. But Trisha seemed pleased by the small gift. She especially liked the feather that came out of its head and linked her arm lightly in Moira's as they walked back to the car.

It was a natural moment between two women, practically strangers and yet there was a bond being formed. Trisha's touch was slight, yet that casual contact propelled Moira into another place, into an image of a boy falling through the air. In one instant she walked along, arm in arm with Trisha, and in the next another scene unfolded. She kept walking forward, but it was as though she had suddenly covered her eyes and her ears and kept walking, because she could see only the image of the boy falling through the air in red paisley swimming trunks. She kept stepping forward, somehow seeing or feeling both places at once. The boy fell from a diving board again, but this time the image continued until he hit the perfectly blue chlorinated water of a pool below. He never surfaced. Moira understood more than saw that his neck had been broken at the moment of impact.

"You're homesick, aren't you?" Trisha said.

The image fled and Moira caught her breath. "So are you," she replied. "Both of us are a long way from home. Why don't you call your sister?" Until she heard what she said she had no idea what it would be. The world felt askew, at risk.

Without questioning, Trisha responded. "Maybe I will. A lot has happened. She lost her son. He was eleven. I was only just there with them in August, for Josh's funeral."

"I'm sorry," Moira said, fearing what she might learn next, yet needing to know. "What happened?" she asked gently.

"He broke his neck. He broke his neck at the most exclusive country club you can imagine. Thirty-six holes of designer geese and ponds and creeks and an Olympic-sized swimming pool. Josh was diving and something went wrong. A freak accident."

Moira was silent. Or rather she was stunned. There was a long pause and then Trisha said, "I never told you I had a sister."

"You must have," Moira said.

"You knew about Josh, didn't you?"

Moira didn't answer.

Trisha let it drop with only a short, penetrating look passing between them. They drove back in silence most of the way. As they eased off the exit ramp for her house, Moira watched for the hill that formed a border along one side of the neighborhood. It comforted her to see it, reminding her of the mountain back in Virginia that had cast its shadow into her house on moonlit nights. But this hill was strewn with dark boulders and studded with creosote bushes, mesquite, occasional junipers and cat's claw. Moira had looked up all of the plants to identify them, but she hadn't yet found the name of the mountain. She asked Trisha if she knew its name.

"Owl Mountain, I think."

"Why the fence?" Moira asked. Moira had wanted to walk closer to the mountain, but had found that a chain-link fence surrounding it.

"It's probably an Indian cultural site."

"Reservation land?"

"Formerly. There are sacred places scattered everywhere. Developers erect a quick fence to hush the protest. It's horrible, really."

"Why don't they give the land back?" Moira asked.

"Yes. Why not?" Trisha said. "Except that there are these white men who think they own everything. Little details like that."

"Can anyone walk up the path?"

"They'd be trespassing. But you might be able to get permission. I'll see if anyone knows anything about it."

"I'd appreciate it," Moira said.

"Could you do something for me, then?" Trisha asked.

"I hope so," Moira said. "This has been a wonderful day for me. I've needed to get away from the house."

Trisha turned the full force of her prancing monkeys toward Moira and looked her in the eye without wavering. "Would you be willing to visit a psychic friend of mine?"

The word sounded strange, like "cipher." Moira's stomach lurched, choosing this moment to protest the sushi. If she pictured the multi-colored tidy packages of raw fish and their progeny she would throw up.

"Someone like you," Trisha said succinctly. "With strong antennae."

Moira gathered a deep breath, still saying nothing.

"I think you'll like her. She's really—down to earth." Trisha laughed.

"Please don't tell anyone about this," Moira said. "I don't know what's been happening to me. Ever since the move—"

"I doubt it's the move, but don't worry. Not a word to anyone but Regina," Trisha said, pulling the Volare into Moira's driveway.

"The psychic?" Moira asked.

"You'll like her. She's from Baltimore. I'll set it up and call you."

Moira let herself out of the car and watched Trisha drive away. For a moment she stood at her own front door, wondering how she could go back in and start her life again.

Seigle's Sunday Drive

Seigle arrived at Turner's property and found Jeff's jeep already there, parked alongside the barbed wire fence. Seigle had left directions on Jessy's answering machine in case she could join them; he had not heard back from her before it was time to leave. In fact, he hadn't heard anything from her again since their first, brief meeting. Seigle felt the hood of Jeff's jeep and it was cold, already colder than the air. Maybe he hadn't understood that Seigle was coming after all.

He waited a few minutes, alternately surveying the field for Jeff and the road for Jessy, before he gave up on both of them, setting out across a stretch of Turner's uncultivated orchard, in the general direction Seigle had mapped for Jeff over the phone. Maybe he'd catch up to him. It was hard for him to remember, in that slap of cold wind, that only a few days before he had lain on the ground with no ill effects. Not even a scratchy throat afterward. This morning he had looked for his scarf before leaving home and hadn't been able to find it.

Over his head stretched the gnarled and knotted limbs of apple trees that had gone without pruning for years. But where the branches were sound the trees had continued to produce. Seigle padded over a brown, soupy mulch of rotting apples. The air held the heady scent of fermenting fruit. Breathing it was like sipping sharp cider. The apple trees sprawled over a few rolling acres. Before Seigle had walked the whole length of the orchard, he cut toward the woods and started climbing a narrow cow path. Not another soul in sight.

From a hundred yards up he had a good view of the orchard and the fields beyond, planted with rye grass, which still appeared very green in contrast to the chopped, brown hay fields. Due to some optical effect, the rye fields appeared to be rising toward him. His high angle flattened out the whole area, though he knew for a fact that the land sloped and rolled. He had walked it. A black adolescent calf bounded from a copse of cedars and scrub pines and galloped toward or away from something he could not see. He followed its zigzagging until he saw it find its mark, its mother, a broad auburn cow that scuttled away from its approaching offspring. The mother cow tried, without shame, to get out of range. But the calf had more energy and let out a moan, its nascent moo, and thrust its head to her teats. After shuffling a little the thick mother cow stood still. Her head bobbed subtly and her eyes seemed to be roving toward the hill, but she stood for the nursing.

Seigle turned his head from the scene and walked on. But almost immediately the loud crack of gunfire stopped him. The shot passed so close to him it might have grazed his nose if he'd taken another step forward. The nursing calf and mother spooked and ran. He knew that deer season had not yet begun, the legal part of it anyway. He didn't know whether to go forward or back, or to stand still and shout. He took the last option as he felt his knees almost buckle from the shock. "Hey!" he shouted. "Hey, there's somebody out here on two legs!" He made his presence known. As he shouted his fear left and the anger rose. Seigle felt like tracking the bullet along its trajectory, back to its source, until he came face to face with the poor sportsman, the asshole, who had fired it. He had tried to think generously about hunting—necessary harvesting— mindful of the good press about donating the meat to the food bank. But it didn't change the fact that the hunters he encountered were likely to be cruising with Old Milwaukee and would just as soon spotlight a deer from their trucks as take it fair and square. Trophy hunters, who cut off the head with the rack and threw the rejected hoofs, tails, and internal organs over the bank of the road to stink—he had no use for them. Only the bow hunters made any sense to him. They made the hunt more balanced by training for it, some going so far as to use bows and arrows made by their own hands. That, he could almost admire. Bow hunters had to stalk their prey and wait in the cold damp early light when the moon was still high without moving a muscle or popping open a can.

No one answered his shouting. He opted next for motion and hurried up a worn foot trail toward The Skull. In its shadow the air turned even colder and darker and in a few moments the sky let go of the rain it had been hoarding. The drizzle escalated rapidly into a steady downpour. Some bit of motion, a rustling in the understory stopped him short again. As he turned his gaze toward the sound, a startled line of deer leaped after each other, back legs high, white plume tails at attention, like feathers in a headdress. One, two, three, four, five, six, the deer kept bounding, moving down the hill toward an open, green field. They were clearly racing from pursuit, and when the seventh deer caught his eye he heard another shot. The gunman picked off the last deer; the rest rippled forward, white tails blazing their escape route. Seigle stood still and waited. The deer was down. Nothing stirred. He was too far away to be sure that the shot had killed it cleanly. He didn't want to know, and yet he needed to see for himself. If it were not yet dead, though, he knew he could do nothing for it. He wasn't packing a pistol and he wasn't about to pound a wounded deer to death with a stone. Seigle turned his attention to the thick cover, searching for the hunter he knew was there.

Pivoting, seeking any slight movement or sound, he shouted again, "Hey, you asshole! You could have killed someone!" into the trees. The rain dripped steadily over his glasses. He took them off and tried to wipe them clear. *Someone*, he thought. Why hadn't he said *me*? Though *asshole* might have been pushing it. If he was a target, let the fucker shoot.

In answer he heard his own loud breaths punctuating the sound of rain as it pelted dying leaves, splattering the ground. Seigle took off walking again, and he was quickly soaked through, clothes riveted to skin. Simultaneously, a long moment of contradictory sun shook out behind the granite eyeholes of The Skull. The sharp contrast of the flare of sunlight during the squall gave an eerie effect to the outcropping's shape.

Seigle reached the site where the deer was taken down. Its tawny flank was shedding rain as he came upon it. Why had this animal been killed out of season if not for meat? Or perhaps his shouting had interrupted the hunter, caused him to flee before collecting his kill. Nothing made sense on this Sunday. The deer had been shot through the heart—at least it had died quickly. A clean kill, whatever that meant.

Disgusted, he made his way back to his jeep. He didn't know what he had come for anymore. Jeff's jeep was gone when he got back to the road. Seigle started up his engine, switched on the headlights, heat, wipers to clear the windshield. He was shivering. A piece of paper fluttered across beneath one of the wiper blades. He switched them off and reached through the window to the windshield, trying to retrieve the paper. He had to get out of the jeep to reach the paper, but he managed to get what was left of it. "I had to—" he read. The block printing looked like Jeff's. Seigle fished another torn bit of paper from the mud beside the front tire. All of the words had bled badly in the rain. He made out this much: "Seagull, you come around...." The note was signed by Turner, the old farmer.

Seigle drove up the rutted road to Turner's crude house. There was a car in the driveway, and he parked beside it. The woodpile was nearly as large as the house, and the split ash and locust logs looked a lot better than the rotted lumber of the sagging porch. Seigle stepped up to the door and knocked. Curling from the chimney, the wood smoke permeated the heavy air. He wondered if he should tell Turner about the deer lying dead in the rain. It might still be good for butchering, but for all Seigle knew Turner had shot it himself, and, after waiting for Seigle to leave, was out there right now, carving the tenderloin. If Turner had shot it he wouldn't appreciate Seigle's drawing attention to the fact. And if by any chance it had been Jeff? It didn't make any sense that Jeff would take the chance of being barred from Turner's land. Seigle tramped back to his jeep, turning up his collar. He didn't like this sort of uncertainty. So far it was a day with one bookend. His beard was soaked with rain. Just as he opened his door a voice shouted his name.

He turned back toward the house and saw Jessy coming around it. She was dressed in spotless hiking boots and a red and yellow nylon shell that could be seen across a long distance. And she was smoking a cigarette.

"There you are," she said. "There's nobody home. I was getting ready to leave. Thought I had the wrong place."

"You are in the wrong place. This is the owner's house. We park down the road. I'm here because he left me a note."

"Am I too late?"

"I missed Jeff. He was here and left. Didn't really have much of a day today. I'm sorry."

"You're going home, then?" Jessy tossed her butt to the ground.

Taking a step toward Jessy, Seigle crushed it with his boot.

"Thanks, Smokey," Jessy said.

Smart ass, he thought. He wanted to say that he was on

his way home; he was tired and wet and hungry, but the intensity of her gaze caused him to say something different. "In a little while," he said. "If you're still willing, we could walk a bit. But there was a hunter out there. It might not be such a good idea. I saw a deer go down."

"I'd rather stay alive today. If they shoot deer out of season no telling what they do with their own kind—or reporters." After a pause she asked him, "Are you hungry by any chance?"

They got in their vehicles and drove in tandem to his favorite dive, where they shoveled down hash browns and eggs, because the "Retreat and Eat" was the kind of place where breakfast never ended. Jessy started out asking Seigle a series of questions, but when his responses dwindled into few words she stopped trying to make conversation. As the silence lengthened they both made their peace with it and left it alone.

As they walked to their cars, Jessy said, "Give me some notice next time, if you can. I might be on a story, okay?"

"I will," Seigle said, not knowing whether he would or he wouldn't. Maybe he'd spent his last Sunday chasing his tail through the woods.

Driving back home, he made a conscious effort not to think about her. He didn't think about her several times, as bits of snow swirled through the air, glowing like fireflies on a summer night. It was as though he could see the earth tilting as the rain turned white, a decisive seasonal shift, a magic trick.

A Legend of the Turtle Tribe:
Falling and Rising

Far beneath the world we know, when time was as raw as the yolk of an egg, the Turtle tribe still lived inside the earth, and the earth was still quickening, turning from the inside out, to spew mountains onto its face. Only illusory, all surfaces might at any moment be changed. In the process of the earth's turning inside out, various features rose and receded. Deserts replaced oceans, so that gradually more and more land appeared that could be walked on. It was as if the earth were waking up from a long, tumultuous trance and giving evidence of its dream life by making irrefutable statements on the tongue of creation. Words like mountain, flume, mesa, plateau, canyon, cavern, river, arroyo; *like* Great Divide, San Andreas Fault, Blue Ridge Mountains, Sierra Nevada, *a chain of names repeated in many languages, spoken around the world. Although there were very few witnesses, there was also no going back on these words once the earth had spoken.*

For all generations the Turtle tribe had dwelled in the cavern under the earth, where pale fish and acrid white tea made up their diet. Their eyes were so small, in the early times, that they knew each other more by voice and touch than by sight. They caught their fish in hollowed rock traps not by hook or spear. The blind fish swam onto the rock and then the rock was lifted onto another underwater rock pedestal, with the fish caught fast in the small pond of the pounded hollow, kept alive until needed.

And in this time and place below the touch of sunlight, the ancestral Turtle tribe developed a hesitant stance and way of walking, because they bruised so easily. Their worst fear, then, was not of enemies or of disease—these were to come later—but of falling down and of being too roughly touched by someone who professed to love them.

Deep inside the cavern was a far chamber closed off by edict of the elders and sealed with a rock cairn. Inside the far chamber, behind the door of a thousand heavy stones, were the soft, decomposing bodies of Turtle people who had lost their footing, slipped or tripped, skidded, or tumbled off balance without explanation. The Turtle word for accident *also meant* death. *And the word for* love *was not spoken aloud.*

Sometimes there was laid to rest the wounded body of one who had been loved almost to death. Custom dictated a seven-day vigil, during which time the thousand stones were removed from death's chamber door, and then, whether the injured Turtle was dead or alive, removal to the far chamber if the one who had fallen could not rise on his or her own.

When a member of the tribe was placed in the far chamber still breathing, the cavern formations would grow more rapidly, at a pace visible to the eye. Solid columns would connect in the center within the space of a week's time, when stalagmites and stalactites suddenly grew together after having hesitated, inches apart, for eons. The cavern grew dense with moisture, and through every part of it water dripped as regularly as a heartbeat. Then without warning the heartbeat of dripping water stopped, and life returned to its slow pace.

The tribesmen or women laid into the far chamber to complete their transitions seldom cried out, but if the tribe were asleep when the dying one drew his last breath, the whole tribe spontaneously awoke as one and gathered in the ante-chamber, on the living side of the rock cairn. If the last breath were drawn during waking hours, every Turtle stopped work and migrated, by silent consensus, to the ante-chamber. Each member of the tribe offered a few phrases, sung or spoken, about the transitioned one. Their sentences or song fragments, characteristically brief and kind, spoke to the best qualities of the Turtle who had passed. When one Turtle stumbled, every Turtle left alive would speak and sing a memory chain that became the official story of the transitioned one's life:

"She loved her children and made sweet tea for them," one Turtle might offer.

"She helped me learn to sing the fishing song," another sang.

"She cooked excellent pale fish," said another.

"She washed her bowls until they shone."

"She kept watch when her youngest skinned his knee and lay until the fifth day before rising."

"She studied well the ancient scrolls."

"She spoke these wise words: 'the seeker of Truth must be true.'"

On and on, the voices wove memory upon memory, until each facet of the departed's life had been included in the fabric. As the voices sang and spoke praise upon praise, a rustling sound moved through the cavern that was interpreted as the transitional soul seeking the way up to the legendary blue air, above which no living Turtle had yet seen. A formation of tiny limestone buds called "kernels sprouting" grew against the direction of that upper air, and as the soul passed over the formation it made the rustling sound. Tribe members who were standing with their backs braced against the cavern's knobby walls felt a whoosh of energy moving past them.

It was said that a Turtle elder lay transitioning in the far chamber the day the world cracked open. The sound and *force of that rushing air knocked everyone from sleep and some bumped their mats onto the hard stone floor. Without warning, rifts opened in the cavern ceiling, as the world of the Turtle tribe cracked open from its shell. Light split the darkness within, and a stunned and blinking people set forth, stumbling through the opening, because up was the only way, and life depended on their passage.*

There was one who led the way; there is always a first one. But this one was the same one who had lain dying, whose transition had caused a swoosh of sound to accompany the first cracking. Frail and blind, this old Turtle stepped out onto mounds of green, rolling land. Many Turtles followed without recognizing who had led them. These followers collapsed with fear when they heard the distinctive laughter, like water rippling fast through a hand, of the one who had been left for dead, laid in the far chamber not long before. The dying Turtle, who was now as alive as anyone, smiled in the sunlight, opening sealed eyes, holding no grudges.

Every tongue began speaking and singing at once of this elder Turtle, who had made the transition, and yet lived—who had fallen and risen. And it felt as if the whole tribe, all of the dead and living, were finally joined.

In time, the Turtle people's eyes grew to accommodate bright sunlight. Their diet shifted to green plants that they learned to plant with a fish and harvest with the full moon. Their backs hardened, allowing them to stand upright, to go and come with steady strides, to fall and rise unharmed, sometimes even laughing from joy. The Turtles learned to cleave in love without the ancient fear of dying, though custom continued to favor group cohesion over the coupling of marriage.

The elder who had climbed through the opening, to first set a trembling foot on green terra firma, became known as Transcendent One. Tales of this Turtle spread, told in every tongue. It was said that when Transcendent One was a child a prophet had spoken saying, "Many will rise from falling because of this child."

Ironically, when the stories were finally written and collected in the ancient book, Tales of the Metempsychosis, *they began to be forgotten—that is, their truth was no longer believed. The stories became nothing more than amusing tales of a fragile, ancient people, wary of touch, who had lived beneath the earth and made their way to the surface.*

In modern times there remains one true book. The tissue-thin leaves of this tome, like droplets of water in the sea or stars in a loved one's eyes, cannot be numbered. Its spine is as sturdy as bone, with curved covers of meticulously metered shell, reminiscent of the hollows of the old stone fish traps. Within the pages of this book, the truth is caught and kept alive, whether or not anyone still believes.

The Quaking

—The figure of a man crouches down to a door and pushes through....Moira has been here before but she does not remember. She will not enter after the man, she thinks. But when the door opens, the wind sucks her into the space beyond the door. Recognizing the smell, she clamps her nose shut. She will not breathe this odor. She holds her breath until she faints, but when she wakes it is in the same, stinking place.

The dark, deformed figure stands over her; huddled beneath the mass of him, she sinks into his humpbacked shadow. His skin, crusty and wrinkled as old elephant hide, oozes from a thatch-work of sores. He points her attention toward a smoldering heap of trash. Whatever she can imagine as the detritus of human life is what the manmade mountain contains: plastic containers that once held detergent, oil, soap, mustard, milk, orange juice; shreds of rusting metal; burned portions of box springs; washing machines, stoves, the crushed shells of cars, unidentifiable manmade fibers with no beginning and no end. And human bodies piled so inconspicuously, layered between the other debris, that until her eyes meet the frozen features of a face with eyes permanently staring back at her, she does not even notice the human remains mixed into the rubbish heap.

Then the mountain of discarded things recedes. She still sees it, but as if from a great distance, or through a thick mist. The mountain turns around, like a thought revising, righting itself from a hundred wrong angles. The shape that was the mountain is spinning, blue, and whirling—

Paul was looking down at her from over the bed, "We just had a tremor, did you feel it, are you awake?"

Without replying, Moira threw back the covers and raced to Ian's room.

—She sees the blue, spinning shape turn to burning. Soon it is a burnt sphere, a cinder-planet, the earth itself. She wonders where she is, from what vantage point she views this scene, because she is looking at where she lives, the only place she knows, yet she is separate enough to see it from a distance. All at once she feels herself falling. It is like the rush of self into self just before sleep, when the body catches fast in the shift from waking into sleep and jerks to attention once more before finally letting down its guard and meeting its dreams—

She opened her eyes again, or for the first time? Paul was hovering over her, speaking excitedly, "We just had a tremor, did you feel it?"

Without replying, she threw back the covers and raced to Ian's room. This time she reached her son.

Ian was sitting up in bed, rubbing sleep from an eye. His stuffed rhino had tumbled onto the rug, his plastic cup lay beside it.

"There's an earthquake," Moira said, moving quickly toward her son.

"There is? We are so lucky, Mommy." Ian's voice was amazed, cheerful. He looked around his room, searching the corners as though he might find the earthquake. All of the vibration had already stopped.

Moira wrapped her arms around her son, giving or seeking comfort.

Ian wriggled successfully from her embrace. He jumped up and padded past her, into his bathroom.

Her heart was caged too high in her chest, like a fish

bone lodged in her throat. She drew each breath with difficulty, pulling the air around the fist of intractable weight. Slowly, she walked back to her bedroom, feeling the steady tug of too much gravity.

The usual voices crackled news from the bedside radio with no mention of the earthquake. She waited for the local news. She could hear Paul showering. The announcers reported a fire near Malibu. No mention of the earthquake. Moira fell back on the bed. She felt that she could not make herself rise again; a heaviness almost pinned her to the bed. It seemed such an easy concept, that she should go downstairs and start some breakfast, but something disturbing was fluttering in her chest where her calm center used to be. She felt unhinged, without a point of reference. And although she did not wish to acknowledge it, she had learned just now that she couldn't trust even time to move in its proper sequence.

Where the center *used to be*. She didn't know how long she had been wobbling, when her un-centering had begun. Before the move had everything felt right? During the last six months, the last year, had she felt something change? If she were honest, the wobble went back much further. It had started before the incident with Chicago radio. Perhaps it had begun in earnest with her mother's death, or earlier, when she had grown up with one visible and one invisible parent, so that she felt striped down the middle with presence and absence. But none of the usual sort of self-reflection was authentic for her in this moment. Then she must be in denial, she thought. What other choice did she have?

The psychoanalytic language meant to provide comfortable categories for individual internal workings eluded her, while she tried to tell herself that this was only due to her overreaching ego. Her ego must be compelling her to invent new explanations, helping her to evade her own mental grasp. She could think herself thoroughly in circles and where would she be at the end of the turning? She wasn't yet ready to acknowledge that this place where she had arrived without effort was so foreign as to have no name on any map she had ever used for steering. Even her body felt alien, her breasts too tender to brush against a feather pillow. The sky's blue might as well have turned to black, and the air become stone.

She heard Paul shut off the shower, the sliding door bang back. In a moment he would be in the room.

She wanted to think that Paul would believe her and not label her, if she told him she had started hearing voices that came at her unexpectedly, as if magnetized through the air only for her ears. The voices held life stories—of the teen-aged girl, who contemplated elopement on a daily basis, or of the husband who kept his thumb firmly on his wife's head. And if Moira contemplated the girl, reversing the magnetism so that it fell on the subject, making subject object, then she could pick up even more. But the events she gleaned were dislocated in time: the pregnancy of the girl, the rejection of her by her parents, the sex of the baby, a boy. These were things Moira *knew*, but she didn't know whether these events had happened, would happen, or if they were only possibilities. The one thing that she did understand was that her absolute knowledge of these facts was not based on her own projections.

Something had caused time to twist, enfold on itself like a Möbius strip. She wanted time to plod in one direction, move forward again, as it always had. She wanted the boundaries back that had allowed her to live without the weight of unknown people's stories bombarding her until she did not know where she began and ended. During a flash flood back in Virginia, she had learned that moving water could be more treacherous than it appeared. One of her neighbors had drowned in her car, determined to cross a bridge that the creek had already flooded and was rippling across.

Misjudging the depth and the strength of the current, the woman drove onto the bridge, only to be swept over the railings, she and her car carried along as easily as a snapped branch in that chute of fierce water that had looked so tame.

Paul popped from the bathroom, headed for his dresser, and pulled open his underwear drawer with due efficiency. For a month they had been in some kind of moratorium, not speaking of anything important; and, since Martin's party, they had had no sex at all. Six weeks was the longest they had ever gone without sex of some kind. Not long after Ian's birth, even three weeks before he was born, they had managed intimacy. Moira wanted to blame herself or Paul for the distance, but they were both participating. While actively doing nothing, they were gradually locking themselves into an invisible tug of war that prevented their crossing the line between them.

She knew she had to offer some explanation for her withdrawal, the long afternoons she had spent on the couch, unable to rise, feeling herself sinking, while all the time knowing that she was only trying to hide from the voices, to escape their prying into her. It was exhausting.

She opened her mouth to begin paddling across that space and heard her words, "I can't fix breakfast today." That's all that came out.

Paul stood before the mirror knotting his tie with sure hands, the quick motions passed from father to son. It was the flowered tie that Moira had given him. He jerked his head to fling his errant locks out of his eyes.

"What's the matter?' he asked, still facing the mirror. "Are you too busy?"

She turned her head to the pillow. The edge in his voice sliced her to silence.

"For Christ's sake," he continued, "it was just an earthquake!"

She lay still, unable to draw a breath. Could he hear

himself, she wondered. *Just an earthquake.* And it was really worse than he knew.

He turned toward her then and lowered his voice. "What's wrong? You don't seem like yourself."

And this is the moment in which she's supposed to tell him that she is hearing people's energy all around her? That she had knowledge of the problems of the couples living in the houses on either side of theirs? One couple was struggling to leave any stick standing of a twelve-year marriage, while the other was involved in a two-way affair with another couple. Whatever Paul wanted from her in that moment, she knew he didn't want to hear the truth.

"Is it the move?" he asked her.

She nodded.

He pulled her to his chest and hugged her close. "It just takes time," he said. Then he released her and took a step back. "You know I love you."

"I love you, too," Moira answered.

"I've gotta run," he said.

"Are you traveling today?"

"Yep. Down the coast. *Hasta luego.*" Paul gave her a peck on the lips.

When she was about nine years old, Moira and her best friend found a badly scarred golf ball in the yard that had been sliced open by the lawn mower. Using a hammer and a screw driver for a chisel, they succeeded in peeling away the stiff, white shell. Inside they found a hard core consisting of coiled rubber strings that could not be separated without destroying the ball. So they had flung that core against the sidewalk and sent it flying over their heads.

She wanted to call Paul back, but she found she could not do it. She watched him leave the room as if he were receding into distant, vaguely defined space in a painting by an old master. He was entering the atmospheric haze-zone that made perspective possible.

Ground Wire

Bougainvillea hedges bordered the small lots of the coastal village. They pulled in front of Regina's house, a squat, stucco with red tile roof. As Trisha curbed the Volare Moira felt her heart sink. Before they could open the car doors, a side door of the house banged open and three children ran out. They mounted bicycles and headed off down the street, whooping without even a vague show of interest in the old green sedan parked in front of their house.

"I don't know about this," Moira said.

"Relax." Trisha pulled the keys from the ignition and quickly palmed them as if Moira might grab them and bolt. "I was scared, too, when I first came here."

"Why did you come?"

"Low energy. I felt tired all of the time and the doctor couldn't help me. I guess I needed some grounding."

Moira remembered a tree she had seen that was fitted with a ground wire. Even so, that one hundred-year-old Copper Beech had been struck by lightning dozens of times, losing parts of limbs, once splitting off a second trunk but still surviving. By the time Moira saw it there was a plug of concrete in the crotch.

"Regina helped me get centered."

Moira followed Trisha to the house and waited as she rang the bell.

"Then maybe I am in the right place," Moira said.

A brass wind chime twirled over their heads as they stood

on the stoop. Through the screen door Moira could see a small foyer lined with coat hooks, and a staircase beyond the hallway.

Regina unlocked the screen and admitted them, greeting Trisha with a brief, warm hug. The royal blue running suit was not the flowing robe Moira had expected. A generous mound of black frizzy hair provided the only dash of eccentricity. Moira almost wished for some trappings—aroma therapy, at least some candles—instead of the banality of bicycles and jogging suits. She felt in need of some strong mojo.

From behind a door that led to another room, a child was peeking at Moira. Regina's back was turned to her son, but she knew he was there.

"That's Michael," she said. "My youngest. He likes to hang around when I have clients. He's a little spy. Sometimes he falls asleep trying to listen through the door." Regina laughed and Michael came out from behind the door, obviously not embarrassed.

"Hi," he said, beaming. His eyes were the blue of deep water beyond the coastal shelf.

"Hi," Moira said back to him.

Trisha reached down for Michael's hand. "Maybe the two of us could play a game."

Michael immediately pulled her into the room beyond the door.

"We'll take about an hour," Regina said and then thanked Trisha for keeping Michael occupied.

Moira followed Regina into the dining room, took a chair at Regina's invitation and watched as her host promptly disappeared through another door. Too nervous to look at anything too closely, Moira tapped her fingers on the white table and let her eyes scan the numerous family snapshots scattered across the sideboard in no particular order, in no particular style of frame. Where was the incense, the dim light and hollow flute music? Bright afternoon sunlight was streaming through six-foot windows, imprinting the wooden floor with a watery brilliance. The kitchen door flapped open and Regina carried a tray bearing a pitcher and two glasses into the room; she set them on the table. Ah, the magic potion, Moira was thinking, when Regina offered her a glass of water.

Although her throat was dry and constricted, Moira declined the glass.

Regina set it close to her anyway. "If you change your mind. It's good to balance you." Then she plopped down opposite Moira. Her gaze was pleasant but direct.

For Moira, meeting Regina's gaze was difficult. She found it far easier to look away, look at anything else, the mantel behind Regina's head, the water glass, the pendulum clock on the wall, the sun imprinted on the rug and floor. But the silence was receptive and Regina didn't seem to be in any hurry.

Moira reached for the water and took a sip. "I guess Trisha told you something about why I'm here."

"No," Regina said. "Nothing at all."

Moira didn't think she could explain. She didn't want to.

Regina waited, and finally she gently asked, "Did you come with certain questions?"

Moira would not be trapped by this. She had heard how it worked. The so-called psychic would deduce "insights" from the information the client supplied without knowing how much she was giving away. Moira closed her mind tightly. She slammed the door and bolted it.

"Perhaps I will tell you what I see, then?" Regina said.

"Yes," Moira answered in a measured tone. She would give Regina nothing to work with and expected nothing in return.

Regina began with a generic proclamation. "You are

slow to acknowledge the changes that have occurred in your life." Her voice was pitched to statements, not the series of either/or questions Moira was ready for. Regina needed no prodding; she drew in a breath and then took the roof off, all the time speaking in a firm, calm tone. "For instance, you are carrying a child, but you have not let yourself know it."

"No!" Moira shot back without a pause. "I'm not pregnant. I've got a child and I know the signs."

"Yes. And you have experienced them without acknowledging them." Nonplussed and smiling, Regina shifted her hair away from her face with one easy shrug.

Moira silently reviewed her physical rap sheet from the last several weeks: bloating, indigestion, irritability, nausea, a fainting spell, headaches, breast pain. There it was, in spades. When was the last time she'd had her period? As each symptom had occurred she had dismissed it.

"I suppose it's possible," Moira said. Something like relief welled up and a lightness settled over her. Maybe everything, all of it, was due to the pregnancy. She was ready to thank Regina and go home, but Regina made no sign that the session had ended and held Moira in place with steady eye contact.

"You are pregnant with more than a daughter. Your life's path is opening and it's the same path I'm on. That's why you have come. You must enter the house of the self to find your own way of service. You have a strong energy with you, and your guides will help you."

Moira reached for the water glass and gulped. Hot and cold rippled up and down her spine. Clammy sweat drenched her armpits and palms. Nothing about this was funny, but all at once Moira felt herself let go, collapse into laughter, and with it the tension she had been holding was set free for a few moments. Then the laughter shifted and she felt she might be able to cry just as readily. She was coming unglued and wondered where it would end.

"I don't want to change my life," she wailed. "I liked everything the way it was. I didn't want to move here."

Regina heard the words tumble out and let the air settle before she said, "It's not about where you are but *who* you are. In a few months your pregnancy will show. There's no way to tuck the truth inside. It has a way of blooming. You can't stop the rain or a train, you know. And you cannot stop your own blooming." Regina's voice took on more force. "It would be fatal to try."

"And the damn voices, what about them?' Moira said. "How am I supposed to keep up with all of this? I'm not ready."

"You are ready. And once you face the voices squarely instead of trying to stifle them, you will be able to hear them without fear. Then you can better judge what to do—and when to do nothing. Once you are at home in your own house you won't fear what comes to dinner. You know what I mean?"

"I don't want this," Moira said.

"If you didn't want it on some level it would not be coming to you."

"So stop whining, eh?"

"Ah, yes," Regina said, and then laughed lightly.

Moira had to admit to herself that she felt better for having been seen, but it was similar to the relief that children feel when their parents guess the wicked truth they have been hiding, and everything can then be put to rights with a confession and a punishment. Moira was afraid her case called for neither.

"I feel so alone," Moira said. "How can I be so different from who I thought I was?"

"Sometimes truthfulness means loneliness—but it's also freedom. It's the human condition when it comes to finding one's path. You were and now you are. This is only a new facet that will reflect a new pattern of light. Didn't you study religion in college?" Regina asked.

"What's that got to do with this?" Moira asked, taken aback.

"Everything," Regina said simply, elbows on the table, lacing her strong fingers together in front of her chin.

Moira remembered her first trip to Dr. Olds' office, in the basement of the chapel. She had had to seek his permission to enroll in his class, because she was only in her first year. His office was intimidating—not just the mahogany framed diplomas from St. John's and Chicago but the grandchildren smiling from brass frames. Dr. Olds was nearing retirement and Moira didn't want to miss his famous class "Ideas of God."

"Have a seat," he had said, motioning her to the available chair, which was overstuffed but frayed from a generation of such visits.

Moira sat and waited for him to speak. Instead he combed two fingers through his gray-white beard. He was a small, bald man with the demeanor of an old Brethren minister and the learnedness of the classically educated person that he was. In these latter years of his tenure, Dr. Olds was becoming noted for reveries that overtook him without notice. He would send his gaze out any available window and stroke his beard as he was doing now, unsettling his students, and then he would fire off some brilliant analysis about St. Augustine's conversion in the next moment.

Moira had broken the silence. "I'm here to ask about signing up for your class."

"Yes?"

"It's a 300 and it's only my second semester."

"Are you troubled by different ideas of God?" he asked, looking into her eyes.

"Of course not," Moira had answered, although she knew precious little of the various world religions outside of her own. And later she had been scared but fascinated as she was introduced to a world of thought she'd never known was there, to enigmatic figures like Simone Weil. She still remembered one of her phrases—it still chilled her every time it crossed her mind—"We love like cannibals."

Dr. Olds had nodded. And then he posed a simple question that had presented Moira with the best opportunity for lying that she had yet encountered in college. He asked her what church she had attended with her parents. She wanted to say anything but the truth. Weren't most academics atheists? Even this mild man before her was a well-known renegade, who had helped to author a school of humanism that had coined the controversial phrase "God is dead."

"My mother and I are Methodists," she said, as if under oath, thinking that now she had lost all chance of enrolling in his class. She wished she were anything else, even a Mormon, but especially a Jew or a Catholic, something exotic with an intellectual tradition.

"Oh," said Dr. Olds. "The church of my youth."

Moira smiled with relief. "May I take your course?"

"I thought we settled that, my dear. We start Thursday morning."

Moira was right back in school again. She faced her new teacher. "I want someone to tell me I'm not crazy," she told Regina.

Regina's gentle authority fell over her like cool water. "Give yourself permission to know what you know. You can always call me, but it is better to seek your own answers. Ask and you will receive."

"I remember that one from Sunday school."

Regina reached across the table to take Moira's hand. "Do you feel crazy now?"

"No," Moira said. "Just terrified."

Regina smiled. "Good." She leaned back in her chair,

away from the table, and Moira felt they had reached the end of the session. Her thoughts returned to the mundane world.

"What do I owe you?" Moira asked.

"Just keep in touch," Regina said. "In six months you will be reading for me."

"In six months I'll be as big as a house."

Regina laughed. "The body is the best teacher."

Disappearance in the Mojave

> *Needles.* A man was reported missing in Wild Horse Canyon of the East Mojave Scenic Area yesterday, investigators say. He had been hiking in the canyon with a companion when the two separated in order to survey more terrain. The unidentified hiker is the third to go missing in the East Mojave since Labor Day.
>
> Leslee Lyles and Jackie Becker failed to return home from a camping trip on schedule. Police believe the incidents to be unrelated. The remote desert area is known for confusing even experienced wilderness hikers.

"I want to name him Peter," Ian said.

Moira set the newspaper aside. "But what if it's a girl?" she asked him, remembering what Regina had said—that she was carrying a daughter.

"I think a brother would be lucky."

"We will be lucky either way. If it's not a boy you will still have someone to play with," Moira said.

"Yes, girls are very nice, too," Paul said, joining them at the breakfast table. "You can pinch them."

"It's a little early for sibling rivalry, don't you think?" Moira punched her husband playfully on the shoulder.

Ian looked at his parents strangely, puckering his lips as if he were about to speak in guppy.

Moira poured Paul a glass of orange juice from the white pitcher on the table. She got up and filled a plate for him from the stove and set it before him.

Ian asked to be excused. He liked to spend the five or ten minutes before leaving for school in front of the television.

When Moira had told Paul about the pregnancy, he had been almost giddy with happiness and twirled her around the living room, releasing the tension that had built up between them. Moira felt their distance dissolving into one explanation. For her fatigue and listlessness, fainting spells and crying jags, at last a reason. Not crazy but pregnant. The relief was plain in the recent softening of the lines on Paul's forehead. But this morning something was not right with him, Moira could see it in the way he hunched over his plate and absently stabbed at his eggs.

"Is something on your mind?" she asked.

"Maybe, I'm not sure."

"So out with it," She prodded.

"Last week I was driving out near Barstow and thought I'd check out the site of the new project," he began. But he had seen no evidence of construction commencing. Aside from coyote tracks and yucca-covered acreage, he had glimpsed nothing. "It was so deserted not even an idea was stirring," Paul said.

"Are you sure you had the right location?" Moira asked. She had a full plate of eggs and toast and even bacon before her. With Ian she had been sick for the first three months, but with this one the morning sickness had been brief and now she felt like eating everything in sight. Already the skin of her abdomen was pulled taut over a bulge that grew ever rounder. Baseball, grapefruit, then beachball—she knew what was coming. Her breasts had bloated immediately and now she was convinced that her nipples were elongating into bottles. She plucked her robe away from her tender chest. She wasn't imagining it—her breasts had swelled so quickly that she could see blue veins pumping beneath the skin when she looked in the mirror.

"Yes. There was a gate with a company logo chained to it," Paul continued. "I'm beginning to think that Martin has not been entirely up front with me. Every day I go beat the bushes for new contracts—and they keep coming in—" Paul took a few bites of his toast, completely ignoring both the butter and the strawberry jam. This morning, he hadn't even tucked his tie inside his shirt, to protect it from spills.

"Do you want something different?" Moira asked.

"No, it's just too much," He said, pushing away his plate.

"I'll take it," she said, and he shoved his breakfast toward her.

"So what are you telling the clients?" Moira asked, picking the bacon off Paul's plate.

"Just what Martin told me, that as soon as we have a quarter of the capital committed we're good to go. Martin has worked with most of these investors before. You know, I didn't come out here to be a salesman."

"Didn't Martin promise you another assignment as soon as this is done?"

"Yes, he did. I'm not sure why I'm edgy. And you, " he asked suddenly. "How are you doing, *chica*?"

"Everything is fine," she said. And it was—for a week she had heard nothing but her own thoughts. No invading voices. She had rested and eaten well. Each day she had driven out of the neighborhood and followed some direction as far as she felt like driving, just getting her bearings in this new environment. It wasn't yet home, but she had made an internal decision to get to know it. She was determined to give it a chance.

She patted her stomach. "Except that I'm getting fat."

"Naw," he said. "You're beginning to look like a pregnant person."

"Person? I've never seen a pregnant man," she said.

"Maybe I will be the first one," Paul said, smiling

broadly. "But, don't say it, I know. Fat chance."

Moira rolled her eyes. Paul's corny humor always made her laugh. She had something to show him.

"Have you seen that giant wind farm toward the Mojave?" she asked. Row after row of metal windmills were planted like palms, spinning energy from the Santa Ana that blew west from the desert. The windmills were turned to face the wind from the interior when she passed them, reversing what she had always thought—that wind blew in from the ocean. The white twirling paddles flashed in the sun. She had stopped and taken a few quick photographs. On the way home she left the film at the one-hour lab while she drank a latté and got Ian from school. She spread the pictures on the kitchen table for Paul's inspection.

The film speed had stopped the paddles in a position that made the windmills look like supplicants reaching up to their god, or maybe like men wearing antlers or old-fashioned rabbit ears, standing sentinel, ready to receive a signal from the wind. And then it occurred to her that the wind generators resembled something she'd seen nearer to home, the images Ian was scratching on his rocks.

Paul tapped one of the photos. "Yeah, I passed it yesterday. It's not ours, though. The new project will compete with it. Ours is supposed to dwarf it when it's finished." Paul quickly stretched out his arm to pull up his sleeve and checked his watch. "Gotta run," he said and called Ian. "Come on, son. It's time."

WHEN THEY HAD LEFT the house, Moira showered and washed her hair. The tight aching of her breasts was somewhat relieved by the soothing water streaming over them.

Wrapped up in her thick terry robe, she marched right back downstairs to the refrigerator when she had dried her hair. The foil-covered leftover roasted chicken was calling her name along with the macaroni and cheese, Ian's favorite. She would leave him a portion. While she zapped the plate full of food in the microwave, she picked up the newspaper again, rereading the article she had glanced at earlier. Lost hikers in the East Mojave. She hadn't seen the territory. She took a look at her map and found the state land clearly marked, a green line surrounding it. Nothing much there, she noted. It wasn't a popular tourist spot like Palm Springs or Joshua Tree.

And then she heard something—a voice assaulting her from the silence that almost knocked her down with its alacrity. Snapped to attention, she was forced to listen to the harangue.

—"I'm telling you I'm not going to stand here and listen to you for another minute. Go on, tell your mother. I don't care. See if I give a good goddam. I can eat soup alone. If you cooked—but you don't even do that. What good are you, tell me that? What good are you?"

Moira saw no images only heard the voice, but the voice alone created a pretty strong set of pictures. The object of the man's scorn was obviously his wife, some poor mousy-looking woman with a caved-in chest. And the man sounded like a weekend husband, some long-distance trucker or salesman opting for a set description of wifely duty, his measure of comfort. It sounded this way and yet now she remembered where she had heard that voice before. She recognized it as belonging to Mr. Darst, who lived with his wife about five doors down.

Ian and she had knocked on their door, canvassing the neighbors to inquire about the owner of the black and white dog that had been hanging around. Mr. Darst had answered his door wearing a red bow tie. When he held out his hand to greet her he flashed a cufflink. She had thought that no one wore those anymore. His hair was cut in a Marine-style flat top. His grin was broad, but clenched, a taut rubber band of a smile.

"No, I haven't seen a dog by that description," he had told them. "I'd ask my wife, but at the moment she's indisposed." His words had needed security clearance to pass his lips.

It was the same voice now. She knew it by the chill of recognition that drained the blood from her extremities. She had failed to shake his hand upon meeting him, instead stuffing her hands into her pockets in a reflex or recoil for which she had no explanation. She and Ian had left his door. After they'd reached the end of the walkway, she had heard the soft *thunk* of his door behind them, which indicated he had spent a few moments watching them before closing it.

Moira closed her eyes and focused. She saw, in a series of flickering images, a woman in a blue silk dress, hanging on to a telephone. The woman sat alone, in a kitchen abuzz with the chaos of appliances. She had turned on everything at once—food processor, blender, coffee maker, dish washer, mixing bowl. This woman needed something that worked. She was engaged in the phone call of her life, or one her life depended upon.

—"I'm calling you to tell you that I won't be here when you get home," she said.

"Where are you going, to the doctor again?"

"I'm moving out. Don't try to find me, Garnet."

"You ungrateful twit. I can always find you. Don't forget that for a minute. If you have a moment's peace it's because I say so. If I don't find you, it's because I don't want to look."

"I want—a divorce." The woman sucked in air, as if she were coming up from having held her breath underwater way too long.

"I want a divorce," he mimicked, in high playground style.

"I mean it."

"I mean it," he said, mocking her again.

"Goodbye, Garnet." Her voice cracked on goodbye, and that gave him another opening.

"Who are you that you think you can just walk away when you want. I'll find you, honey bunch. And you'll be sorry you pulled this stunt. I'll find you. But I doubt you have the nerve to leave. Even if you have no appreciation for all I've given you. Right now I'm due in a partner's meeting. If you think any lawyer in this community, any judge, will take your side against me, you're crazier than I ever thought. Do you remember what happened the last time you tried this?" He paused. "Do you? Do you?"

"Yes," she whispered.

"Just keep it in mind. And you didn't even call anyone so no one knows. No one. If I were you I'd think twice about what you're doing. You're making me late for my meeting. Why don't you cook something for dinner. Do something with your time."

"You won't let me get a job," she said, crying now.

"I want a steak. Your job? It's to grill me a steak. And bake a potato. I'll be home early. By seven. Get it on the table, okay?"

She said nothing.

"Okay?" he asked, with more volume.

"Yes," she said.

"Good girl." He hung up the phone.

Moira could still see the scene in the kitchen, as Mrs. Darst twirled around on a stool, rocking herself while she cried. Moira tried to stay focused on the woman, on the sound of her tears and the flickering image, but another image overtook it and filled the dark spaces between the fragmented images she had seen. Like a still frame in a movie, each interpolated image interrupted the stream.

—A warm, coiled shape unfurling, brown against even darker edges.

—Two dark shapes peering out from the solid rock face

of a mountain.

—Dim shadows ascending, moving over Moira's eyes like black birds flying between her closed eyes and the sun. Their shadows poured like water, spilling darkness between her and the sky. Placing her between, always between them and an object beyond.

—White scars, scratches, like scratches across film emulsion or through black crayon, the same technique Ian was using to make his pictures. But this pattern became a spiral. Then a fat-bodied figure with stick arms and legs, a triangle head plopped on top like a crude hat.

—A human face amidst black flickering. Then an iris shut down, a lens tightened on the scene. Then black.

Moira opened her eyes still seeing Mrs. Darst in her kitchen—every appliance a prop of her imprisonment. Moira was unable to shake the image. She began mentally speaking to it, projecting only one word, *Leave*. She tried to convey the word through the distance, beaming it like a strong spotlight. Moira knew the house where this woman was sitting. She didn't know if she should go there. On what pretext? How would she explain herself? She could bake a cake, anything. But she wondered if she could ever say anything that would make any difference. What influence could one stranger really ever have upon another? She could see that the intimate knowledge that had come to her was useless—or worse, torture. It was torture to know and have no way to intervene to change the wrongs she witnessed. Moira had heard much, it was true, but still it was only partial; she didn't know whether Garnet Darst's threats alluded to some previous violence on his part toward his wife or to a breakdown of hers. For everything she had heard, for what she knew, there was a mountain of buried information.

Before she had considered it further, she found herself mixing cookie dough because cookies were quicker than cake. One at a time she dropped two eggs into the sugar and shortening, mixed in the dry ingredients and the cocoa. For the last few strokes, Moira used a wooden spoon. Stained dark with many baking battles and chipped a bit, it had been her grandmother's lucky spoon; she'd never made anything good without it, nothing bad that it had touched. As Moira stirred, loosing batter from the sides of the bowl, a flashing image stopped the motion of her hand.

—A room with whorled walls, like the slick interior of a seashell. A wet rock room unfolding beneath shafts dripping liquid calcium.

Moira shook the image from her and began dropping batter onto a cookie sheet. It was the first time she had felt in control of an image when it reached her. She managed somehow to turn it back from the reception end. She felt stronger. She was more than a blank screen, more than a giant ear set up to catch whatever came to her.

THE WOMAN'S BLUE, SILK DRESS had been exchanged for blue jeans, but otherwise the tall brunette who answered the door matched the woman whose image had reached Moira earlier. Indeed, it was Mrs. Darst. Nowhere was the mousy, sunken creature Moira had first imagined. A slight red cast to the woman's nose and puffiness beneath her eyes were the only outward signs of her unhappiness.

With the plate of cookies before her, her badge of domestic harmony, Moira introduced herself in a honeyed Southern voice, referring to her earlier encounter with Mr. Darst.

"Oh really," Mrs. Darst said. "And did you find your dog?"

"It isn't ours—or anyone's it appears."

"I am Renée," the woman said, extending her hand. She managed to produce a patently forced smile that strained the edges of her make-up, dark lip liner around frosty mauve lipstick.

Moira took the cold hand briefly and released it, as she introduced herself again. Renée issued one of those routine, polite invitations that were really meaningless, and yet Moira accepted. She stepped inside, still holding the plate of cookies before her like a shield.

"Would you like some coffee?" Renée asked, taking the cookies.

"Yes, please." Moira followed her into the kitchen. She seated herself on one of the stools she had seen Renée twisting while she talked with Garnet. The kitchen had all of its appliances in place, but they sat quietly now. The cord from the wall phone dangled beside her ear. Moira chatted with Renée about her move west, about Paul's job that had brought them here.

"My husband's a lawyer," was all Renée revealed.

Renée poured the coffee into black, octagon cups; she placed the cookies, coffee, cream and sugar on a natural bamboo tray and led Moira to the living room. A high ceiling peaked to a skylight above white furniture and a cool-blue rug. Huge avocado and ficus trees framed a wall of glass blocks. A lap pool glistened beyond it. The impression of the whole was balanced somewhere between *House and Garden* and *Architectural Digest*. The room had no distinctive identity—it only mirrored a packaged style that left its owner's taste anonymous.

"How old is your son?" Renée asked.

"A precocious five. Ian loves school, but he's a little smaller than most everyone else."

Renée said nothing.

Moira filled the gap before she could stop herself. "Do you have children?"

The response was swift, in a word, "No." Renée looked down at her hands, then reached for a cookie and stuffed most of it into her mouth.

Moira reviewed the Heimlich Maneuver, watching

Renée. But she was still coughing into a napkin. That meant she was breathing. "Are you all right?" Moira asked. That's all she needed—to kill Garnet Darst's wife with one of her cookies.

Renée took a sip of coffee. "I'm fine. Sometimes when I eat it goes down wrong."

Moira was thinking that she should clear out before something really did go wrong. "I'd better be getting home," she said. She pushed herself up from the deep sofa cushions. Her head swam from the caffeine; she had forgotten to ask for decaf. This pregnancy was hard to remember. Aside from her expanding appetite and waistline, she felt normal.

"Oh, don't go," Renée said, with feeling.

The entreaty tugged at Moira. Renée's dour expression pulled Moira down to the couch, where she felt her weight sinking, sinking. She didn't want to stay and yet she had initiated the visit. Unbidden or not, it was her psyche that had picked up Renée's energy. Regina's admonitions echoed: "You do not want to acknowledge that you have already changed." There's no stopping a river. Divert the stream and the first hard rains will bring the waters back where they belong. Dam it up and you will spend a lifetime spackling the cracks in the cement, eternally vigilant, and then the truth will slip through anyway. That's just how it is. "Know what you know," Regina had said.

But how did Regina expect her to live? She would not spend the rest of her life as an unconscious voyeur, an unwilling witness to the worst moments in the lives of strangers, with these moments interrupting her own life, barreling into her, while she, in turn, invaded others.

If she could define responsibility, she might know where to begin. She hadn't asked for this knowledge, yet now that she had it she couldn't wish it away. She saw that Renée was crying.

"Can I get you something?" Moira asked.

"No, nothing. I'm sorry."

"Don't apologize."

"I guess you want an explanation," Renée said.

"No—that's not necessary."

"I'm just so far from home," Renée continued. "This might as well be the moon compared to Oregon. I didn't plan to live here. It's Garnet who had to be in California."

"Oregon's not that far. Maybe you should go for a visit."

"Oh, we're so busy all of the time," Renée said in one breath, exhaling.

Moira paused and then plunged ahead. "Won't Garnet let you go?"

"What do you mean?" Renée bristled. "I just can't spare the time."

Moira let the conversation rest for several silent moments and then rose again to leave, knowing she had blown it. "I really should get home."

They exchanged stiff goodbyes with hollow promises to get together. A few days later Moira found the cookie platter propped against her front door.

Over the following days a cacophony of voices came back toward her, and Moira tried to filter them, to make the contact by her choice. If she had to accept the fact that she heard voices, Moira wanted to be in charge of when she received them. She also wanted to know why this was happening to her, regardless of Regina's words, "The cause is unknown. And it really doesn't matter. Knowing the cause wouldn't change the effect."

It helped her to think of her situation as a growing thing rather than some kind of freakish curse. Her gift must have a root system that could not be imagined from the green stem glimpsed above the ground. Nor even from the brief flower. And when that flower dropped and the green shoot withered the unseen roots could stay healthy and strong.

Some plants wouldn't thrive without a freeze, while a frost would kill others. The shallow root systems of Giant Sequoias were disproportionate to the huge trees. Those trees reached hundreds of feet high if they managed to thrive in the right environment, yet a strong wind could topple them if they were caught outside of their narrow, sheltered valleys. Who could know this by looking? She would have to be patient if she wanted to learn the ways of this path of insight, eyes being one thing and seeing quite another.

Forecast: Snow

Truth told: it was damn cold outside. Seigle had been sniffling and sneezing, beset with low energy, but that usually wouldn't have been enough to keep him in. Fact was he felt like half a heart trying to beat and the forecast called for snow. He thought it would be a relief to see the brown leaf-litter buried, the brown crust whited out. Maybe he'd make a snowman, dress it in his own clothes, call it his alter ego. Grim joke. For six weeks while nothing had changed on its face, the earth had been pulling into its shell, adapting for the whittling of winter's knife, and now it was here, this day balancing on the solstice like a word on the tongue's tip. The shortest day of the year.

In his plaid wool shirt, Seigle looked the part of a mountain man, but his sensitive skin was irritated, itchy, and red in gaps where the tee shirt didn't mediate. He thought he might feel better attached to the human race if he shaved his shaggy face and went out to mingle a bit with the last minute Christmas shoppers, not that he had any gifts left to buy. He'd given his secretary a bottle of bourbon—that's what she wanted. It was easy enough to wrap the bottle, and he had only used a little of the giant rolls of paper and curling ribbon he had bought. At this rate the jolly Santa faces would fade from the paper before he could use it all. He'd thought briefly about a gift for Jeff, abandoned the thought. Thought about sending Jessy a card. Too late.

He sat down on the couch and plucked the newspaper

off the floor. In Boca Raton a couple was saved from a nocturnal alligator attack by their parrot. The parrot shrieked what it could, which was a continual chorus of "Goodbye! Goodbye!," finally waking them up to discover a seven-foot alligator trying to smash through a floor to ceiling window. Whether the alligator was attempting to mate with its reflection or hunting for a midnight snack was unclear. A bullet solved the quandary. Result: one heroic parrot.

A story closer to home also caught his eye. A family woke to find their house settling heavily, thudding down in spasms and then briefly free falling before another jarring halt. When the sun came up the light revealed that a giant sinkhole was trying to swallow the house. A mouth with teeth of quartz had chomped away the foundation. The hole kept growing and the first floor was vanishing, engulfed before their eyes. The family dog could not be found. All gone, including the bark. Result: unknown.

Seigle reread the story. One detail had escaped him the first time through, the family had recently drilled a new well. Their foundation must have been perched on a thin limestone crust. And once the water level dropped enough the crust collapsed. Neighbors 400 yards away could now smell gas. Not natural gas but petroleum. Seigle knew of a storage facility, suspected it wasn't far from that house. He scanned the article for an address but none was supplied. The earth is honeycombed with subsurface water, which is gradually being depleted. A leak anywhere in the storage tanks and gasoline could seep into the water table and be carried along for miles.

Norbert Casteret, an inveterate caver in the early part of the century, had located the source of the Garonne River with fluorescent dye, to prove that a proposed Spanish power project would affect the river's tributary on the French side of the border. That happened back in 1926, three years after he swam two sumps in Montespan to discover the world's oldest sculpture, a headless clay bear made by hand 20,000 years ago. Casteret gave up his law practice to follow his passion; it was all he had and he followed it every day. How could anyone forget that the earth was only one sphere, that the same waters began and ended somewhere?

Some Indian tribes, Seigle had heard, refused to recycle their bottles, cans, and paper, because they said it was the white man's burden. What one brings into this world he must carry out. But there was another tribe he had read about that wanted to use its reservation lands for a toxic waste dump, the land unfit for anything else. Some stubborn irony. Some fatalism.

His thoughts meandered. When an underground river re-surges, air rushes out with the stream. The river can run for miles and centuries, slowly eroding the rock beneath the surface. No one sees this happen, sees time become space: over time the water carves a dimensional space, a cave so large a man can panic in its vastness. If a caver moves beyond formations, shapes named for the world he knows, like "fried eggs"—a formation of large crystals that reflect a yellow yolk, surrounded by smaller crystals that reflect white; or other speleothems resembling the Statue of Liberty, the Empire State Building, a pipe organ, wedding cake and bells, famous profiles and even bacon strips—he or she might be lost among curved walls extending around, over, and through a darkness so enveloping as to be completely disorienting. You might as well be suspended upside down underwater without even a bubble trail to show you *up*. If a caver finds his bearing by compass to the center of a massive underground chamber, fear of open spaces, agoraphobia, can grip him. The young guy from the university who had joined them, Buck Simmons, had never tried caving again; and he had felt only an inkling of the terror that was possible, which could make your ticker leap, skip, or stop altogether.

But wasn't the fear what they were hoping for or against? By belaying, prusiking, rappelling? On the inside of the caver's skull there are no stars to guide the way as he picks through preserved records of rainfall, mineral deposits, temperature fluctuations from over thousands of years. All he's armed with is curiosity—a crude measure of a man. If palpitations begin and blood pounds in his chest, he stands in the darkness alone. He'd better be whole there, complete in himself, with every layer echoing until the cave exfoliates, heaves to light, a thin crust crackling like spring ice.

Seigle figured the sinkhole was in an area he knew; the incident told him he wasn't far off his mark. He could feel his old dark blood returning, the darkness that ran in his veins because of his passion for the underground. He knew the lesson of sinkholes well. If he didn't go out to meet his fear he would be eaten from within.

ON CHRISTMAS MORNING Seigle sat drinking his coffee at the usual grim hour. It felt like a workday with no work. He waited a decent amount of time and called his siblings to wish them a happy holiday. Then he went out to his private appointment—to walk for his heart. He found his buckskin gloves but not his red scarf, turned up the collar of his jacket and stepped out of the house. Then all at once he remembered: he'd tied it around that little boy's neck, Ian Robbins, back in September.

No driving to the woods today, to tramp among the ghost stalks of fall, over the last stains where the berries dropped. He set himself in motion, picked up the pace, and soon the sidewalk ran out, leaving him with a choice. He could turn back or plunge into a field marked "No Trespassing." The neighborhood was so empty of inhabitants at this hour that he might have been a tourist on earth the day after a nuclear disaster. He had no company but his own trails of smoky breath. He didn't feel like retracing his steps, so he climbed the fence against his better judgment, thinking he would be all right on this day of all days. No one would shoot him on Christmas morning.

One Christmas he had driven into town and watched three movies in a row. He only remembered one of them, *A Fish Called Wanda*. He had laughed until he had to rub his face to release smiling cramps. It was quiet there in the dark with the flickering projections. When there's nothing to be done about one's solitary condition, why make a bother. Simple is best. He had bought a large popcorn and enjoyed himself.

He picked a spot near a sturdy fence post but felt the sag of wire beneath his boot. With one leg poised on the top wire, he balanced for a second before making the short jump to the ground, into the field where he didn't belong. The *thump* of his boots landing with all of his weight on the ground sounded like the plunking of a ripe watermelon. *Mea culpa*, he thought, a bit cheerfully. For each of those movies he had paid full price, waiting in line and buying another large popcorn. He wasn't a rule-breaker, but it didn't feel so bad right now.

Mown close, the last hay baled back in November, the grassy field held nothing now but scattered clumps of straw, artificially green in arcs from fertilizer applied by machine. He stood for a moment beneath an overgrown apple tree and watched some cows sending up steamy flares while crunching their X of hay, which had been laid down by a tractor. The cow field was less than three miles from his house. Before long, probably, there would be nothing here but tract homes planted in tidy rows, with tiny lawns bordered by fences, each with its own abandoned dog barking all day. Next thing he knew he was scrambling up into that solitary apple tree, sending down a black soot of bark. As he pulled himself aloft, he squinted to keep the flakes out of his eyes. Branches broke as he climbed to the crotch where twin trunks split, fanning. He was only eight feet off the ground, but still two feet taller than his usual height. *Ass in a sling*, he thought. *Perfect*. Nothing to watch but cud-chewing critters, whistling up steam like copper kettles.

He remembered how the last woman had left him, leaving casseroles in the freezer with instructions on the kitchen table instead of a goodbye note. For once, he had done what she wanted and heated up the food slowly in the oven. He knew that now she was living alone, just as he was. A sad sort of symmetry. He wondered if he had ruined her. If she thought he had done that with his silence—which he had thought meant peace between them. He hadn't been with another woman since. Five years and not even a one-night stand. There was something about having been rejected without explanation that liberated him and something that had nailed down the lid. He didn't know whether he was afraid for himself or the hypothetical person on the other end, or whether it was just cowardice, the kind he felt when he sometimes unplugged his answering machine before leaving the house, because he didn't want to know at the end of the day that no one had called him. Some days it would be too much knowledge. In apple boughs, he sat precariously while the feeling drained out of his hands, which were holding on to limbs higher than his heart.

He had a mad urge to jump down from his perch and run across the field scattering the cows in every direction. With flailing arms he'd cut a swath through the morning stillness of a cold Christmas day that promised him nothing, not even a good snowstorm. The sky was lightening up. There'd be no white cover for this scarred ground. He did let himself down from the tree then, but slowly, slowly, while gently hugging the trunk. *You old tree hugger,* he thought. And the small thud of his weight rejoining ground disturbed nothing—not even a last brittle leaf twirled to the ground from a trembling branch.

The Land Between

Through the miserable, ghostly field Seigle resumed his walk. Thought about Turner, the old farmer—or whatever he was. Wondered what this day must be like for him. Seigle tried to picture him surrounded by grandchildren, even great-grandchildren, with twinkling eyes, each presenting the old grizzled cuss a handmade gift. He wanted Turner to be seated at the table's head. Steaming platters heaped with vegetables and roasted meat. Part of the food grown by his children on land he had given them. It would be soft food—potatoes, corn pudding, overcooked roast—that he could chew with the few strong teeth he had left that didn't pain him. Gradually the truth edged in. And Seigle knew how it probably was for Turner. Rising alone to shake the ash-coated coals to life again, fanning a glow into a flame. Shuffling outside for logs with sleep still heavy between his ears. Scratching through a crust of beard when he stroked his chin. Bending to stoke the wood stove and feeling an ache low in his back that never fully left him. Waiting for coffee. Pouring canned milk into the chipped cup for which the matching saucer was long broken. Christmas day like any other.

Seigle felt jabs of cold air in his lungs. Then he had to run, to escape his own thoughts. He startled the cows and flushed birds he hadn't known were there. The wings fanned into the air and scattered in a burst of sound and motion. Jogging most of the way he reached his house breathless, throat and chest knotted with a lump of cold air lodged high in his throat.

Inside again, his eyes fell on the row of colorful Christmas cards staggered across his mantel—cards sent mostly out of obligation from people he hardly knew. Workers at the plant and old college friends whose lives he had fallen out of years ago. They sent pictures of their children. Each year he watched their children grow taller, finally develop into teenagers, and then the Christmas letter said that they had gotten their driver's licenses, gone to college, taken first jobs. It was Christmas day and Seigle opened his freezer to see if he had anything stashed away that he could put into a pot and call stew or soup. He'd forgotten to get to the grocery store and now they were closed.

One half bag of corn, a dinner that had gone to freezer burn, and a whole pound of coffee beans. He decided to stay in motion, to get into his jeep and search for an open restaurant. He decided this and one other thing. He picked up the phone before his mind could reject the thought. He dialed. Five times it rang and he forced himself to hold on to the receiver, to refrain from hanging up. An answering machine clicked into Janis Joplin belting out her freedom anthem and again he struggled against instinct, counter-intuitive, wanting to dash the handset back onto the phone.

"Jessy," he began. "It's Seigle, Randy Seigle—"

Before he could form the sentence Jessy said, "Hello." She was back early from her parents'. They had opened their presents last night, Christmas Eve, because she had a story to write, a deadline. But later in the day she would go with him—where, it didn't matter. He arranged to pick her up.

THEY ENDED UP driving to look at lights. There was a house Jessy knew that was outlined in blue and red, the front yard filled with plywood angels and mangers and wise men and two-dimensional Santas with piped-in carols recorded by choirs no one had ever heard of. Frosty the snowman stood on the diving board, ready to belly-flop into the drained pool.

Turning down random roads, guided by nothing but whim, they followed the brightest lights and stopped to ogle. Farther and farther, they drove, finding a tiny little house with each window outlined in multi-colored bulbs, each tree obsessively strung with lights, and they wondered how the family could afford the extravagance. Crackling through an old drive-in speaker, Elvis was singing, "Blue Christmas."

"Some things are necessities," Jessy said. "Lights or ham—I'd take lights."

"I'd take the ham," Seigle said, admitting he was half-starved.

And then they took a turn and another, in search of a main road that would take them to a restaurant. What they found instead was a dark dead-end where a temporary barricade stopped them from going any farther. The jeep lights hit the reflective yellow and black stripes of a police barricade and then illuminated a sunken portion of a white house. Seigle got out of the jeep with his flashlight.

"Be careful," he said, as Jessy opened her door to take a look for herself.

The asphalt had given way about ten feet on the other side of the barricade. Seigle's beam fell on the house that was being swallowed.

"Jesus," Jessy said. "It's the sinkhole house."

"And it's still falling." Seigle shone his light into a cauldron of mud where some slowly moving earth was trailing down, disappearing into the giant hole that had opened. Only the second story and parts of the roof that hadn't caved in were above ground now. The rest had been eaten by the jaws of something too enormous to see. Seigle stood without speaking, shining his flashlight into the pit. Earth was shifting, little bit by bit, but constantly falling down. The hole was growing incrementally larger as they watched.

"If we stand here long enough, it will swallow us, too," Jessy said. She stepped back around the barricade and got into the jeep. "Come on. It gives me the creeps."

Seigle followed her, slipping behind the wheel. There was a long pause that took no measurable time. It was that pause in which two people look away from each other's eyes, deciding whether or not they could be lovers. Each knows the moment of decision has not yet arrived, but that it will. Each is living in the possibility, in that pause before heading into the dance or out the door.

Then Seigle started up the engine. His headlights flashed across the windows of the sinking house as he turned around.

THE UPHEAVAL: from *Tales of the Metempsychosis*

TRANSCENDENT ONE *was almost ready to die when the tale of Upheaval was finally told. Since that time the tale has been retold many times. No matter who tells the tale, it is Transcendent One's voice that guides the teller. No one knows the gender of Transcendent One, so the tale adapts to each teller. No matter who hears the tale, it is Transcendent One whose voice reaches the listener.*

So it was that when Transcendent One was lying on her straw mat moving closer to death with each breath, the shaman hovered over her waving a blue-black raven's feather.

"The past is before us," spoke the shaman. "But there is a piece missing from the picture. How can we turn around and face the future without the completion? Transcendent One, you must tell us our story of Upheaval."

Transcendent One's voice sounded strong, though her skin was a cracked carapace. "No matter how fast I go I hear something approaching. It is the truth giving the lie to the story."

"Your riddles are wise," spoke the shaman. "But show us the other side."

Transcendent One's eyes shone, flecked with mica. "Storytelling strings truth along until it catches up. The story of Upheaval has never been told, because the truth would beset the story like a wild dog, gnashing and leaping, and all the past would be in danger. The place of Upheaval is the first link. You call it history. But what comes before alters the meaning of what came afterward." The old one closed her eyes and rested.

But morning came again, and again the shaman requested that the first story be told. *"The past is all we can know. We must fashion the first link before you pass. You are the shield, Transcendent One, held between our past and our future, the known and the unknown, truth and fiction. You must tell us of our emergence."*

"When you know the place you will be more vulnerable, not less. For the present balances between truth and story, and once all stories are told, all time will be as one." The wise one shook her head in a knowing way and said, *"Confusion."*

"You cannot take our story with you!"

"I cannot?"

The shaman bowed and spoke more softly. *"We hope that you will not. It belongs to all of us."*

"As you wish. Perhaps you will learn the wisdom of listening and holding your tongues." Transcendent One began to speak. Here the voice of the old story takes over.

TRANSCENDENT ONE *lay as though dead, in the far chamber underground when the Upheaval cracked open the cavern ceiling. It was as though she flew, then, through the top of her head. The burst of light was that sudden and odd. She who had been left for dead climbed from the cavern, following swords of sunlight. She thought she had died, until she felt her muscles' aching and saw the blood rise from scrapes she suffered as she scaled higher and higher. The skeletons of all those who had been left for dead glistened beneath her, bright bones flooded with light. She was obviously not dead. She kept moving.*

One way of transcendence is through the body, not around it or without. As a woman, this was something Transcendent One already understood. She had given birth to three children in the cavern, and with each birth her belief strengthened. Her body made a space for life. Her body taught her spirit of the world within the world, the invisible world that bursts forth. When Strong Fist, her first son, was born, she knew the truth of the body meant responsibility. She, who had given life, embraced it with fierce protection. For reasons unknown, the slow up-thrusting of mountains began. The crust of the world cracked and became convoluted, sending waters plunging away from the inner places. Where seas had flowed basins were left, dry playas, empty sinks full of residual salt where the deep blue bodies had been pulled by the tides. The crystal bodies sparkled in the basin lands, and many people were cured by rubbing these sparkling salts over their skins.

Where the crack had opened there was now a steep mountain studded with dark boulders that appeared to be spilling down its slopes. It was here that the tribe's new life above ground had begun.

Transcendent One had long recognized the mountain as the place of the first crack, but because she had been feared as the one who had come back from the far chamber, the old ones had deferred to her, allowing her to keep her silence until she was the last of them left alive to speak of it. Now this young shaman wanted to know the exact location of the tribe's sacred ground. Until her last day Transcendent One had only said that the place was alive and therefore subject to change. Transcendent One feared that the earth itself would become an idol for her race—or worse, that the tribe would strip away the soil, little bit by little bit, each seeking a fistful of its special power. Knowing that faith in what is seen can only disappoint, Transcendent One gave instruction along with the facts the shaman craved.

"The black, knobby mountain is the mouthpiece of the world. Ascend this mountain and at the summit you should give thanks on the very angle that first turned up. Lift your

arms there and feel the air in your hair. Turn and bless the four directions—White, Red, Yellow, Black—and beware of the illusion under your feet." Transcendent One closed her eyes then and never opened them.

The pyre of Transcendent One's passage was still billowing when the shaman led the first group up the slopes of the black, knobby mountain. Many arguments had broken out concerning who would make the pilgrimage and whether it should be limited to those of a certain age or restricted to those who believed in the shaman's blessings. Some even said that if you were half turtle not whole you should not be included. Finally, consensus decreed a lottery, so the first group contained women, men, and children of all descriptions. Their journey took a whole day, sunup to sunset.

Upon reaching the summit, the party found that their water skins were empty and their throats parched, yet they followed the shaman's directions when he told them, "Lift up your arms and feel the air stir your hair." The shaman led them in prayer, blessing the four directions. He omitted or forgot to repeat Transcendent One's most important words, "Beware of the illusion beneath your feet."

On the slopes of the black, knobby mountain, the Turtle tribe began leaving signs of its passage. Here, on the dark volcanic boulders, they incised their first stories. As years passed, more and more stories found their way onto the boulders, chiseled and scratched onto dark rock. The light stone beneath the dark patina shone out of the rocks to be read in figures and words.

When Turtle children came of age they were brought to black, knobby mountain to learn the early stories and to start the story of their lives. Each boulder held the story of one member of the tribe, the version of that life that he or she wanted to tell. No one knew whether the stories held up the mountain or the mountain held up the stories.

Thus, the instruction of Transcendent One, to "beware

the illusion beneath your feet" was carried out despite the shaman's negligence.

At the Foot of Owl Mountain

SHE WAS WALKING to the edge of the neighborhood, past the houses and their neat, watered squares of misplaced grass, along the sidewalk, to the far end of the community park. The fence was not high, chest level, yet no one crossed it. A "No Trespassing: Keep out" sign hung on the top wire. Even the children had lost curiosity. The fence at the far end of their playing field had become an invisible border. To cross it would be to travel beyond the limits of order. So far no one had hit a ball hard enough to send it over. Moira paused before the fence, briefly hesitating. Beyond the fence stood the craggy shape of Owl Mountain, loose buff-colored soil strewn with dark, varnished boulders.

Once she had hoisted herself across the fence, over that barrier, she began following an overgrown path toward the base of Owl Mountain. Creosote bushes hunkered along her route. Some dry, green thorny cat's claw bushes pricked at her jacket sleeves. She kept walking.

At the foot of Owl Mountain, she came to the first cluster of dark volcanic rocks. This grouping was small and looked almost staged. They reminded her of the paper boulders shouldered and hurled with accompanying grunts by Ben Hur. But when she leaned against them they held her weight; they were solid. Their odd markings beckoned her to squat beside them. In her knees and spine she felt the pull of gravity and nearly toppled backward. The one who chiseled this parallel zigzag pattern into the rock must have squatted here, pitched forward on the balls of his feet while he worked. The other rock was etched with a lone, fat-bodied figure: triangle head atop stick limbs. It looked something like a turtle balanced on hind legs, walking with its shell before it like a shield. But if a turtle walked forward, upright, the soft shell of its belly would greet the world. Like a human being, she thought. Stone parts guard the back and the stomach proceeds where the arms could wield a shield and a club.

She rose and followed the path, winding up, feeling the strain in her calves as the climb grew steeper. The water in each cell of her body pooled, pulling down sharply. Each of her steps felt perilous, though determined, a strategy of hard-won moves against a wicked incline. The boulders thickened, then rose higher, stacked irregularly in giant mounds. Moira could not see beyond them and walked quickly between angled walls that sheltered the path but created a hazard of jutting edges. And from that living rock a thorny weed reached out and scratched her forehead bringing forth a seam of blood she didn't pause to stanch. As she walked the walls of rock closed in on her; she was losing breath and orientation, pushing herself faster than she felt able to go. Panic rose through her chest, and when it reached heart level she pushed back at it, caught with no choice but to go forward. Then she popped out, free of the claustrophobic maze.

Tilting her head back, inhaling deeply, she glimpsed the pinnacle of Owl Mountain, no more than a dark shape of stone silhouetted by fierce shafts of bitter sun. Squinting, she shaded her eyes, yet discerned no more detail at the top. All along her passage random petroglyphs appeared on the massive boulders, so many that her eyes darted between them without settling for long on any one pattern. She saw a spiral. A hunter with raised spear. A snail. Rain clouds pouring rain. An elk. A lizard. A turtle with cracked shell, each half on one side of a crack in the rock. Her eye lingered in the crack, where something essential was missing.

Into the space of the crack, she looked. She peered so searchingly she forgot her reason for being there, for having begun to look, for initiating this climb up Owl Mountain. From the crack and the darkness within it, she heard her name being called, "Moira." This is when she thought, *I must be dreaming.*

Space. Emptiness. She searched but saw nothing more. The communication formed internally, unspoken. She heard it clearly. It was a plaintive voice that issued from a deep juncture in the petroglyph, from the crack in the rock, between the two halves of the turtle's shell.

"You must help."

"Who are you?" Moira asked.

"I was born once, but I am not of your world. I have returned to mine. My tribe has survived many lifetimes. Long ago we migrated from inside your earth. Eventually we took refuge in the greater lights."

"The stars?" she asked.

"Something like that."

Moira saw the cracked shell open farther, the two halves breaking apart. The acne-scarred face of a man, pocked as the surface of a pond in a patter of raindrops, appeared to her. He pulled his arms around his body to conserve what strength he had left.

"Many of my race are dying," the voice continued. "Enough will survive by burrowing into our new earth, by conservation of moisture. The harsh heat of the sun has been killing us, our skins are cracking open. Our sun has turned cruel. A hole opened in the top of our world and the sun pours in without a filter now. It is time for your planet to find another fuel, or your race will go the way of mine. We will survive, but you will not."

The acne-scarred face receded, replaced by an image of

two women. One lay face down and did not stir. Slowly the other woman placed a rock on her back, and then, while weeping, stacked rock after rock until the pile of rocks had covered the body beneath them.

"Moira." She heard her name again, the images faded away, and she felt Paul shaking her awake. He had returned from taking Ian for a Christmas night drive to look at the lights; they had left Moira to rest on the couch.

Torn paper, box lids and bows were still strewn about the room along with the gifts they had given each other. She had fallen asleep before she could clean up. Christmas fell a little hard on her—it was the time of year her father had left. His leaving was a body-memory that recurred. And going through the motions of preparation, especially decorating the tree with the ornaments that she had known since childhood, always made her think of her mother. How she missed her. But the way she felt now was due to more than exhaustion, and different from holiday blues.

She could hear everything Paul said, but her eyes would not open. She couldn't force them, although she could feel her eyeballs fluttering, jerking beneath the lids. Her vocal chords felt cramped around a word, locked down. She struggled to produce a sound.

"I—" she said

"Open your eyes," Paul directed her.

"Mom," Ian said and touched her hand.

Moira struggled to move her hand to acknowledge her son, but it rested limply at her side.

Paul sent Ian to his room.

"But Dad..."

"Go, please, now."

Paul whispered into Moira's ear. "You're scaring me. Should I call an ambulance?"

"No—" The word edged past her constricted throat.

She could feel her eyes twitching beneath the lids and

Paul's light touches on her arms and hands. She listened to his breathing close to her and saw orange flickers beneath her eyelids. She waited, suspended between sleep and waking.

"I can see your eyes working—you're in R.E.M., but you're not asleep," Paul said.

She opened her eyes briefly, and they fell closed. Paul touched her hand and she was able to grasp it and squeeze back. She struggled to sit up in bed.

"You look pale. Put your head down if you can before you pass out."

With Paul's help, Moira was able to shift to the edge of the bed and let her head drop between her legs. The blood rush made her eyes feel heavier. After a time she slowly raised her head, seeing lights beneath her still closed eyelids. Something like bright stars jittered in a pool of moving water. All of her cells collected at the top of her skull.

"Small sips." Paul helped her take some water.

She took a bit of water. But she was still unable to open her eyes.

"Moira, what's happening to you? I think we should call Dr. Ross."

Moira concentrated on her breath.

She had been approximating the motions of normalcy, while she walked the border between her old self and a new self she hardly knew. Had she reached the point of no return? The spontaneity had leached out of her every action and response. Whatever excuse she offered for her distant behavior, Paul had accepted. He'd look at her oddly and then she could see the wheels of rationalization turn in her favor. After all, she was pregnant. Any excuse at all—"My ankles are swollen," "My head's swimming," "I feel like a water buffalo"—and he latched onto it, smiled with indulgence. "I'll cook tonight," he would offer, keeping their lives on a steady course, as though nothing essential had changed.

Now she felt a hole opening dangerously beneath her. Over it, she balanced without a net, aware of the distance she could fall and letting go of more and more of herself in order to appear unchanged.

"You can talk to me," Paul said. He took one of her cold hands and warmed it between his palms. He reached for the other hand and warmed it gently.

Moira opened her eyes and found her voice. Between sips of water, she let the story spill out. She told him about the voices she heard, the dreams she could remember, her fainting spell with Trisha. Her visit to Renée's.

Paul listened to everything without interrupting or questioning. A wrinkle of concern deepened in his forehead. When she had finished, he said, "I don't know what to say. I believe what you're telling me, yet how can it be true?"

Moira rested her eyes. This is what she had feared. The scientist in Paul. She tried to keep herself calm. "I'm asking you to trust me. I know this is hard to believe. I don't believe it myself, but it's happening. I have no choice. When Regina told me I was pregnant—"

"Regina?"

"—it all clicked into place. Yes. Regina. She's a psychic-friend of Trisha's."

"She left a message for you. She's in the hospital." All at once Paul burst into nervous laughter.

"What's so funny?"

"She's calling you on the phone. Why didn't she just wiggle her nose?"

"Because that's not how it works. Is she all right?"

Paul stopped laughing. "She sounded fine."

"I trust you when you talk about Nonlinear Dynamics, or Godel's Incompleteness Theorem," Moira said.

"But those are scientific theories."

"Yes, and I can repeat a theory without understanding it. Like, incompleteness posits that no system can ever fully describe itself, because to do so would mean that it could fully separate from itself."

"Exactly," Paul said. "And I'll give you another one. The laws of physics dictate that no signals of any kind can travel faster than the speed of light. As signals travel, they lose strength."

She knew he was pleading with her now, though on the surface he tried to stay matter of fact. "Meaning?" she asked.

"It's impossible for you—or anyone—to pick up conversations out of the air at those distances, or to hear them before they happen. Come on, Moira, you understand this as well as I do." Paul was pacing the room.

"Actually I don't. And I never have. I have to trust you."

"But it's not me you're trusting—it's science."

"For me, it's trust in something I cannot see."

Paul sat down on the bed beside her. "What am I supposed to do about all of this? What you're telling me defies everything I know."

"I don't think so. What about Chaos Theory—didn't you tell me it tracks repetitions and variables? This is a variable, but it's still part of the system." Moira grabbed his hand, held on. "And what about Bell's Theorem, doesn't that say something about effects at a distance?"

"Hold on," Paul said. "Just because a butterfly wing flutters in Africa and produces weather changes in Peoria, that doesn't mean that Newtonian physics doesn't cover 99.9% of daily life. Our material lives operate within fixed limits. If I knock something off the dresser it falls on the floor, and if I need to talk to someone outside of this house, I have to either go there or pick up the phone."

"There's a tenth of a percent left over, and I'm living in that percentage for some reason. I'm asking you to trust me."

Paul's eyes opened wider. She could feel his urge to fix everything, shore up the changes. He shook his head. "I don't know if I can," he said.

"Paul, this is about who I am."

"What about our family?"

"We're still a family."

"I wanted you to see a professional—and now I insist. We need some expert advice. What if you're in danger? What if one of these trances, if that's what it is, hits you when you're driving the car, driving Ian?"

"I will do anything to help you accept this—to help myself."

Paul gathered Moira into his arms, clinging to her. "You'll go then, you'll see someone?"

"A psychiatrist, you mean?"

"I suppose so."

"I said I would go." Moira fought the urge to stiffen. She relaxed in Paul's embrace, wanting to believe that there could be a bond between two people that was so strong that no circumstance dare break it.

It was Paul who pulled away first. "Let me just go check on Ian," he said.

Moira heard Carlos barking at the back door. In a few minutes he came careering into the living room, bounding toward Moira's ready lap. She wrapped her arms around him and rubbed his floppy ears. He was real, like the Velveteen Rabbit, with patches of fur loved away, as limp as a sleepy kitten. He'd gotten a bowl for Christmas with his name painted on the side.

Paul came back into the room and grabbed Carlos by the collar, pulling him off Moira. "My turn, pal." Paul lay down on the couch and slipped his head into Moira's lap. Carlos slunk off to his new bed.

"How's Ian?" Moira asked, stroking Paul's hair.

"Already asleep. He'd put himself to bed." Paul pulled Moira beside him, kissing her, pressing against her chest.

"Easy," Moira said. "Those hurt."

"Too much?" Paul asked.

"I'm fat," Moira said.

"You're perfect."

"I'm perfectly fat, then."

"And I'm the King of Spam. Hey, Baby, let me lick your can."

"You're terrible."

Paul reached for the buttons on her blouse. He sank his teeth around one, attempting to push it loose from the buttonhole with his tongue. "Tough little button you have there," he said.

"Not so tough." Moira helped him with the buttons, letting her blouse fall from her shoulders. "Shouldn't we head to the bedroom?"

Paul reached to unclasp her bra.

"Careful," she said.

"I'll treat them like royalty. You can always tell royalty by their noses," Paul said. His tongue played over her breasts.

Carlos appeared over Paul's shoulder.

"Go to bed," Paul told him. "Bedtime, pal, you're breaking my stride."

"Go on, Carlos," Moira said.

"Why did Ian name him that?" Paul asked.

"There's a Carlos in his class. Go on, boy."

Carlos trotted off. Moira heard him settle into his bed again, rustling the cedar shavings.

Paul reached for her, slipping his hand beneath her waistband. They undressed fully then and rolled toward each other like planets in gravitational correction. The pull was still strong and favored two bodies over one. Paul and Moira knew each other's rhythms well, but with pregnancy an air of the unfamiliar heightened the excitement. The third body growing between them stirred at the center of their lovemaking.

They eased to the floor, making space amidst the torn

Christmas wrappings. Paul pressed into Moira as if he were searching for the one who slept behind the wall, gently probing the membrane that separated that small life from the whirling systems holding it in place.

Moira felt herself giving way, shuttering quickly toward a final convulsion of pleasure. Each of them was holding off, waiting for the other. She wanted all of Paul and she raised herself toward his thrusts until they rocked together, breathless. Layer upon layer shifted within her, gripped her with spasms of relief and joy. Since Ian's birth she'd been able to feel long rippling orgasms that drenched her, wave after wave.

She opened her eyes to the blinking Christmas tree lights. Fires seemed to ignite and travel down the tree from the gold foil star Ian had made. The light moved all around the limbs until it illumined the branches near her face.

"Looks like we nearly knocked down the tree," Moira said.

"You rock my tree, that's for sure." Paul grinned at her like a kid.

The lights kept blinking, sending twinkling colors over the ceiling and walls, and over the features of the lovers who were too tired to move off the floor.

Dinosaur Tattoos

"I TAKE IT you enjoyed the caver's company?" Moira asked, holding the phone to her ear.

"Do you realize that caves have to be discovered on foot? No aerial instruments can detect them. Randy Seigle told me about this cave in Borneo—more than a dozen football fields could fit inside it, and it was just discovered less than twenty years ago."

"Fascinating." Moira laughed.

"Sorry, woman. You could say it's been a long dry spell here in the nunnery. You might say I've been immured."

"Sounds like you've roused some interest."

"I wish. We didn't get that far. It was only one date in the height of the religious season. But you know it was perfect somehow. Weird, but perfect. No groping, just driving around looking at lights and sinkholes."

"You're kidding about the sinkhole, I hope."

"Well, not exactly. It's a long story. I just hope he calls again."

"He will. Give it some room to breathe."

"You know, sometimes your sympathy makes me feel like a loser. He's top of the line, wolfhound, you know."

"So are you," Moira said. "Top of the line something else."

"There you go again. So what's new with you?"

"Nothing much. I'm pregnant."

Jessy sucked in air. "I didn't know you all were trying.

Congratulations."

"No plan, but everyone's happy with the idea."

Jessy cut to the chase. "What about you. Are you happy, too?"

"What else am I going to do?"

"Lots of things. But you are a good mother. Remember when that ancient photographer—what's her name—was interviewed about whether her children had interfered with her work and she said that parenting had only taken twenty years of her life. *Only twenty years*! Chin up."

"And what would you know about it?" Moira said.

"Nothing at all, but I know you—and you will figure it out."

Moira wanted to say more, but she didn't know how to begin. It wasn't something you could drop into a conversation. How would she phrase it exactly, *and by the way I'm clairvoyant*? Instead, she said, "You're the gorgeous one with the interesting career. And a mysterious caveman calling you. All I do is bake cookies."

"You know that's not true. I miss you," Jessy said.

No, it wasn't true, Moira thought. "I miss you, too," she said.

They signed off, promising to call more often.

MOIRA HAD MADE AN APPOINTMENT with a psychiatrist recommended by their new family physician. She hadn't told him why she needed one, only that she was anxious. Great impression she was making on the new doctor. Part of her resented Paul for urging this on her and part of her was still hoping for a cure. Until the appointment date she threw herself into making their home complete. With Ian off from school and Paul undertaking a lighter schedule in the week after Christmas it reminded her of the old days, when the three of them together made a world.

Ian was still heavily interested in Indian lore. Every day

they spent time reading from a book of legends. She propped the book on her subtly swelling belly. She read a story of a hummingbird that hovered over the world as if it were a sweet flower. When the hummingbird dove for its nectar, its long beak pierced through the world and stuck fast. The world started tilting, and the seasons were born. Ice and snow, wind and rain were added to the sunshine the world had known before. *Whenever an earthquake rumbles,* she read, *it is the hummingbird trying to let go.*

Ian's favorite story was a particularly frightening creation myth about a chief whose wife gave birth to four monsters. He asked Moira to read it over and over again. The monster-children grew to terrorize their tribe and were eventually destroyed by a turtle that burrowed beneath them so that they were carried off in four directions, becoming the points of the compass: North, South, East, and West.

"Why do you like this story so much?" Moira asked Ian.

On the page facing the last paragraph of the story was a human figure with antler protrusions on its head. Ian pointed to the antlers. "Broder saw them like this."

Broder had become Ian's regular sitter and the local representative of everything cool. "Indians with headdresses?" Moira asked. "Where?"

"Broder said they were like horns that glowed in the dark." Ian traced the antlers with his index finger. "Broder said they were in an orange grove."

"I'd like to see some petroglyphs," Moira said. "Were they near here?"

"Broder saw the other people, in the antlers," Ian nearly whispered.

"What other people?" Moira placed her hand over Ian's. His idle rubbing of the image was getting on her nerves.

"I'm not sure," Ian said.

"Where did he see them?"

"Don't be mad at me." Ian turned suddenly from the book and looked at her.

"I'm not mad at you," Moira said. "But Broder shouldn't tell you scary stories like that."

"I'm not scared," Ian said. "You know those stories you read to me about the Turtle tribe?"

Moira nodded.

"I tried to find them for my teacher in the book at school and they're not there."

Moira turned the page of the book in her lap to its table of contents. Each Turtle tale was listed. "It must be a different book," she said.

"It's not," Ian said. "It's this same book. I took it to school and she couldn't find any Turtle tales."

Moira didn't respond, didn't know how to. Ian had to be mistaken. She closed the book and suggested that Ian try out the press-on dinosaur tattoos Santa had left in his stocking. When Paul came home from work he found his wife and son bearing prehistoric reptiles on their faces, hands, and arms.

The Butterfly Effect

The good doctor's office was located on the ninth floor. The last button on the elevator panel was labeled "ROOF GARD," which Moira took to be a garden while picturing an armed guard stationed on the roof. A garden on the roof—this was what the natural world was coming to, what too much of it was already. *They really did pave paradise.*

No receptionist greeted her. She had her choice of three overstuffed wing-backed chairs tastefully done in a pattern of crewel flowers on muslin. An aquarium held a gulping Oscar that was outgrowing his tank. In the small waiting room Moira flipped through a slick issue of *Architectural Digest*. She was almost glad to be seeing this shrink. Regina had called her again and the call had left Moira more than uneasy. "There's something I need to talk with you about that cannot wait any longer—why haven't you called me back?" Regina had begun.

The opulence of the magazine photographs—the wrought iron and expensive fabrics, the oriental rugs, followed by endless glass and wood—like rich food, made her slightly sick to her stomach. But maybe it was her nerves. In less than five minutes the door opened. A small pale man in an excellent suit extended his hand.

"I'm Dr. Skruncmaren."

One of the corner windows she had seen from outside the building occupied the far end of the doctor's long, rectangular office. They sat opposite a coffee table in the darker end of the room. One small window behind Dr. Skruncmaren lent him a backlighted halo-effect, and prevented Moira from closely observing his expressions. She was trying hard to meet his eyes, to speak in an easy, familiar tone that would signify equanimity and mental health.

"Dr. Hanson referred you for anxiety, is that right?"

Absolutely not, Moira was thinking. "That's right," she said.

"Why don't you tell me about it," he said brightly. His light eyebrows were beginning to grow haywire, the mark of a man in middle age, yet his skin remained unlined, forehead uncannily devoid of wrinkles or mobility. Moira wondered if he had indulged in a little self-administered aesthetic medicine—or maybe a lobotomy.

"I'm here because my husband suggested I come. I'm pregnant and I haven't been feeling like myself the last few months." She thought that sounded neutral enough.

"How were you feeling before the pregnancy?" he asked.

"About the same—without the morning sickness." Moira laughed, but the doctor did not. He just gazed at her expectantly. Did he know it was a joke? She laughed too loudly. "I don't really have morning sickness," she said, into dead air.

"When did your feelings begin to change, then?"

"Right after we moved out here, I suppose."

"Before the pregnancy?"

"Yes." Moira stared away from the doctor, toward the far corner window. She could see nothing but sky. Regina had asked her to help the police in the East Mojave. The man and two women who had vanished still hadn't been found, and Regina's energy level was too low after having had a cyst removed. "Call Detective Taylor at the Needles police station. I've worked with him before." Moira didn't even know where Needles was, she told Regina, and then she remembered she had seen it on the map. "Don't let this drop," Regina had said. "It's not something you can pick up and put down."

"Why don't you tell me how you've been feeling," the doctor said.

"I really don't think I can do that," Moira said, composure vanishing.

The doctor held his hands in his lap. He was waiting.

"It's not so much a question of my feelings as of what has been happening to me," Moira said.

"Why don't you describe your experiences then."

She was here for Paul, she told herself. And if this man gave her the right prescription her life could go back to normal, despite what Regina had said, "This isn't a hobby, Moira, God's hand is on you. Think about what kind of holiday those families had not knowing what happened."

"I—" she stopped herself. She focused on the patch of light sky she could see outside, out the corner window. She could not look at him, but she began. "Sometimes, I hear voices that are not in the room."

"What do the voices say?"

"They are having conversations."

"About you?"

"No. Not about me, about their own lives. They're just having a conversation, and I happen to overhear them somehow." Moira took a deep breath and paused. She looked at him now. His expression gave away nothing.

"At first the voices mixed together," she said, "but now I can hear them distinctly." She told him about hearing Renée and her husband, and about her frustrating but confirming visit to her neighbor's the same day. "I couldn't help her," Moira said. "She wouldn't talk to me."

Dr. Skuncmaren nodded. "How did that make you feel?"

"Helpless. I know something about people that they haven't told me. And then what do I do with that? I just want to live my own life, but I don't know how to do that anymore."

"You must be a very empathetic listener," he said. "People give off a thousand subtle clues in conversation—that you must pick up on without even knowing how you do it."

"Are you telling me that I hear voices at a distance—because I'm a good listener?" Moira felt her adrenaline surge.

"Why do you think it is happening?" He remained poised.

Maybe she should make up some story about how her mother locked her in the closet with the family dog when she was barely two. Or what about that potty-training incident when she was forced to swallow goldfish? She looked the doctor squarely in the eye. "I came here so you could tell me why this is happening to me. If you have no earthly idea, just say so."

"I think we can get to the bottom of these phenomena, but it's going to take some time. And some diagnostic tests would be useful."

Moira sank into her chair. This was just the kind of thing Paul felt comfortable relying on, something smeared on a slide. "What kind of tests?" she asked.

"We'll look at the matrixes created by your preferences, nothing stressful. You'll choose answers that best reflect your feelings about yourself and people close to you. Some of my patients consider the tests a pleasant activity."

Which ones, she wondered. The sociopaths or the agoraphobics? Question: would you rather ax your father (mother) or go on a cruise? Question: If you could steal twenty dollars and never be caught, would you do it? Question: Do you ever feel constipated? This was the trick question, the baseline, which would show up unexpectedly to gauge your honesty.

"I don't think so," Moira said.

"Your insurance will cover the expense."

"You don't seem to understand this any better than I do," Moira said.

"The tests could prove more useful than you think."

"You haven't heard me," Moira said.

"You can understand what is happening to you if you're willing to process the causes," he said. His little pink tongue clicked against perfectly capped teeth when he spoke.

Every summer Moira's mother had taken her to the beach, even if it they could only afford a weekend. She remembered having dived beneath waves, trying for perfect timing. Once, she had dived beneath a wave and been caught, slung up feet first, while her head sought the wrong direction. It was like being born feet first, like floating in gray darkness forever. Thinking down was up, she was using every ounce of strength. The more she flailed and kicked against the current the more her lungs felt ready to explode. With her air running out, she had clung to nothing but her own will, clinging with all of her strength to her original plan: that the arc of her diving would pop her up just as the wave crashed over her. She couldn't let go of that notion and continued to struggle in the wrong direction. In time, her air did run out and she had to let go, stop kicking, stop thrashing, stop breathing, stop. Her limp body surrendered. And then the surf spit her out on the shore with its graceful treachery. She had saved herself by letting go. Coughing salt water, she had raised her head off the sand and gulped the stinging air.

Moira knew then that no one could possibly explain herself to herself, and that she could spend all of her own energy defying who she was if she were not careful. Regina's explanation was probably better than most. "God's hand." When Moira had insisted that her life was her own, god damn it, Regina had said, "Your life is a gift, one part of the whole fabric." Moira had to act on the knowledge she was given, live through her own experience. What, then, had been stopping her? She was no different from anyone else. All she had was one moment at a time. The rest was illusion, or the price of listening to fear. Each butterfly wing beat to its own rhythm, but the air stirred because of the wings, changing weather patterns continents away. She would be a pebble dropped in a pond; she would be a moving wing.

"If this shit were happening to you," Moira stared the doctor down, "maybe you wouldn't be so fucking condescending."

Dr. Skruncmaren's mouth hung open like a tiny bird's, but he uttered not a peep.

Moira rose from the chair onto her swollen ankles and smoothed her dress. It was an old paisley sack that had the advantage of being unbelted. She had worn it when she was pregnant with Ian, and thank god she had saved it from the ragbag. The dress would expand as she did. She found her own way out of the office.

Moira walked steadily to her car. She drew in a deep breath, all the way to the pit of her stomach. Letting it out gently, she felt the calm of her body. No twitching muscles or tightened neck, her back was straight and shoulders level. At ease. It was as if she had everything she needed in one place.

She got out her phone and called information.

"What city?"

"Needles. The police station there," Moira said.

WITHOUT A MAP

"MOIRA, DON'T DO THIS. I'll be worried all day. You've never even met this man, Taylor." Paul's defiant lock of hair drifted over his eye.

"I have to go." Moira reached out to touch Paul's arms that were strapped across his chest protectively.

"It's such a long drive out there."

"That's why I have to get started early."

"Jesus, it's not even dawn."

"I'll be fine." Moira hugged him while he hugged his chest. At the last second he unwrapped one arm to lightly pat her on the back. She was giving him a full hug and receiving less than half a hug in return. Moira felt his distance tug at her decisions. "Paul, I didn't choose this. It chose me."

"You could say no."

"I have tried and it doesn't work. I have to live the life I'm given." Moira released him.

"What about my life, *our* lives, Ian's? The baby's?" One by one, Paul was pulling out all the stops.

"We'll have to figure it out as we go along. I don't know how we'll do it, but I know we can figure it out." Moira had never worn the shell bracelet after Martin and Cindy had given it to her at the welcome party. Today, she had slipped the unbroken circle over her wrist.

Paul didn't answer. Maybe he didn't want to say what he was thinking then, but his arms were tightly folded over his chest again. Moira walked past him toward the garage. Before she had backed out there was a peck on the glass. She lowered the window.

"Call me," Paul said. "I want to know you're all right. Call me tonight."

"I will." She remembered all of the times she had waited for him—and later he had said he was too busy to call.

Ian had given her a geode for Christmas. She placed it on the passenger seat and occasionally reached over to touch it. Brushing her finger across the rough interior crystals, she drove toward the morning sun, along the route that so many had driven in the opposite direction, west from Texas and the whole dust bowl into California.

The sun caught her eyes and she fought the glare with a visor that was just this side of long enough. Or maybe she wasn't quite tall enough in the seat. The road unfurled like a fire-eating dragon, as she squinted, trying to stay inside the lines. She felt she was driving outside of any town or time. No one seemed to have lived along this road, and yet it was filled with moving cars and trucks. Right up to the gateway to California there was constant movement along old Route 66, which defined the American highway: constant movement along an axis of pure desire.

In a tangle of juniper and yucca an old black truck rested on its hood. Rust outlined all of its seams, like iron ore in a seam of earth. No visible tires, and probably no engine beneath the crumpled, upside down hood. Any usable parts had been long stripped. The truck probably wasn't much older than some of the vehicles traveling alongside her, rust on wheels. After the next century's turn, she wondered if the abandoned truck would still be balanced on its cab, eternally emptying its load.

How were so many people, who had lost so much—more than shreds of rubber and shards of glass—able to arrive at their destinations? Up on the ridge a wind farm's twirling paddles and spindles caught her eye. The motion tossed streamers of sunlight in its wake, making the sun seemingly the prime mover instead of the invisible wind. Paul had said that late spring and summer were peak seasons for the production of wind energy, but now it was mid-winter and the wheels still spun to an unheard percussion. The obelisks with wings might have been dreamcatchers, woven circles spun by unseen energy. Ian was making one now, weaving colored yarn around a black, center eye.

From the antenna of an abandoned red station wagon, she saw a white T-shirt waving in distress or surrender. She kept driving.

The East Mojave

THE VISITOR'S CENTER crouched before pitted walls of burnished, volcanic rock. Beneath its overhanging roof was a large wrap-around porch. In the parking lot, wind was whipping loose earth into clouds of dust. There was only one other parked vehicle, a small truck filled with hay.

Moira threw open her door and felt the cold, dry air hit her lungs. She clutched her collar as she walked, to close the gap between it and the red scarf she had hastily looped at her throat. She'd been meaning to send the red, hand-knitted scrap of a scarf back to Seigle via Jessy but kept forgetting.

The young man pulled his boots off the desk when the door banged back. "Welcome to Hole-in-the-Wall," he said, running his hand over the scant sprouts atop his head. He was one of those pale, baby-faced men who had probably been balding from birth. What kind of dog would Jessy call this one, Moira wondered. She couldn't think of any nearly hairless breeds, but she knew they must exist.

A well-used kerosene heater was cranking out the only heat. Near it lay a sleeping, ninety-pound Golden Retriever. "Down boy," the young man joked, when Moira glanced toward the dog.

"I'm meeting Detective Taylor here," Moira said.

"It's Charles," the young man said, extending his hand. "Taylor? He's been out here a few times."

Moira shook it quickly and introduced herself.

"Dave," he said in response, leaving Moira uncertain of which name went with the man and which with the dog.

"It's sure cold up here," she said.

"By afternoon it might warm up to fifty. Up at Midhills elevation it's always ten or fifteen degrees colder. We've got it good down here."

Moira moved toward one of the large bulletin boards that caught her eye. "Tips for Desert Survival," she read.

"Yeah, like you're going to remember those." Dave or Charles shook his head, and laughed. It sounded more like a spastic attack.

Moira read the rest of the notice silently: "1) When planning a trip into the desert, always inform someone as to where you are going, your route and when you expect to return. Stick to your plan. 2) Carry at least one gallon of water per person per day. 3) Be sure your vehicle is in good condition. 4) Keep your eye on the sky. Flash floods may occur in a wash any time thunderheads are in sight, even though it may not rain a drop where you are...."

In all, twenty items of helpful information made her skin crawl. She was wondering who would ever leave a vehicle for the comforts of bajadas and alluvial fans when she read "a vehicle can be seen for miles, but a person on foot is very difficult to find. Do not sit or lie directly on the ground. It may be 30 degrees hotter than the air. Do not remove shoes. You may not be able to get them back on swollen feet."

"I won't have to worry about the heat today," she said.

"You'll notice there's no mention of snakes—"

"Snakes?"

"But it's not because we don't have them. The Mojave green is deadly," Dave or Charles said.

"Won't it be hibernating now?"

"I'd step lightly. You wouldn't want to disturb a dreaming snake." He rubbed his hand quickly over his fuzzy head, brushing some imaginary strands from his eyes.

The Golden woke up, stretched, ambled over, and began sniffing vigorously at Moira's crotch.

"Friendly dog," Moira said, trying to push his nose away as she patted his head.

The door seemed to blow open on its own, as a large broad-shouldered man with polished skin the color of a Kenyan coffee bean entered with the gust of wind. His loud sneezing was incongruous with his taut, muscular build.

"Yo, Taylor," the young man greeted him.

"Yo, Dave," Taylor said wryly, clearing up one mystery for Moira.

Dipping a long finger into the pocket of his parka, Taylor pulled out a handkerchief. "They told me my allergies would clear up once I moved to California. I'm from Cleveland. Turned out it was dust and pollution I was allergic to." Taylor croaked a laugh. "And cat dander."

"Well, at least you're safe from that," Moira said and introduced herself.

"Cats came from the desert originally," Dave interjected.

"I don't know if I can be of any help," Moira said.

"Don't worry about it. I respect results, and Regina gets the job done. If she recommended you, we'll give it a shot. Myself, I've got about as much resonance as a rock." Taylor wiped at his nose with the still neatly folded handkerchief.

"Got my wheels stuck on Wildhorse Canyon road yesterday. Couple of hunters pulled me out," Dave said.

Taylor raised his eyebrows.

"They hadn't seen crap. I asked."

Taylor turned to Moira, all business. "Let's go have a look at the Midhills camp site, with a stop along the way. If you're ready."

The significance of this was lost on Moira, but she answered, "Of course." Her eyes wavered back to the bulletin board and briefly surveyed a crude map of the whole area.

"We give those away. More detail on the wall opposite." Dave led her to the large topographical maps posted behind his desk. It was warmer there, nearer the heater.

"Isn't Wildhorse Canyon where the man disappeared?" Moira asked.

"Here's the loop road," Dave said, tracing it with his finger. "It's eleven miles. Drops 1,000 feet from Midhills to about where you're standing. You'll see an interesting change in the flora." He seemed to have lost track of Moira's question. "Large evergreen perennials, Joshua trees, and then—nada—only some stippling of wolfberry and rhatany down here, small cacti and creosote bushes. Only about two million years ago the Mojave lifted as a block and became a transitional desert, excluding warm climate species. Basin and range topography's more marked here than in the Sonoran to the south. Over here—" his finger trailed off the black dotted line, "was where the two men separated, according to the one who's left."

"It doesn't look that far off the road," Moira said.

"Out here, a mile off, and you might as well be on another planet. Disorientation can happen like that," he said, snapping his fingers. When he did, Charles rolled over. "It's like getting lost on the moon—or something." Dave grinned. "Not that I've been, you know." He laughed his oily-hinge laugh.

"It's definitely close to the end of the world out here," Taylor said, hovering over their shoulders as they surveyed the map.

"It has its appeal," Dave said flatly.

Moira pointed to a spot miles below Wildhorse Canyon labeled Mitchell Cavern. When she touched the map a sensation of warmth coursed through her hand, from her fingertips.

"We can take the Mitchell tour later, if you want," Taylor said. "If you think it'd be worthwhile." Taylor's tone struck a note somewhere between impatience and anticipation.

"I'm not sure," Moira said. "But maybe we should go there."

Moira followed Taylor outside to his towering SUV, which was dwarfing her car parked beside it. As she stepped onto the running board she remembered her purse.

"I forgot something."

Taylor waited while she retrieved her shoulder bag from the office, locked her car doors, and climbed back into the truck. Moira felt sure that Taylor was not the kind of man who forgot things. But he appeared patient.

Not far up the road Taylor pulled off and entered a loop. He parked and got out. Moira followed him down a short, well-worn path that ended at an overlook. The steep, narrow canyon beyond was pitted with the shadows of natural nooks and shallow caves. Moira leaned over the railing and searched down plummeting walls to the desert floor where a sliver of sunlight pried away at the shadow, as if the sun were emerging from an eclipse. Her neck seized up from the awkward angle and, eerily, the sheer walls shimmied and erased the tinges of reflected light. Having just closed her eyes and gripped the railing hard to keep from swaying towards the drop-off, she nearly jumped when Taylor spoke.

"*Thought* you needed to see this." His first word was spoken with such emphasis that it echoed off the rock walls, entered the canyon, and slid away as a chorus: *thought, thought, thought.*

Moira gripped the steel rails. Taylor had already turned back and was headed up the path to his truck.

In church, when she was a little girl, she had studied her mother's hands lightly placed on the pew in front of them when they stood for singing or prayer. Her small hands had reached up to hold the back of the pew while her mother's hands reached down. Moira had wondered when she would grow tall enough to balance herself by reaching down instead of up, wondered when the skin of her own hands would be as marked by traceries of veins and visible bones. Now they were. With effort, she loosed her fingers from the railing.

Without looking back at the brown walls of rock, she stepped quickly after Taylor. The path wavered before her eyes, then solidified. Her vision was trained on the back of Taylor's burgundy parka. Taylor bypassed the truck and started up the opposite path. It descended to where it was choked by large boulders and then dropped out of sight between two huge standing stones. She couldn't see Taylor, but his voice billowed up, barking an order.

"Climb down the metal rings."

Edging closer to the drop-off, Moira caught sight of a ladder of metal rings spaced down the rock and there she hesitated, reminding herself of her pregnancy and her swollen ankles. Nonetheless, she lowered herself backward and slipped her right foot into the first ring.

"Other foot," Taylor coached from below. "And take your time." Then he sneezed.

Moira pulled herself back to the starting point and glanced below her. He was right. The second ring was tapped into the opposite wall and she could not very well cross one leg over the other to reach it. This time, like a good dance partner, she began by stepping backward with her left foot, found the first ring and lowered herself with minimal effort. She turned around at the bottom, pleased with herself, but Taylor had gone on to the next set of rings and descended again out of sight.

After a third set of rings they emerged on the canyon floor. There was little flora in view except sparsely scattered bur-sage and low yucca. Occasional flowering thistles protruded from rock walls and must have been thriving on air alone. As Moira and Detective Taylor wound out of the shelter of the canyon they dodged pile upon pile of horse droppings. In the distance a bajada rose out of the soil. Exposed deadwood on the shrubs grayed the landscape.

"How do you think the horses climbed down those metal rings?" Moira asked.

Taylor laughed or snorted a couple of times and returned no comment. His long even strides easily outpaced Moira's. But she didn't want to ask him to slow the hell down for her.

After following a dusty trail for about twenty minutes, Taylor stopped. "This is where Steve Hogarth said he and his buddy Carl Ingram split up."

"But this is right on the trail," Moira said. All of the intersecting equestrian and hiking trails were clearly marked by wooden posts. No distances to destinations were given, but it would seem easy to at least stay on a trail.

"No, it isn't far. And Hogarth looks like a football player. Says Carl could take care of himself. Carl was a swimmer—two miles a day."

"What else do you know about him?"

"Fiancée, adoptive parents, mother still living, father dead of a heart attack several years ago. He and Steve Hogarth came out here every few months, had since high school. Tent camping, hiking. Quiet guys, really. Nature Conservancy. No hunting. Just boy scouts without the military-macho, survivalist stripe."

Moira squatted and touched the desert. "Does anything live out here?" The only living thing she had seen so far, aside from the few plants, was a rabbit hiding in a thatch of yucca.

"Night lizards. No eyelids on them. They hide in the shade during the day. But I'm biased. The guide books will tell you this place is teeming with life."

Moira scrubbed her empty hands over the trail, not knowing why. No images. Nothing came to her.

"I guess I'm just not comfortable with the forms it takes out here," Taylor added.

The rough surface almost abraded her palms before she stopped rubbing her hand across it. "I'm sorry," she said. "What did you say?" Although she had heard his voice, it had sounded far away.

"No matter. You know Carl Ingram's family had a funeral, but there wasn't anything to bury. Haven't even found a bone, not one bone. I hate that."

"And what about the women?" Moira asked.

"We'll go up there and take a look at where they told their husbands they were camping." Taylor gestured in the distance.

"You think they weren't there?"

"You never know," Taylor said. "Their camper's gone and so are they."

Moira noticed that he wore no wedding band. They retraced their steps through the canyon and climbed the series of metal rings. When they reached the rim of the canyon Moira felt a cold wind.

Back in the truck, Moira gladly accepted Taylor's offer of coffee from his Thermos. Inside the truck, without the whipping wind, the sun pouring through the windshield felt deceptively warm.

"How long have you been in California?" Moira asked. "You said you were from Cleveland?"

"Fifteen years. And you?"

"Fifteen minutes." Moira laughed. "We moved from Virginia in the fall."

"Beautiful state, Virginia," Taylor said and Moira agreed. "I drove part of the Blue Ridge Parkway once. In Cleveland," Taylor paused, a wistful tone creeping into his voice, "there was a little restaurant in the precinct with the best borscht I've ever eaten. Can't get that in Needles. We've got a Chinese diner run by a Korean. What's a black dude with

Jewish taste buds supposed to do for his soul food?"

Taylor offered Moira half of his sandwich and they silently munched corned beef together. The coffee made its way quickly through Moira's system, and she had to resort to the portable potty. Down the path she went while Taylor waited for her yet again.

The pre-fab fiberglass dome was a poor excuse for an igloo. Even in winter the pungent odor of human waste struck her in the face as she opened the door. She sucked in a breath of fresh air before ducking into the chamber.

"WE'LL HEAD UP to Midhills," Taylor said, starting up the truck. "The women's camp slot."

"Please tell me about them," Moira asked.

"Leslee Lyles and Jackie Becker, 38 and 33. Lyles had a little girl, nine years old. Becker had only been married a year, no children. Her husband's a real charmer—a pencil-pushing piranha. On my case night and day for a while, until he announced that he was going to sue us. But we haven't heard from him lately."

The pavement gave way to gravel washboard that jittered Moira to the bone. "Some road," she said.

"Actually this isn't so bad. You should see the 4x4 trails."

"I'm beginning to appreciate how easily someone could get lost out here." Moira gazed out the window. Twisted trees looked like supplicants to a punishing god.

"Mojave yuccas," Taylor said. "Just north of here at Cima there's the largest stand in North America."

"I thought they were farther south."

"In Joshua Tree, you mean? Well, those yuccas are slightly different from these, but I guess the yuccas just didn't know where the National Park Service was planning to locate. These trees wanted to be under state supervision instead." Taylor pulled off onto another road that was strictly dirt and packed gravel. He drove past a number of campsites, including one occupied by a classic old silver Airstream. Whatever had pulled it there was not at home right now. The site where Taylor parked looked similar to all of the others, except for the yellow police tape that bordered it: picnic table, fire-box grill, some sheltering cedars and mesquite trees.

Moira hopped to the ground.

Taylor was already out on the other side with an unlit cigarette dangling from his lips. "I'm not going to light it," he said. Taylor spat out the cigarette and fairly stomped it into the ground. "I hate being controlled by anything," he said.

"I think you killed it," Moira said. "Maybe you should surrender instead."

Taylor gave a quizzical look. "Aren't you lobbying for everyone to stop?"

"My best friend smokes." Moira bent to touch a clump of weed. An image invaded her so quickly that she fell off balance. And the next thing she knew was that she was opening her eyes. She lay curled on her right hip and shoulder. With Taylor kneeling beside her.

He helped her rise and walk to the picnic table and sat her down on the bench. He offered her a drink of water.

Her legs were heavy and numb beneath the picnic table. She propped her elbows on the table and caught her chin in her hands. Like this, she could almost sit upright. Mouth open. No words. It was as if a deep stutter held language in check. Her tongue felt heavy, her throat barred by a chokehold to the windpipe.

Moira labored over each word. "They were here."

"Take your time," Taylor said.

Taylor's dark eyes appeared to her as a dark space too vast to plumb. Moira closed her eyes, lids like weights. Immediately a series of images flashed back across her mind, and when she saw them, she recognized that she was seeing them for the second time:

A woman piled stones over the body of another woman. She was crying as she piled the stones atop the body. As she slowly piled stone upon stone her strength was giving out.

Moira's throat opened enough for her to say, "One of them had to bury the other."

"Which one was alive?"

"The dark-haired one."

"Leslee," Taylor said, taking a note in his notebook. "How did Jackie die?"

"She was attacked."

"By what?"

"I'm not sure. She's buried beneath a cairn."

"What about Leslee?

Moira sounded her depths and brought up nothing—no image, no sound. Nothing to confirm and yet she knew. "Yes. She died, too."

"Do you think you could find their bodies?" Taylor said softly, waiting with notebook in hand.

Combing the image she had been given. Moira tried to press her vision to the periphery of the burial scene for landmarks, anything to identify that vast, colorless place. "There's a shadow on the ground with a sharp edge. A cone-shaped rock with a jagged top is right behind the cairn. Maybe thirty feet high."

"Out here?" Taylor asked

"Yes."

"Any other landmarks?"

"Not nearby." Moira could hear the scratches of Taylor's pen against the notepad, as her mind cleared and opened like a box. There was nothing else inside the box. She opened her eyes then. The blood had crept back into her legs, all the way to her toes.

"Do you feel like going on with this today?" Taylor asked.

"I think so," Moira said. "I hope I didn't scare you."

"I've worked with Regina enough that it doesn't faze me. Are you strong enough?"

Moira shook her head yes. "I think so, but I scared myself," Moira said. "Does it hit her like this?"

"She told me it felt like running into a tree blindfolded," Taylor said. "You seem to recover quickly. Let's drive down Wildhorse Canyon Road, take in the scenery, then loop back to the visitor's center. Maybe Dave has a line on the rock formation you described. He's done a lot of field work for his geology dissertation at Irvine."

The truck bounced down the sand-covered road. Moira identified cedar trees sprinkled over the sloping high desert. The gnarled limbs of yuccas grew unpredictably toward sun or soil, or even horizontally, defying architecture, only to raise or lower a limb in a sudden angle. These trees had all the presence of a breathing animal. They watched and waited, appeared to think and feel.

"You know yuccas aren't really trees," Taylor said.

"I know," Moira said. They looked ancient to her, ancient and human.

For several miles the truck bounced down the incline Dave had described, tires bumping the ruts. It seemed to happen suddenly, as if they had crossed an invisible boundary. The stands of yuccas shrank, and the cedar and mesquite, barrel and deerhorn cacti vanished. What was left was sparse brush and some razor-bladed grasses hugging close to the ground, just as Dave had described it. Taylor identified the hymenoclea bush when Moira pointed at it and asked its name.

As they neared the two-mile post, having traced the scenic byway, a large volcanic hill rose on their left. The dark, varnished boulders spilled down the hill like huge building blocks thrown from a desperate height. The rocks heaped in places, leaving other spots relatively bare. Toward the top of the hill the boulders clumped together with no surface of grass for the eye to rest upon. Everything was jagged rock, dark rock, bare rock.

DAVE HAD HIS HAND on the topo map behind his desk. Charles hadn't even gotten up when they came in; the dog was either too decrepit or deaf. Dave walked his fingers east of Midhills. "Sounds like Totem rock to me. Over near Rock Spring."

"A familiar landmark?" Taylor asked.

"Not really. I named it myself, if it's the rock I think it is. Matches your description anyway. But I haven't been out there since August. Been too busy with schoolwork and office work when I'm here."

"Tomorrow," Taylor said. "I'll call for back-up."

"It'll take you a good three hours one way to hike in from Rock Spring," Dave cautioned. "Are you good for it?" he asked Moira.

"I can make it," she said.

Taylor nodded. "I need you, too, Dave."

"I think they can spare me here," Dave said with a shrug. "Tell your men to bring their cameras. There's a spiral petroglyph on the way that'll blow your mind." Dave trailed them to the door. "One fine example of a season-marking glyph. Sunlight pours through a notched rock and hits the spiral right in the center on the first day of summer. The shaft will be way off the center spiral now. You'll dig it," he told Moira, rubbing his head and blinking his enthusiasm.

"They'll have their cameras," Taylor said. "We'll head on down to Mitchell Cavern this afternoon." His somber tone made Moira shudder; her thoughts leapt ahead toward tomorrow.

Mitchell Cavern

AFTER NEGOTIATION with Jenny, the guide, who thought she had finished her last tour of the day right before Taylor and Moira arrived, the three of them hiked the ascending half-mile path to the locked gate of Mitchell Cavern.

Somewhere in her early twenties, with spiked blonde hair, wearing the standard-issue park service greens, Jenny began her usual spiel despite the small audience. "This entrance was known by local tribes as 'the eyes of the mountain.' Spirits were thought to inhabit the cave, so it was entered only by Shamans—"

"Our schedule is rather tight," Taylor interjected.

Jenny unlocked the gate and led them through one of the "eyes."

Inside the first room, Jenny's robotic lecture clicked on again, and this time Taylor listened long enough for Moira to glean the simple facts that explained the cavern's formation: a layer of limestone (karst) plus calcium carbonate and more time than human imagination can grasp. As the surface water seeps through tiny fissures in the rock it slowly dissolves them, moving the calcium carbonate down to the water table where it must seek an outlet. The water grows so acidic that it flushes through limestone; eventually the waters drain and the seeping surface begins to deposit calcite in its wake, making formations in tediously slow drips. Mitchell Cavern was inactive now, Jenny told them. It was a dry cavern, unlike the wet, still forming caverns familiar to Moira—the Luray and Dixie of Virginia.

While they still stood in the first room, Jenny pointed out one defiant stalactite that was forming on a low overhang by slow dropper measures of calcium carbonate. In fifty years the new formation's progress might equal the length of one's little finger. Moira wondered how many tourists had been tempted to lean out and interrupt the tiny water bud, to taste the acidic solution and alter the future. Even in this so-called dead cave, living water held on.

Every formation was named for its shape. Taylor grew more and more impatient but held his tongue as they passed "soda straws" and "draperies," "curtains," and "popcorn," a stippling of irregular lumps that always grew toward air.

"Columns are formed when stalagmites and stalactites meet; they're rare. So are cave shields," said Jenny, pointing to a flat gravity-defying disc between ceiling and wall.

As they followed their guide along the well-trod path, she pointed out the many cracks, horizontal faults in the bulky formations where earthquakes had interrupted the steady sculpting. "Caverns are especially stable in earthquakes. They have to be—they form on faults." Jenny checked Taylor's face for a reaction.

"That's interesting," Moira said and tightened Seigle's red scarf around her neck as she felt the air grow colder.

They were edging through a keyhole passageway when Jenny stopped them, shining her strong flashlight into the darkness that surrounded the bridge at their feet. The chasm they were suspended over appeared bottomless. "Mitchell himself used to fool people by throwing a lighted flare into this pit," Jenny said. "He'd time it perfectly to burn out before it hit the bottom. Even so, it's deep enough, don't you think?"

From the darkness below her feet Moira felt a sudden surge that knocked her onto her knees. Taylor knelt beside her and loosened her scarf. Jenny shone her light toward them.

"Get that light out of my eyes," Taylor barked.

Moira could hear everything around her, yet drifted away as an image hurtled toward her, overtaking her consciousness. It hit her squarely, no glancing blow, and seemed to suction her through the solid rock. As sure as she was of anything, she knew that where this chasm emptied they would find a man. A snapshot floated toward her and she tried to register its every detail. Ragged clothes. Holes ripped in elbows, knees. A layer of dirt like a mask across his features. As hard as she tried she could not bring his face into focus, but she saw a spark of wildness flare in his eyes. She could only see his eyes, their passionate glow. Then she dug deeper, without knowing whether she was going into the earth or into herself. The man was standing in water. He was breathing from an air pocket. He was not alone. And there was not much time left.

And then she saw the man she had seen in her dreams many times and forgotten. The man crouched before a door and pushed through. This time she followed him willingly as he showed her the trash heap she recognized as her planet, Earth.

From the top of the mountain of trash she scanned all directions, above and below, even into space to see that the spinning of the mound was splitting off chunks of debris and hurling them into the darkness beyond. This space was filled with other beings, other worlds, not emptiness at all. And her planet was a most rudimentary landfill, spewing poisonous smoke, its own crude waste, into the face of the universe.

The being takes her by the hand.

She looks into his face, which had appeared before to be pocked with scars. Now his unknowable face opens to her. This ancient being's face is so wrinkled that she can only distinguish bright, black eyes. Though old, the being is lithe and limber, with long legs and a firm grip on her hand. His voice seems to be coming from inside her, their communion completely internal.

"How do I know you?" Moira asks.

"My name is Carl Ingram. I was raised on your planet, but I am not entirely of your race. I've returned to mine. We will survive by becoming troglobites once again, by Turtle oil, but your race cannot. It is time to find another fuel," he tells her. "Photosynthesis has supported your food chain, but there is another way to convert energy. My people are conservationists, self-contained, able to adapt like your cavefish, which is deaf and blind but thriving underground. Each stroke of its fins propels it twice as far as an ordinary fish.

"The energy reserves that took the earth and the sun eons to produce—deposits of coal, oil, natural gas—cannot keep pace. The sun's conversion and storage of energy, and its purification process, is too slow for your consumption. The foods you eat, sprinkled with pesticides and synthetic fertilizers, offer less and less energy for your bodies. And there are other threats, other tribes who are not so benevolent. They have no attachment to Earth—they have not made pilgrimages as my tribe has—and they make no pledge to care for all sentient life. They would let the Earth vanish for its recklessness before it poisons them too."

Moira felt the urgency in his message, the concern, and trusted it. But everything he said raised more and more questions. It was beyond comprehension, and yet she had no choice but to believe this creature.

"Energy is free, neither created nor destroyed. You must live in this breathing space where there is energy without waste. Every interaction is a translation of light."

She saw then that the man's head bore two horns of light, like a headdress of luminous antennae. He began to write a formula in the air, and instructed her to remember.

Moira felt her hand being gripped. The touch tugged her from her floating on the waters of pure receptivity, and she returned the pressure, squeezing the hand.

"She's responding," Taylor said. He loosed the scarf completely from her neck, and she felt her chest rise, balloon from top to bottom as she gasped.

"I'll get some help," Jenny said. "She's fainted."

"She'll be all right in a few minutes," Taylor said.

Jenny pulled her mobile phone from a cargo pocket. "I'm calling the rescue squad."

"I'll tell you when we need them," Taylor snapped.

Moira felt the gravity of muscle tension return to her tingling legs and arms. Her head pounded, as if she were waking from a massive hangover. Taylor helped her to sit up.

"You're overloaded," he said.

She leaned heavily on him.

"What happened?" Jenny asked.

Taylor didn't explain, and Moira could not. Her tongue lolled in her mouth like a lump of half-cooked potato.

After a pause of ten minutes or more, the three of them inched along, Jenny supporting Moira on one side, Detective Taylor on the other, until they made their way out of the cavern and back down the path to the ranger station.

Moira remembered the small geode in her car, how she had run her fingertips over the rough hollow space inside. Sitting inside the station, she rested one empty hand inside the other, feeling nothing but the coldness of her own skin. After half an hour of rest and two cups of Jenny's herbal tea, Taylor judged they were ready to leave and drove the sixty miles back to Needles, leaving Moira's car parked overnight at Hole-in-the-Wall.

He checked her into a motel and instructed her to take a hot bath and be ready for dinner at eight. They would talk then, he said. But although she tried to concentrate, she couldn't remember anything but a phrase from the episode inside Mitchell Cavern, not one image. And the phrase was too silly to repeat. What would Taylor make of it? *Turtle oil?*

All she knew to tell Taylor was that Carl Ingram's body would never be found. She felt sure of it, yet she had no evidence to offer, nothing but her conviction.

Recovery

WITH MOIRA BESIDE HIM, Taylor pulled his truck into the Hole-in-the-Wall parking lot. The rest of his convoy was right behind him—two officers in another 4x4 truck with a covered long bed. Taylor rolled out of his truck and joined his men. Moira stepped out, too, and Taylor introduced her to Rick, a slim, freckled man still in his twenties and Will Slaughter, who was probably older than Taylor, with the shoulders of a bull and black coarse hair.

Dave and Charles rode with Taylor and Moira. The other two drove in tandem to Rock Spring, where Dave suggested they begin hiking and Taylor suggested they four-wheel farther in.

"About two miles from here, we'll hit the canyon rim," Dave said. "And there's no way down there but to hoof it. Between here and there we could disturb a lot of desert crust."

"That's four miles saved each way," Taylor countered. "It could mean a lot more on the way back."

A compromise meant that Will Slaughter would drive his truck the two miles, with Moira riding with him while the rest of the party walked. Will Slaughter drove without talking, but Moira broke the silence.

"Have you done many rescues?" she asked.

"I have done more recovery than rescue," he said in an even tone. "Things being how they are."

The parties met up at the rim. The four-hundred-foot

descent to the canyon floor was a scramble but easy by comparison with slogging through the sandy arroyo below. Moira's heels sank into the loose silt and her calves ached from pulling forward step by step. Each of the officers wore a frame pack; Taylor and Dave carried water, marching through the sand as if it were solid ground. Charles ran ahead of the pack, occasionally barking over his shoulder, setting a pace not even Will Slaughter could match, as Moira fell farther behind. Stopping to catch her breath, Moira saw the future coming back at her, as if she were passing it in a certain spot: *two heavy body bags, like canoes being portaged, suspended between two pairs of men. Moira would be carrying the water.* Knowing the story's end, she still had to walk the whole distance, there and back. The sand gave way beneath her weight. The past and the future slid into each other, closing off the present. She had already passed herself returning, and yet she had to keep walking ahead.

Dave stopped them all before a cluster of rocks and pointed to a chiseled circle with a spiral ending in a 'c' clearly etched within its perimeter. "Here's the season-telling petroglyph." He then directed their gaze toward a boulder opposite. "There's the notch where the sun projects." A narrow shaft of illumination was slanting off the smaller boulder, well off center of the encircled 'c'.

Quietly observing the petroglyph, Will Slaughter said, "There are only two kinds of time, there's right *now*, and then there's all the other time—the *not* right now." He bent down to examine some fresh animal droppings no one else had noticed. "Bobcat scats," he said.

Dave tilted his head back and resumed his academic spiel. "I've observed that the shaft of sunlight marks the circle exactly dead center on the summer solstice, when the sun reaches its northernmost position."

"I think ancient science was called worship by my people," Will said. "Human life is as brief as a summer."

Something in the thought cast a contented smile across Will's face.

Dave's mouth dropped open as if he would argue, but he fell silent and pulled off his cap to run his fingers over his sprouting scalp a few times.

As the procession resumed, Will fell back, giving up the second spot behind Charles' wagging tail to Dave. Will walked with Moira. His upper body was bound by his uniform shirt; the pack he was carrying cut into his arms. Otherwise, Moira thought, his bunched muscles might expand to fill a country or a world. While everyone else had donned parkas against the blowing dust and chill air, Will had worked up a sweat that seeped through his shirt. After pacing her for several minutes he asked how she liked the desert.

"I'm not sure," she said. "It appears empty, but it's full. I grew up surrounded by mountains and green trees."

"Yes, a paradox," Will said, pleased by her answer. "The desert only appears empty, but turtles are sleeping at our feet."

Moira took in what she thought was a tidbit of Indian wisdom. Will must have caught her expression, because he added, "It's true. The turtles burrow through the winter, preferring old river beds. This is the season of the Turtle Dance. Mid-winter you prepare for spring. Everything turns on the thing that comes before it. A good circle dance makes the brown earth green. Like your bracelet," Will observed. "The shell was hollowed without breaking the rim. Time circles without beginning or end."

While Moira had been listening only to Will, unmindful of the others, Dave had dropped back to walk near them. "Karma," Dave interjected. "What you do now and who you will become."

"Fertility," Will said, eyes on Moira. "The earth in full bloom—like a pregnant woman."

Dave let out a whoop. He had spotted his Totem rock

and began to lope along with Charles, the first to reach it.

When Moira touched the rock, Rick whipped out his camera and took her picture.

Taylor scowled.

"Just checking the light," Rick said.

"Where's Charles?" Dave asked, looking around. "He was here a second ago."

They walked a few hundred yards, rounding the rock. Moira felt her knees turn watery. Charles had bounded ahead and now stood sniffing beside a mound of rock.

"Call your dog," Taylor said sharply.

Dave shouted for Charles and leaned down to him. "Easy boy."

"Stand back," Taylor instructed. "Rick, get your shots before we move in."

Rick circumnavigated the site, his camera focused on each part of a decaying body that had been reduced to bones nestled in shreds of cloth. A face half-eaten away was upturned, frozen in what might have been permanent astonishment, though there were no longer any eyes to clarify the expression. Beside the body rose a rock cairn.

When Rick had recorded each angle, Taylor instructed Will and Rick to unfold a body bag and fill it. Then they settled in to remove the rocks of the cairn.

Beneath the rocks they found another body, decayed but seemingly intact.

"Jackie Becker," Taylor said, having bent to examine the remains. "Her throat was cut. Her wrists have rope burns."

The skin of her face was burned and blistered, as if the sun had tried to break the body apart, flay it by means of light alone before she had met her death. Beneath one of the rocks, Rick found a large hunting knife. And a length of belaying cord. He tagged both and collected the knife in a plastic evidence bag. He wound the rope around his arm.

The brand of satisfaction Moira felt in having been right was cold comfort by definition. Cold enough to be numbing. She fell silent as a stone as they hiked back to where the truck was parked above the canyon rim. She carried one of the backpacks now. Inside it was the evidence: the knife, the camera, and the cord. The four men carried the two bodies between them, stopping to rest every ten minutes. They had to struggle to get the bodies up the ascent from the canyon floor. Finally Rick and Dave, Taylor and Will hefted their cargo into the covered truck bed and collapsed beside it to catch their breath.

Moira felt tears well up. And in a second she was sobbing.

"I feel like crying myself," Will said.

"You have no idea how relieved these families will be—just to have something to put to rest. And an idea of what happened." Taylor mopped his brow, directing his words to Moira. "You've done a good thing here. Don't forget it. I don't know how you did it, but you did." Taylor paced a few steps, rocked back on his heels, and turned toward her again. "But the job's not finished. We have to find the man who did this."

"I have to go home," Moira said.

Detective Taylor nodded.

THERE WAS SCANT TRAFFIC on the road, but Moira gripped the steering wheel tightly. Before today she had never seen a dead body except for her mother's. And then the casket had been quickly closed. Her mother hadn't wanted anyone to see what the illness had done to her. Even so, her mother's body had been sanitized by the mortician before she had to see it again outside of the hospital room where she had slipped away; her hair had been curled and make-up applied as if she were going out. And she was going out...

Moira watched the red taillights of the cars that whipped

past her vanish into distance like glowing cigarettes. The more she understood of life the more she saw. She had seen the dead weight of two bodies straining the muscles of four men. Even though she didn't like to use it while she drove, she picked up the phone and called Paul. Before she could say much of anything, ask for the support she sorely needed from him, his anger tumbled freely. She had forgotten to call him. "We had an agreement," Paul said.

She told him she was sorry, sorry, sorry, and asked him if they could talk about it when she got home.

Before she left, Taylor had leaned into her car window and said, "If you think of anything else—you call me right away. There's a man free who shouldn't be. Carl Ingram didn't just vanish without a trace, and neither has our killer."

Now the steering wheel slid through her hands as she neared the exit for home. She could not shake the feeling of having forgotten something of great importance. Something dropped down a well, just out of reach of the bucket, like a word lost in the mind's folds just as the tongue begins to speak.

The One Who Was Half Turtle

HALF TURTLE WAS BORN of a Turtle woman, but his father came from the land of Green Trees. In the first five weeks after conception, Half Turtle, like any other embryo, was female. Every male of the Turtle race begins as the other sex. Still, Half Turtle's childhood was a mixed-up affair. Raised as a member of the Turtle tribe, beloved and treated as their own, yet he was called Half Turtle because he was physically different.

The age of initiation—which was the age of reason—was approaching for Half Turtle. In part of the ceremony, the initiates were given to the fire by their fathers. A small circle burned on the upper arm, branded by a hot stick, marked a man. Half Turtle, who was already taller than any of the Turtles, went to his mother. "Where is my father?" he asked her. The ceremony demanded a real father not the surrogates who had taught him thus far.

At first his mother, Pokil, turned her back on his question and wouldn't speak. Then she went for advice, to the spirit pit where Old-Time Turtle, a descendent of Transcendent One, sat vigil between worlds. Old-Time Turtle guarded the passageway connecting this world and the next. When someone died or was born, he would smoke his pipe to ease the transition. Old-Time Turtle fulfilled an essential function, though some considered his presence to be more ceremonial than necessary.

Pokil let herself slowly down the ladder into the spirit

pit and found Old Turtle sleeping. She cleared her throat and stood well back, where the light from above would clearly illuminate her for Old Turtle's failing vision. She did not want to startle him. This revered Turtle was known to be cantankerous.

Without seeming to wake from his slumber, and without opening either red eye, Old-Time Turtle began speaking: "Daughter, it seems like only yesterday that I piped you into this world. You brought us Half Turtle. I piped for him, too. Now Half Turtle must take his place in the circle, but there is no marked path for him."

"Old-Time Turtle," said Pokil, gathering courage from Old Turtle's gentle voice. "Must I tell my son of his Green Tree father?"

"Green Tree has marked Half Turtle as much as we. His legs are not our legs, his heart only half ours. To become a man, Half Turtle must use his legs to find his father."

"But Old-Time Turtle, he is my only son." Pokil bowed her head and the tears flowed.

His voice soft but firm, Old-Time Turtle said, "You gave him birth, but Half Turtle must live his own life. You have helped with the first half, now he must do the second half on his own or he will never be whole."

Old Turtle's words hit Pokil hard, though she felt the wisdom in them, and the kindness in their truth. "Old Turtle," Pokil said. "Why do they say you are gruff?"

"Because they come here with stupid questions."

Pokil turned and climbed the ladder then, almost laughing. Before she reached the top she heard Old Turtle resume his snoring.

She found her son beneath a Pinyon tree and told him the story of his father. "I do not know where to find him," Pokil finished.

"I must go to the land of Green Trees," Half Turtle said.

"I cannot even tell you the first direction. In my whole

life, I've been no farther than the spring."

"My legs will direct me," Half Turtle said. "They have been growing for a purpose."

"You are brave." Pokil placed a hand on her son's shoulder.

"I can never walk like a Turtle," Half Turtle said, "until I find my father in the Green Trees."

"Perhaps you must walk your own walk," said his mother. She cried again, because she saw the loneliness crouched ahead of her son, waiting for him in the darkness, like a lynx. If she had never lain with the one from the Green Trees, she might have had a whole Turtle son who could enter the circle without this dangerous journey. She feared that her son would never know the completion of the circle and never feel the burn of manhood. But perhaps, had she not lain with the stranger, she might never have had a son at all.

"Mother," spoke Half Turtle, "I will return. Perhaps my father will show me the ways of Green Trees. And I will know two tribes, two ways."

Pokil did not wish to burden his pack with her tears. Instead, she filled his bundle with supplies and taught him to recognize nettles, berries, and edible nuts. She pointed out the poison roots to be avoided and showed him how to divine water with a forked branch. After his mentors had taught him the old rituals for survival away from the caves, she watched him climb down the wall and walk away.

Half Turtle set out alone across the basin scattered with healing salts known as the Crystal Body. His long strides led him, but sand blew to erase his footprints with each step. When he grew afraid he looked up and found the Turtle stars and sang his gratitude to his mother and the tribe that had raised him as their own.

Years of wandering trained Half Turtle to await the night with expectancy. What had saddened him in the early part of his journey now gave him pleasure and rest. After walking as far as he could each day, he made a bed of needles or moss or grass and lay down with the stars as his blanket. He listened for the night owls. He fell asleep thanking each of the stars over his head. By taking one step at a time, he learned to walk without anxiety. After a while, it did not matter that years were passing as he searched for his father. At the break of each day, Half Turtle walked. At sunset, Half Turtle slept. By walking and sleeping, Half Turtle came into his own. Somehow he reached the trunk of the great tree where his father lived.

Half Turtle climbed the tree without fear. The muscles of his long legs were hard, conditioned by years and miles of walking. The day Half Turtle found his father in the Green Trees he was already a man. Into the leafy light, Half Turtle climbed higher than any Turtle had ever climbed. When he had left the earth and trusted the tree, he remembered the many starry nights that had stretched over him, binding him in gratitude to the sky. He knew he was also a creature of these heights, born to search the ground yet seek the sun.

At the top of the great tree, Half Turtle's father held out his hand, "I have been waiting for you, my son, offering thanks for you, for whom I had no reason to hope."

Now Half Turtle's two hearts healed into one strong beat. And ever afterward he was called Turtle of the Trees.

The Ides of March

Seigle, holed up hearthside, at the ragtag end of a sunspot cycle, with his feet propped up, was reading one of his favorite authors. Forty-foot pines had been uprooted by the weight of ice; power and phone lines had snapped beneath cracking branches in the previous days. On his way home from work he had seen a dog let out to pee on a cord, slide on its back like a seal, slipping on the ice down the slope of a yard. A kind of strange bungee jump. His secretary had been hobbled by a fall taken as she entered the grocery store, and now she limped to her desk and used a cane. Everything and everyone who wouldn't bend had been breaking. Seigle reread a passage from Thoreau.

"*Two or three of us could have pulled over one thirty feet high and six or seven inches thick. They were easily rocked, lifting the horizontal roots each time, which reminded me of what is said about the Indians sometimes bending over a young tree, burying a chief under its roots, and letting it spring back for his monument and protection.*"

His cellphone rang and Seigle picked it up without leaving his chair. Jessy, calling to see how his day went, to ask him to meet her for a drink. He said he would. Hung up the phone and lifted himself out of his easy chair to wash his face and find his shoes. Jessy's voice. His chest almost ached when he heard it, as if it were thawing. Two nights before he had stood in her living room and held her to him a good, long time. Then he had left her standing there, waiting for him to fully connect. He hoped she would wait a while longer so that he could work his way around his fear. He didn't even know if his system still worked; like a shriveled leaf, it had been too long without water. To disappoint her—he couldn't do it. Would rather do nothing at all.

He fished out the shoes he'd thrown into the closet after work. Hiking boots were wedged in the back corner of the closet. Stuck there for two months. He'd been to the gym, walked the treadmill but not the woods. Excuses of time or weather, he had made these to himself, but he knew the truth of it was that his energy had changed direction. He could get to the gym quickly and then meet up with Jessy for a meal.

TUESDAY NIGHT and the place should by all rights be dead, but spring or cabin fever had packed all of the booths where Seigle and Jessy liked to hide. They looked at each other, shrugged, and took side by side bar stools, ordered up two Jamesons on the rocks and settled into conversation, holding hands beneath the bar. His hand rested on her leg, then hers on his. Fifty workers had been recalled to fill a government order at the plant, he told her. Jessy said she was skeptical about the product—stick propellant to charge howitzer cannons.

"I was just happy for the workers, being called in," Seigle said. "I hate it when I have to lay them off." Before the munitions plant he had done plant engineering for private industry; had left because the government's benefits and pension plan were better. The motives didn't interest him. But it was all Jessy could think about.

Jeff Stacey came up from behind, grabbed Seigle's shoulder and whirled his stool around. Seigle introduced Jeff to Jessy. Jeff swayed over his boots, face set in a hard-edged frown. Jessy's eyes were set on Jeff's hand, which was still gripping Seigle hard by the shoulder. He tried to shrug it off.

"Buddy," Seigle said to Jeff, keeping his voice light, rising from his stool, "Let's go for a stroll."

Seigle led Jeff back to the jukebox and the cigarette machine between the last booths and the rest rooms. Someone's quarter had resurrected Johnny Cash's "Ring of Fire."

Jeff balanced his weight, gripping either side of the jukebox as if it were a pinball machine. "You got a lot of nerve," he said, eyes slowly scrolling the song titles to avoid Seigle's eyes.

"What do you mean?" Seigle asked him.

"Sucking me into your goddam treasure hunt and then dropping me like a rock." Jeff pushed off the jukebox and squared his shoulders.

"I haven't been out lately, or I'd have called." Seigle put a hand on Jeff's arm and felt it shaken off.

"Like hell. You got pussy fever," Jeff said loudly. "Sucking up to the press. You college boys are all alike."

"Listen, you asshole, there isn't any treasure, just a hole in the ground and only a maybe on that. I didn't promise you anything." Seigle thought he should have decked him right then and there, but it was too ridiculous. He could smell the mix of paranoia and beer on Jeff's breath and stepped back. Had he thought their "cave" was going to be the next tourist trap along the Blue Ridge Parkway? Seigle felt sorry for the guy, even as Jeff's glassy eyes flashed toward him and he hauled back and flailed at Seigle, punching wild and hard.

"You bastard," Jeff said as his ring grazed Seigle's jaw.

Seigle tried to walk away but Jeff held him and took another swing. Then Seigle got angry and decked him, connecting with Jeff's nose. He went down spewing blood. Adrenaline coursed through Seigle like electricity. Knuckles scraped raw and bleeding—but he had won. In the seconds after he had hit Jeff he forgot why they had been fighting. It only felt good to have connected and dropped him.

Seigle hovered over Jeff, ready to kick him if need be.

Like a turtle flipped on its back, Jeff was rolling side to side, unable to right himself. He was holding his nose.

L.T. bent down to Jeff, then turned his head up at Seigle, "Get outta here, jack. You kicked the man when he's down."

"I didn't kick him." Seigle turned to head back to the bar when the bouncer, bare-armed and dressed in black, a referee without the stripes, took his arm and showed him the rear exit.

"My girlfriend's in there," Seigle stammered.

With a firm hold on Seigle's upper arm, the bouncer deadpanned, "She went home with someone else."

"The other guy started it," Seigle said.

The bouncer just rolled his eyes.

Seigle could hear him chuckling as he padlocked the back door. Out in the alley, Seigle took a breath of cold air into his lungs. His back straightened, shoulders relaxed. He had won the fight and could still feel the energy surging down through his arms. All he needed was a little celebratory drink, but the bar was off-limits to him now.

He walked to his jeep and saw the empty parking space next to it where Jessy had parked. Back home, after pouring his two fingers of whisky, he called her. An ice bag was wrapped around the skinned knuckles of his right hand. Leaning back in his chair, he listened to the ringing of Jessy's phone. She'd had ample time to get home.

The answering machine sang its usual song, but this time he studied the words, *nothing left to lose*. After the beep, Seigle said, "Hi, it's me," hung up the phone, settled back, and waited for her to return his call.

Sometime in the middle of the night he woke up in his chair with a plastic bag full of water in his lap and a fresh scab across his jawline.

"Are you proud of yourself?" Jessy asked Seigle, days later when she finally returned his call. "Is that what happens when you get frustrated? You were enjoying yourself. It scared the crap out of me."

"It had nothing to do with you," Seigle said. "He asked for it."

"You're serious, aren't you?" Jessy said.

"Listen, I was kind of defending your honor."

"Oh Popeye," Jessy said, in a fair imitation of Olive Oil. "Spare me the swagger."

"I've never hit a woman in my life and I never will," Seigle said, finally catching her drift. "How could you even think that I would?"

"How can I be sure?"

"It'll never happen again—with anyone, if that's how you feel."

"It's already happened," Jessy said.

"What do you want me to do?"

"Nothing."

"Jessy, please don't make a federal case after the fact. Jeff was pissed. I'm not some redneck bully and you know it."

"Well, you could've fooled me." Jessy's voice was ratcheted up a few notches, so Seigle concentrated and lowered his.

"So you'd rather I'd wound up on the floor, is that it?"

Jessy issued a theatrical sigh and hung up.

Seigle held the phone out from his ear, hoping she'd reconsider and turn hers back on before they lost the connection. She didn't. There's nothing like winning the battle and losing the war. He firmly believed that if he'd landed on his ass with a bloody nose Jessy would have been there wiping it. He slammed down the phone. Even Jeff knew he had it coming. There'd be no hard feelings there. Irony and women go hand in hand. He'd give her a few days to cool off.

NOT LONG AFTER, Seigle heard from Cap that Jeff had gotten laid off at the furniture plant and had practically been living at the bar. When Seigle showed up Jeff had already tried to pick a fight with most everyone else, including L.T., but Seigle was the one who fell right into the trap. Something about Jessy's reaction seemed right as rain to him then. But he wasn't quite ready to admit what a fool he'd been, so he thought he'd stretch it out a few more days before he called her, hoping she'd call him first. It could be a long wait, proving whose honor he had been defending. In the meantime, there was something he'd been putting off that he had to do.

Vernal Equinox

Snow spit at his windshield. He imagined a dragon with breath of ice instead of fire, as the wind slurred outside the windows like water shooting through a tunnel. Every thought pulled Jessy in its wake. He hadn't heard from her yet. It had been a long week. And now he was teetering on the edge of spring. 4:55 PM would bring it in. He glanced at his watch—3:30. The tendons along his arms tingled as he tensed and released his muscles while gripping the wheel.

He signaled off the main road and swung onto Turner's driveway. Just as he slowed, a line of deer leapt in front of his jeep, just feet ahead of his front bumper. For once his timing was perfect, and he slipped effortlessly between two leaping does.

The gravel beneath his tires crumbled like old teeth as he pulled toward the disheveled cottage. The string of bad weather had nearly whittled Turner's woodpile back to earth. It was hard for Seigle to open the door of his jeep, climb down to the ground, and ask advice of an old man who lived alone in a falling-down shack. Even Turner's dog lumbered from old age. Deaf and blind, it never even let out a warning. With the porch boards creaking beneath his boots and snow finding the gap between his upturned collar and throat, Randy Seigle raised his fist and knocked lightly. Pretty soon he stamped his feet in the cold and pounded the door. He raised nothing but the old white-faced coon hound that finally ambled closer and let out a throaty bark.

Uncle, Seigle thought. Whatever had brought him here could as easily take him home. But instead of going straight to his jeep he stepped around behind the house. Between his footsteps and the whining of the dog, now nipping at his heels in a show of territoriality, he could hear the swift clean stroke of metal through wood.

About twenty yards off, beside a ramshackle shed with a roof peeled back like a sardine can, he could see Turner bending to throw the split halves away from the block. Without moving a muscle too much, the old man balanced another log on the block, tapped in the wedge, pulled the maul back over his shoulder and hinged it forward, thwacking clean through the wood. The log sang out as it opened through its core. Seigle had split wood before and recognized a yogin with a maul when he saw one. The essence of a good stroke was not to be found in the force, but in the placement and follow-through, the intent of the man. Turner's stooped posture didn't hinder his masterstroke through the wood's heart. Turner picked up a half log, propped it on the block, and split it cleanly with his long-handled ax.

"Hey there," Seigle called as he approached.

Twaack. The ax blade broke the other half log in two with hardly a splinter.

Seigle called again, only ten feet now from Turner's back. The old man was absorbed in his work. The cur stood between the two men and yipped, drawing the old man's attention. Turner turned around and showed no surprise. His watery eyes widened in a tight face hatched with wrinkles. He set his lips and paused without giving out a greeting.

"How's the wood business?" Seigle said. "Do you think this winter's ever going to let up?"

"I'm just about two days ahead and two days is all."

"Doesn't feel like spring, does it?"

Turner looked at the sky, then back at Seigle. "It ain't—

yet." Turner placed another round on the block. "Watch now," he said, more to his dog than to Seigle. The wedge ran true. The log split beneath the maul as if liberating a force from inside the dead tree.

"What you come for?" Turner said, loading one of the half rounds onto the block to meet his ax blade.

Seigle pitched his voice as loudly as he could to keep himself from choking on the word. "Advice," Seigle said, nearly shouting.

Turner blinked, expressionless. "Let's go on in the house," he said. Turner dropped his ax beside the wedge and the maul, leaving the wood waiting on the block.

Seigle followed Turner toward the back door. They had to step over the dog, which had just lain down and did not budge from the back stoop.

Across the dim room, Seigle saw the lid of a large black pot quaking rhythmically on the stove, releasing the pungent warmth of simmering roots: onions and garlic, turnips, and potatoes, and an herb Seigle could not identify. His mouth began to water as the simple, strong aromas hit the back of his throat.

"Soup's on," Turner said. He ladled soup into blue bowls and set them on the plain, warped table that had been worn smooth and oiled by years of hands. From the oven he retrieved a loaf of fresh bread and cut some slices for them both. The crude, wobbly chair creaked beneath Seigle's weight but held him. He hadn't even taken off his coat before he was spooning the old man's soup to his lips. Soon the heat was fogging his glasses and he pulled them off along with his coat. Nothing would have been different had they been sitting in the nineteenth century instead of the twenty-first.

The two men exchanged no words while eating. Turner's bachelor etiquette suited Seigle. Steaming soup, the rhythm of spoon to lips, thick cuts of potato and buttery broth.

Dill, that was the herb.

Turner rose once from the table and fed a split log into the old cookstove.

When Seigle had finished another bowl of soup Turner set down a glass of cool spring water before him.

"I don't make coffee but oncet a day," Turner said.

Seigle sipped the water and it was almost sweet. He thought he preferred it over dessert.

But then Turner said, "There's an apple pie in the oven."

On the wall opposite the table hung a large shield. In the dim light, Seigle's eyes traced the uneven oval until Turner said, "Twas that turtle that like to scarred my daddy to death." Turner had a good laugh before he went on.

"He was a kid fishing in a pond—pond's filled in now, smooth as the day is long. Daddy threw in his hook, and that turtle," Turner gestured toward the shield on the wall, "that turtle took a notion and raised its head and spat. My daddy toppled right into the water. Heh." Turner had to laugh again before he could continue.

"Daddy never could forgive that turtle. Grew himself taller, like he was growing to spite the turtle, kept on fishing that pond, all along brooding on old Mr. Turtle, who had spooked him good."

Seigle traced the broad, scalloped turtle shell with his eye, listening to the story.

Some of the merriment went out of Turner's voice. "Must have been ten years later, but my daddy weren't one to forget. One day he lured that old wrinkled reptile to the edge with a chicken neck and hoisted it clean out with a homemade net. Muddy from head to toe, my daddy carried that big old turtle home, built up a blaze beneath the lard pot and threw it in headfirst without a blessing or a curse. That's how its shell come down to me."

"It's a beauty," Seigle said.

"You could say it. Some day I think that old turtle's

going to stick out his head, take a look at what things has come to and get the last laugh." Turner paused and wiped his mouth. "What about yours? Your daddy. Was he the snapping kind?"

"Didn't snap—but didn't say much of anything," Seigle said. He reached for some dark, dried fruit in a bowl on the table.

"You got the arthritis?" Turner asked.

"No, why?"

"You're eating my pokeberry cure."

Seigle spat the berries out into his hand, while Turner laughed, wiped his mouth of the purple stain and said, "I thought they were poisonous."

"Heh. They's poor man's peyote. Now what was it, son, you come here to ask me?"

"Thank you for the soup," Seigle said.

"Good Lord, I plumb forgot about that pie." Turner rose and dished out the pie and settled in at the table again. They ate in silence until Turner pushed back his pie plate and said, "You come here for my cooking then, I suppose."

"You make a hell of an apple pie."

"I ain't much of a cook, but you live long enough you learn a little bit about everything. Jack of all trades, master of none is the way my daddy would put it." Turner set his hands in his lap and waited.

"I've been wondering what you know about a cavern around here," Seigle said.

"So you ain't found it yet?"

"No sir," Seigle said. "I think it could be large, if I could find the way in."

Turner scratched at his white bristled chin. "You ever shaved yorn?"

"Not since college, half my life," Seigle said.

"Shave sometime," Turner said. "Start it all over again. Stranger to your own face if you never look." Turner looked at Seigle kindly, but straight into him and through.

"You know my girlfriend said she'd like to see my face," Seigle blurted and then stopped cold.

Turner raised his bushy brows but didn't comment. "Likely there's a cavern," Turner said. "As big as Mammoth, could be, don't see why not. I believe I stumbled on its mouth—long time back, before you were a twinkle. When I weren't nothing but a boy myself and in some hot water with my daddy. I can't say exactly where I was, but it weren't far from here. Seemed like as foreign a place as the stars. Folks used to tell children you could dig a hole deep enough to find China, come out on the other side of the world. That's what it was like, son. I guess I fell through."

"Would you tell me about it?" Seigle asked.

"I'll tell you what I can remember—but most of my life's on this side of that hole." Turner took some water and swallowed with a gulping sound. Seigle could see the liquid trembling from Turner's slight palsy as the glass found the table top again. Turner wiped his mouth and began.

"It happened long about the time I was making my way up from short pants to long, and running over these fields in every direction I could think on. My daddy caught me with an old leather bridle from the barn over the hill—that barn rotted, it's been took down—and told me not to step foot back into his house, not to eat or sleep again under his roof until I'd figured out how to be an honest man."

"Your father was a hard man," Seigle said.

"Heh. Hard as nails. You know that old bridle weren't no use. I just wanted it to play with my little pony, and it wouldn't fit him anyway. The reins was about dried and cracked in two. Same with the headstall. And the bit, it was made for a quarter horse, not a little ole pony, to start with. I wouldn't a-kept that bridle but just slipped back into the barn and hung it up on the tool wall that was full of useless and rusty odds and ends, if my daddy hadn't come along, right when I was trying to slip the headstall over little Roy's ears, and asked me where it came from and what in Sam Hill I thought I was doing.

"I was so scared that the first thing out of my mouth was the truth. The bridle come from Falkner's barn. That day I learned how the inside turns out on you as you grow on up and try to squeeze through the straight gate. My daddy, he was nothing but strict and honest and never had two cents to rub together. That's what happens when a man chooses what he thinks is all white over black and can't see to steer through the gray days, when fog hangs low on the mountain over there and inches down so heavy, on down to the creek, that a man would need to crawl on his belly like an asp to escape it, to keep his head out of the fog.

"My daddy, oncet he caught me like a thief, he just left and went on back to our house. The time was late in the day and the temperature was dropping off, and my job was to pump water up from the well for Mama's cooking and washing up the supper plates. I didn't want to make matters worse, so I pumped that water and set it on the front porch. Then I chopped some wood for the stove. And even though I couldn't see Daddy right then, I didn't dare go inside. I saw through the window that Mama was stirring something and singing to my little brother, still in diapers at that time. Mama never looked over her shoulder or through the window while I was looking in and watching her. I knew my daddy wouldn't even tell her why I was gone, and she'd likely worry herself sick, thinking one thing and another that could have happened to me. I didn't know where on earth I was going to sleep. Only place I could think of was where I'd gotten caught up in the first place, Falkner's barn. So I left my mama making supper that my daddy would smack his lips over, and I headed toward the barn before the night come on altogether. I thought I'd get up my nerve and go knock on Falkner's front door oncet I'd given him time to eat his supper. Why I didn't go straight on up to his house and confess my crime, I don't know. Guess I thought it'd go easier on me if I stretched out the time a bit and let Mr. Falkner fill his stomach with his cook's famous biscuits. Boy logic ain't a man's, so I really can't tell you why, just tell you what I did.

"Everyone said Mr. Falkner was a good man, though he drank a little whiskey. He worshipped with the foot-washing Baptists like we did, and he was baptized in the creek like I had been. I was sorry I'd borrowed that bridle, but you know I weren't planning to keep it, and there my daddy—who was always at the ready to prove I weren't worthy of my mama's love—caught me with my hand on another man's property. I couldn't think of a way out, because I knew if I didn't confess to stealing my daddy wouldn't be satisfied, and if I confessed, well, it weren't the full truth. And how was Mr. Falkner going to feel about a man managing his farm who had a son stealing from him? I didn't want to get Daddy fired. My stomach was all knotted up with confusion, and with being hungry for the stew Mama was probably feeding to my little brother right then. If I just got that fool confession over with I could have my share. Wouldn't my mama know I was still a good boy?

"My head like to hung so low I was feeling nothing but pitiful and hungry, whilst dragging that old bridle along behind me by the reins like my ball and chain. One of the first crisp nights was falling as I walked to the barn, and I wished I had on my long johns that I wore all winter under my britches and for sleeping snug in my bed in the loft. I climbed a ladder up there and it was just my room, big enough for a narrow cot and two feet on the floor, but it was mine. Little Greg had a thief for a big brother before I could even talk to him proper. Fear got a-hold on me, inside deep, and dug in. And oncet that happened I couldn't think straight on what I should do. Everything seemed wrong. I got to feeling so low and scared that I thought maybe it'd go better on everyone if I just went on down the road like a hobo. I'd seen their signs on the fence posts and seen where they slept in the hay.

"I heard later on that the Great Depression made hoboes of a load of good men, but all I heard from my daddy was how those scruffy drunks didn't know how to work for their keep like God-fearing men, how they were the grasshoppers, thinking the world owed them a living. When my daddy said these things, he looked me in the eye just a-daring me to ask for something I ain't worked for, and me not twelve years old. Maybe I should walk on down the road till I met up with the railroad tracks and catch me a freight train and chug to the end of the line. I could get off the train and start all over again, and nobody would know I weren't as honest as they come. I could work hard and send back some money for Mama and little Greg. If I stayed here I would always be no better than a thief.

"About that time I got to the barn and stepped inside. I hung the bridle back on its rusty nail and wished I'd never seen or heard tell of it before. I stood in the barn listening to the animals for a long minute. In the dimness I could hear the cows kind of moaning and rustling, and the manure smell tightened against my nose like a muzzle. I hate to say it, but a flicker of a thought ran through my mind about Mr. Falkner's quarter horse. With a horse I could get myself as far away as I wanted to travel. Whilst I was thinking on that and fighting the temptation, I began to ponder all over again just what kind of a man it looked like I was turning out to be. My daddy was right to be hard on me if I weren't no better than a low-down horse thief. I stepped outside the barn into the cold air to get myself clear.

"Electric lights were burning in Mr. Falkner's house, though the moon weren't even up. I knew my daddy had yet to light the gas lamps, miser that he was. A dollar saved is a dollar earned, he always said, and he didn't care if it meant we had to eat in the dark and never read a book come evening, not even the Bible. We could recite, he said.

"I looked toward Mr. Falkner's house and started in the direction of it, but something took a-holt of me, like to yank me back and set me running the other way, away from it, but I weren't sure where I was. And I mean I was flying, in just a second or two, running like a convict with a pack of dogs on his trail. Running like a crazy person, like a mountain lion after prey, running every which way you can think. I didn't care about nothing but running, just running and running and running, until I fell down hard on my face and probably fell out for a spell.

"When I got myself awake I sat up and it seemed like I couldn't stop crying. So shook up, I was crying like a baby, but louder, and I was so mad at myself. You know how boys can be about weakness. Night had fallen and it was the dark phase of the moon, too, and purt soon I sensed that I weren't nowhere, nowhere at all. I knew I couldn't find my way home until morning, even if I had a-been welcome there. I knew I couldn't just sit there crying, so I picked myself up and started walking slowly, putting one foot in front of the other like a blind man picking his way through the brambles. Where I was going I didn't know, but I was going to stay on my feet instead of bawling like a crybaby.

"Branches scratched at my arms, and every now and then I twisted my ankle in a sudden dip or rut in the ground. But I kept right on going, going, kept right on. After a while I stopped sniffling. My steps were measured for the dark, and I was beginning to see that I ought to just stop walking and find some place to sleep through the night. Maybe things would look better in the morning, that was one of Mama's thoughts. My eyes adjusted as the darkness come on, so that I could see just a little ways in front of my face, but not far. Like I said, there weren't no moon. I guess I'd forgotten about wanting to leave, because all I could do was think about going home in the morning. I was hoping for hotcakes after I talked to my mama and set things to rights.

"Cheering myself up, I started whistling a tune, and the next step I remember unbalanced me so that I fell headlong. My foot took a step into nothing but air. I tumbled down for so long, rolling ass over teakettle, that down didn't mean a damn any more. I flailed my arms trying to grab a-hold of something, but nothing stopped me for a very long time. So far did I fall, then, that when I stopped I would have thought I was dead if my stomach hadn't been churning so bad that I heaved. Nothing came up but bile as I was so hungry. All my strength about give out on me then. I was struggling like a tipped-over tortoise to right myself. Arms and legs and hurt places—I was waving them all in the air to find my balance again. And as soon as I got myself turned over I fell into an achy, fitful sleep, almost like I had took chamomile.

"Those dreams I had that night were filled with faces and words. Faces from all over the world, and some all colors, with eyes like almonds, some with little bitty slit eyes, some with tilting eyes. Everywhere eyes. Words hurled toward me, more like something you saw than something you heard. I can do figures in my head, and I've always been able to spell, but all the same it weren't possible to recognize the words in the air coming toward me fast as baseballs.

"An old bent woman was walking along carrying a knapsack of belongings on her back. She stopped, reached to the ground in front of her, and palmed a big, black, rock. If a boy picked up a rock and then the next day two rocks and the third day three, and on like that, purt soon he'd be as strong as an ox. That wrinkled old woman, she pulled her arm back like a stiff bow string and flung that black rock, sent it sailing at least a quarter mile down the dirt road. Well, the rock hit a bird on the wing, and the bird fell straight to the ground like it'd been shot. I went to see it and what I found was an orange and white striped tropical fish, big as a mallard duck, lying dead in the road. My jaw dropped open. I looked toward the old woman, but all I could see was another black rock, so I picked it up and threw it with all my strength. That rock was a sight heavier than it looked, with a mind stronger than gravity. It tried to fall right back on my head, though I had thrown it away from myself. Seems I spent the rest of that long night trying to hurl that rock away from my own head. Oh the dreams I dreamed that night....

"Dreamed I was crawling, like to crawled for miles. If a man could crawl around the belt of the earth itself, that's how far I had to crawl that night. And I couldn't raise myself up no matter how hard I tried, and I couldn't see nothing but my hands pressing down on the dirt as I dragged myself forward and up, through something like a tunnel. Even though I could scarcely see, I felt through things as I moved. I crawled over mounds of skeleton bones. I could feel them breaking apart beneath me. Sometimes I felt some soft moss and wanted to stop and sleep, but I didn't dare stop. Other times it felt like I was crawling over animal fur, thick pelts. And their musk was strong in my nose, almost smothering my breath.

"The next morning I woke on the rim of a hole in the ground, biggest damn sinkhole I ever saw. Must have been more than a hundred yards across. And so deep that when I looked down into it all I saw was blackness. I raised myself up, bruised and sore and started walking away from that hole, looking to find the creek that ran all through the valley, so I could find my way home like I was water, like I was running to a river and on to the sea.

"My mama met me at the door of our house and reached for me and pulled me to her. But I never could feel that safe again, like my mama always made the world for me before.

She said I looked a sight, like the devil had been chasing me and when I found my voice I said, "That's just what happened." Being afraid my daddy would catch me up short for telling lies, I never said no more about that night whilst they were living.

"Later that day my daddy hauled me back to Falkner's farm, made me look Mr. Falkner in the eye and show him the bridle back on its hook and tell him I had taken it. While my daddy offered to switch me senseless in sight of the barn, Mr. Falkner reproved me by saying that I had been on the brink of trouble, but that I had saved myself by my confession. And that was all the reprimand I got or needed, though Daddy seemed less than satisfied.

"I've never found that sinkhole again, though several times I felt drawn to look. I have heard travelers passing North or South, asking after that hole, or something like it. One claimed to have found it and they sent him to me. He was talking some jibberish and tried to take me there, but I have no need of going back to where a boy fell in what folks around here call the Murder Hole and crawled out a man." Turner leaned back in his chair and took some water. "For all I know it ain't even the same hole. This was years back."

"So you've never been back?" Seigle asked.

"I got no need of it, and there was plenty of other things to think on. Two wars and as many wives and a slew of children that has children and babies that has babies now. If I wanted to, I could give up this farm and live house to house with a different child every month." Turner shook his head. "Like as not I'll stay here and they can carry me out in a pine box."

"You ever feel lonely?" Seigle asked him.

"Oh, hell, I'm never alone for a minute. Two wives in heaven's worse than one in the kitchen. Some days the chatter's something terrible. If I don't cook a good meal for myself, believe me I hear about it. Like to run me ragged, those two old ghosts." Turner shook his head again and laughed.

Seigle stopped cold, not sure whether to laugh or cry, wondering whether he'd wind up as half-baked as Turner or as wise. And without even ghosts to watch over him.

"Why don't you speak up?" Turner said.

"What?" Seigle started.

"Why don't you just ask?" There was a ripple of light in the old man's eyes, as if two skipping stones just danced across their surfaces. "Find it again, I reckon I could."

Seigle felt his blood rush to the top of his head. "Maybe you can point me in the right direction? Lead me there?"

"I'm not too steady on my pins. Fact is, I'm a decripid old goat, and you can't expect me to traipse all over creation like a young buck."

Seigle pushed back from the table and rose with Turner as he started clearing the bowls from the table. Then Turner disappeared into a back room.

In a few minutes Turner came back to the table, wearing a suit vest over his shirt and carrying a long tube beneath one arm and several smooth river stones in his hands. From the tube he drew out a map and unrolled it, weighting each corner with one of the stones. From his watch pocket he fished an inverted pyramid out by a string. It rose from the vest pocket, an heirloom, golden, but not a timepiece.

"I've been dowsing for fifty years, took it up in retirement. Heh." Turner stopped to give a laugh at himself. "Used to walk around with a cherry fork, now I use a map. I guess that's why you're here, I guess somebody told you."

Seigle shook his head, no.

"I can dowse water just as easy as you please. This augury come from my mentor." Turner lifted the gold pyramid, which swung like a fishing weight at the end of the black string. "This was left me when he passed. With this I can dowse most any lost thing."

The augury swung back and forth as Seigle observed it. From the gold augury Seigle thought he saw a spectrum emerge, as if bent through a prism. The colors intertwined and swirled into the air. The old man snapped his fist over the pendulum motion and gathered all of the string into his left hand.

Seigle jerked his head back and blinked.

"Heh," Turner laughed. "Just like hypnotizing chickens. Son, don't you fall out on me, now. Oncet we begin, you attend the map, not the pendulum, you hear?"

Seigle nodded.

"Now tell me your request if I ain't guessed it. You got to state it."

Seigle opened his mouth and nothing came out. His tongue felt like a brick in his mouth, dry and swollen. There was an egg where his Adam's apple used to pump up and down when he talked. He couldn't even swallow.

Turner's head appeared to be bowed. He was silently reading from a strip of Sycamore bark scribbled with words. He'd pulled it from his vest pocket. "Indian paper," Turner said. "My mentor left me this prayer."

Seigle reached for the bark.

"It's for the seer not the one with the question," Turner said and covered it with his hand. "Take your time, but say what you come for. Nothing comes without asking. It's a lesson hard to learn and no way around. Knock and the door shall be opened. It's true, though I ain't one to thump you with the Bible."

Seigle closed his eyes. He let the hum of a thousand and one things quiet in his mind. The emptiness was so real it felt unreal. "I want to know if there's a cavern and where it can be entered." His words rang true in his ears; there was no ambivalence, just a pure question.

The old man nodded, released the gold pendulum so that it dangled from his hand. Except for a perceptible, slight pull in the opposite direction when he slowly steered it across the map, the pendulum appeared stagnant.

"Folk used to fortune tell with tortoise shells. Drop the shell into a fire and interpret the cracks."

"Have you ever read that shell?" Seigle meant the one mounted over their heads.

"Not myself, no. But this is way back I'm discussing, and foreign. My mentor studied on most ancient ways. Used to tell me he was Chinese-Cherokee. Either way he weren't much to look on, ugly as sin and twice as ornery. That man could clear a room of the faint-hearted and bring on the curious like a sideshow just by sitting still." The pendulum lurched and began spinning clockwise. "Whoa, now, I think we've caught something," Turner said.

Seigle looked at his watch. 4:55. Vernal equinox right on the nose.

The old man pressed his mouth into a determined line, closed his eyes, and held his arm steady while the pendulum spiraled, gradually narrowing then widening its concentric circles. If it had been a dog it would have found its spot and lain down to sleep.

Seigle hadn't noticed until that moment how the sun had blasted through the window, dispelling the notion of snow. The sun created whirling shadow from the pendulum on the map below, so that Seigle's eyes followed the shape as it distorted, waxing larger and waning smaller than the augury.

Turner's practiced eye discerned the spot, as the augury traced its spiral once more. The old man placed his index finger on the map. The augury stopped, sending a shudder up the string, and hovered above the spot. Turner set the augury down, picked up a pencil, licked the lead like a schoolboy, and drew an X on the place that his finger had held.

"There, you'll find what you're looking for."

Seigle's hands tingled as he squinted toward the X.

"I've a message for you, though, son," Turner said, summoning Seigle's gaze. "Words sometimes appear like signposts in my head when I'm doing the dowsing. I never ask why, but the words ain't never failed the test of truth. There's a message for you under the earth beneath the X, but you ain't ready to heed it. Some knowledge has to spread on you like sunshine. I advise you to wait. Don't go headlong into this. Your heart, it has to open in its own time. You're a man with a shadow and somehow you've got to set it a-loose before you go into this any further."

"Ah, shit," Seigle said. "What a bunch of hooey."

"You think so. You listen good. You're like a frozen pond. Hold a man's weight in winter, but hard to drink." Turner stood up and removed the four river stones, rolled up the map. His hands quivered again and failed him, so Seigle reached out and tightened the coil and tapped the map back into the tube. Turner deflated like an empty feed sack, all his energy had run out. He was old and stooped and Seigle thought he might fall right over.

"Cat got your tongue?" Turner snapped, in a feisty tone.

Seigle nearly jumped.

"I'm a frazzled old turtle, but I ain't passed. Heh." Turner began to laugh. His cackle spilled beyond the frail borders of the man to fill the kitchen. Seigle laughed, too, in spite of himself. Between himself and this old farmer, the smoke and mirrors of generations had swept a clean path. Seigle gazed into Turner's face, as into his own soul, neither good nor bad, young nor old. They were two halves of heartwood split by a single stroke.

"I'm sorry for being an ass," Seigle said.

"I seen worse."

"How did you learn all this?" Seigle asked.

"I've had good teachers."

Seigle looked squarely into Turner's watery eyes and found that there was still a bit of fire left in them. "How does a man find his teacher?" Seigle asked.

"By loving someone," Turner said. "Here, now, you take this map."

Head reeling, Seigle nearly tumbled out the old man's door and into his jeep. Nothing can be that simple, he thought. The map tube rattled off the passenger seat, onto the floor, as Seigle backed around in the driveway. He had what he'd come for, but he was thinking of something else. Someone else. He had to talk to Jessy, tell her how he felt while she might still listen.

The Shattering

Moira heard Carlos bark, the front door opened, and Paul stepped into the house. He dropped his briefcase and came toward her. "What a week." He drew her into his embrace. "I'm glad it's over." His rough cheek pressed hers, and then she felt a warm kiss greet her neck. It sent a wave of pleasure to her face and down her torso. Then the doorbell rang. Moira unwrapped herself to answer.

It was Renée, dressed radiantly in a blue silk suit. "I won't keep you," she said. "Car's running. But I wanted you to know that I'm leaving."

Moira was stunned. She felt Paul come up behind her.

Renée, all grace and manners, addressed Paul, "I'm one of your neighbors—or I was." She turned to Moira, "Anyway, thank you."

Moira watched Renée walk to her car, get in and drive away.

"What was that all about?" Paul asked.

"I'm not sure," Moira said. "I think she's leaving her husband."

"I hope you didn't have anything to do with it." Paul turned toward the stairs. "I'm going to change."

Generic tacky. That just about covered the restaurant décor. Including the ferns and the fringed sombreros, it reminded Moira of the packages of Mexican jumping beans she had received as party favors when she was a child. But the food was highly touted. She surveyed the menu and tried unsuccessfully to suppress a yawn.

"Bored with my company already?" Paul asked.

"You know that's not the case. Sorry, I can't seem to help it." Five months along, the pregnancy left her tired no matter how religiously she napped each afternoon.

"Would you like for me to order for us both?"

Moira nodded, and that's what Paul did when the waitress reappeared. This was their night on the town. Ian was at a sleepover birthday party—and thank God it wasn't Moira having to host it. Her energy seemed to be turning inward as the baby grew. Even the sensitivity that had sharpened to a point, alarming her and changing everything—she thought—had waned to a low drone, no more than a fuzzy view through curtains that she could shut out at will. She wondered if she could have lost the gift before learning to employ it fully.

Seeing Renée had reminded her of the urgency she had felt. It was already a memory. Taylor had phoned to tell her that both of the women had been assaulted before they died, and she'd asked him, "Do you mean raped?" Assault seemed like a pretty word for it, a euphemism. Yes, that was what he meant by assault. Taylor wanted to know if she had any leads, had she picked up anything more; there was a very dangerous man at large, whose samples didn't match anyone's they had on file. It had given her a helpless gnawing sensation in her gut. What good was her so-called gift if she could only find dead bodies? Any trained dog could do as well.

Detective Taylor applied some pressure on her to return. "Maybe you would pick up on something new. We're dry. We've got nothing. Will you please think about it?" Moira had asked him why he didn't call Regina, and he said that he had, but that she referred him back to Moira. "Why would she do that?" Moira asked him. Detective Taylor had said, "She didn't say. Maybe it's because you're already in."

Paul had yet to ask about her role in the case. Was he afraid it would overshadow their life together? He had been so angry when she'd returned home that the subject was quickly buried along with the hatchet. She felt part of a conspiracy of conformity that deadened her.

"Would you rather we'd stayed home?" Paul asked.

"Oh, of course not."

"I was hoping for some conversation."

"Well, what have you been working on all week?" Moira asked.

"Anything but that—don't remind me."

Moira tried to think of a suitable subject.

"I'll tell you about something amazing," Paul said. "The Tevatron particle accelerator has documented the discovery of the last quark." Paul's voice had come alive.

"The last quark?"

"The top quark—the smallest, oldest piece of the puzzle. The last elementary particle. Isn't that amazing? Seeing its signature is like a glance backward in time."

"Just how far back are we talking about?" Moira asked.

"To the beginning. It's the twelfth note in the scale of creation."

"That's a rather long scale." Moira laughed.

This was Paul's favorite brain candy. "It is. From Newtonian solidity, to energy/matter exchanges, to field theory, to relativity, and so forth." Paul stopped to bite into his giant burrito and gulp some beer.

The conversation, with the exception of the last quark's discovery, was ground they'd been over before, always with Moira far behind and feeling sore. This was Paul's territory, his passion. She liked seeing him come alive in his ideas again. "Great burrito," Paul said, taking another bite.

"Yes, it is. Good choice."

"You see, what we call 'things' are only probabilities that might become events. The way light is both particle and wave."

A question turned inside her, as Moira listened. It was the same old tune, yet this time she found a spark of relevance. "Then why did you tell me that nothing could travel faster than the speed of light?" she demanded more than asked.

"Not that again. We're discussing the theoretical level, not ordinary life—there's a difference."

"What use is a theory without applying it? Instantaneous communication across distances—that can be inferred from your theories. It's a short leap."

"I think you simplify somewhat." Paul wiped his mouth and leaned back in his chair, away from the table.

"I know one thing—you haven't asked me anything about what happened out there. I could have gone to the mall for two days for all the interest you've shown. All you cared about was whether I came home when I said I would."

"Lower your voice." Paul leaned in. "And call—you didn't even call, remember? I read the newspaper. They found two bodies, and there wasn't any mention of psychic intervention. It seems to me that you've been spending your time meddling in other people's business. I think it's time you paid some attention to your own."

"Is there something you want to tell me?" Moira asked. "If I've been neglecting you, please say so. You're the one who has stopped communicating. What are you working on, anyway? That is the reason we're here, isn't it? What's so top secret that you can't share it with me anymore?"

Before Paul could answer or Moira could catch her breath the water erupted out of their glasses. Dishes and silverware sprayed in all directions. In Moira's recurring elevator dream the walls fell away and the floor of the elevator car began tilting, as she struggled to maintain balance and the car kept moving up. Ceiling plaster crashed around their table and onto it, bursting into plumes of dust upon impact. They were like ants on a paper plate being shaken off the flat earth.

When the vibration stopped, they were on the floor. Moira felt Paul lying over her, a human shield. His blood was falling into her eyes. Moira pressed her palm to his forehead covering a gash.

"Are you okay?" he asked, laying a soft hand against her stomach. His face was streaked with blood, like a brave's war paint.

"Yes. I think so. You have a cut above your eye."

They struggled to their feet with the rest of the patrons. No one appeared more than dazed, the victim of cuts and bruises. As they followed the rest of the group out of the restaurant onto the sidewalk, a man in a soiled silk sport coat said, "At least it wasn't the big one."

Their car was unharmed, but the SUV parked right beside theirs had had its windshield smashed in by a concrete cornice.

"I'll drive," Moira said. Before starting the engine she found a roll of paper towels in the backseat and peeled off one for Paul.

Paul was finding his phone. "Ian," he said. "What's the number?"

Moira gave it to him.

"Shit, no service." Paul waited half a minute and punched redial. He pitched the phone into the floor at his feet. "Let's drive over there."

"We've got to get you some stitches," Moira said. "I know Ian is safe. I feel it."

Paul shot her a look. "You'd better be right."

EXTRA WAITING ROOM CHAIRS were lined up in the middle of the room facing forward, as if for a home movie. Fractures, concussions, and contusions limped by, while Moira and Paul waited their turn. Occasionally something more serious was rolled through the double doors on a stretcher and disappeared.

The young man with his arm cradled in a bloody towel had been shot. He was the victim of Saturday night, not the earthquake. A young boy wailed, "Help me! Help me!" as his mother carried him to the check-in desk. His little wrists were locked into toy handcuffs. And there was a wound on one of his feet that trailed droplets of blood.

"Moira," Paul began. "I haven't wanted to tell you this, but I think Martin, the company, may be involved in something illegal. I'm not sure."

Moira's attention left the little boy and riveted on the one word, *illegal*. "What did you say?"

"I'm sorry to tell you now, but I've put it off too long. The customers I've sold contracts to are calling me back, impatient, but Martin won't give me any information to pass along. Oh, Christ, I should never have brought you and Ian out here."

Moira felt her stomach lurch at the panicked tone in Paul's voice.

"I can tell something is wrong," Paul said. "I don't know what, but I suspect Martin is hanging me out to dry. Maybe Polaski, too. The bottom line is that my signature sealed all of those contracts, and they may have been obtained under false pretenses. And some government agents are sniffing after Polaski. Martin says it's just federal bullshit, but I wonder."

"Cindy told me Andrew resigned from the Goldstone Station when they took some cutbacks."

"Maybe he took something with him. I'm sure he had to sign a non-compete, and he had access to everything up there. He probably designed half of it. If Martin's involved in a crime, I won't get out unscathed. I'm scared, Moira."

"Go to the police. You have to."

"With what? I don't have anything concrete."

Eventually, a nurse appeared and read off Paul's name from her clipboard. He followed her down the hall to an examination cubicle formed by a curtain. Moira took a seat in the hallway outside the room.

Right under her nose, she was thinking. Here was something right under her nose and she hadn't had a clue about it. Moira dug out her phone to check on Ian. She needed to know that he was safe.

What she learned was not reassuring. Ian wasn't there. *Not there.* He had left the party with Broder, who had given some story about how Ian had to go home, couldn't stay the night, and that his parents had sent Broder to pick him up. And Broder wasn't even old enough to drive. She called her home number and listened while it rang and then she entered the message code.

She was waiting on her feet when Paul emerged with stitches across his forehead. A patch had been shaved at his hairline where the network of small jagged cuts began in his scalp and spilled down his face toward the bridge of his nose and his left eye. Bandages covered the deepest cuts.

"I'm okay." Paul said. "The doctor said that any leftover glass would work its way to the surface. It's going to take some time. Moira? What is it?"

"It's Ian," Moira said. "Broder picked him up from the party right after dinner. He said he was taking Ian home."

"Broder driving?" Paul shook his head with disbelief.

"Let's go," Moira said.

"Wait a minute. The doctor said he'd check you next. And I want you checked."

"There's a message from Polaski. You better call and listen to it."

The nurse ushered Moira into the room where she was given one of those infuriating gowns that covered nothing.

The doctor was a small man wearing thick glasses, who did not seem to be looking at her as he placed the stethoscope on her swollen stomach and listened to the heartbeat beneath the skin. The doctor didn't listen to Moira's heart.

"Tell your husband everything's fine."

"Everything's fine? I'll tell him." Moira dressed quickly.

The Listening Station

The car bounced up the crude road for more than a mile before the trail just stopped and a chain-link fence barred their passage. There was another car parked nearby, an old convertible with the top down.

About fifty yards away, behind the ten-foot fence festooned with menacing saw-toothed spirals, the headlights revealed a white disk, like a giant funneling ear against a background of gnarled, Mojave yuccas.

Paul cut the engine, and then the lights. "When I was out here before there was nothing, not a thing except the fence." Paul said. "It must be as big as Goldstone."

When their eyes adjusted they saw an enormous swath of constellations behind and above the antenna.

"What are they listening for?" Moira asked.

"Something coming from so far away and long ago that only an antenna as large as this can pick up the frequency," Paul said. "But this is way too costly just for curiosity's sake. And why—" Paul stopped himself. Paul moved to open his door. "You stay here."

"I want to go," Moira said.

"Please, no." Paul got out of the car and toward the gate. He worked his way through several keys. Without satisfaction, he returned to the car. For a second or two Moira thought he was going to start the engine, but instead Paul straightened up in his seat. "I'm going over," he said.

Moira watched from the car as Paul again approached

the fence. The chain fence rattled as Paul started scaling near the gate and dropped to the ground on the other side. As Paul hit the ground Moira felt a sharp pain shoot up her left leg from the ankle. Paul gave a short wave and disappeared into the dark night favoring one leg.

As Paul moved farther away from the car, he pulled Moira with him. Soon it was as though she stood beside him in the shadow of the giant white ear. Invisible pulses sifted through the cold desert air. Moira felt her own receptivity expand, moving out through the night to meet her husband, to be with him. Moira let go the barriers between what she experienced and what she had been taught she could experience. The boundaries fell as she embraced what she loved, in the knowledge that it was love that moved faster than light.

Moira remembered the first time she'd met Paul, at a frat party she had not wanted to attend. He primed the keg for her and pumped out a plastic glass of beer. When he had handed that beer to her and met her eyes for the first time, she had felt a warm certainty shoot through her: she knew he was hers, her partner. In a matter of months he was—and had been ever since.

The white antenna opened to the night like an empty shell, an enormous open possibility. If she held her ear close to that white ear, would she hear the cosmic sea whispering inside? Moira moved with Paul through space and through thought. What he saw, she saw. What he felt, she felt also.

"Moira," Paul addressed her. She could not any longer see him, and yet she heard him clearly. And she knew he was stumbling around in the dark, looking for something, not knowing what. So far all he had found was the antenna itself.

Polaski's rather cryptic message had said that Ian was out at the project, that Broder had shown up with him. Did it mean that Polaski was holding Ian? Moira did not know.

Paul found a trapdoor carved into the rock at his feet, a concrete door that had been roughly concealed by a loose dusting of soil. Paul reached for the steel handle and opened the door. Moira felt that she was remembering this door. Below it, stairs descended sharply. Paul started down, as if into a basement—or a sixties-style fallout shelter.

Moira sent Paul a question, and their conversation shot back and forth instantaneously across the darkness. "How much energy would it take to make a speck of mass?"

"An enormous amount. $E=mc^2$," came Paul's answer.

"What if there were a heavy bit of mass, a speck that—"

"You mean the process in reverse?"

"Yes."

"If there were a new particle, heavier than any we have known so far it might produce untold energy. But no one has seen anything but a trace of the top quark. I told you— It's like a meteor trail across the sky. That quark is a third generation particle that only travels the width of a proton before decaying into other particles, streams of hadrons, muons, electrons, neutrinos. We have only seen the aftermath of the last quark, not the thing itself. But if it could be harnessed, perhaps—"

At the bottom of the steep stairway Paul entered a corridor lit by bands of phosphorescence, like yellow-green smears of fireflies' bellies. He moved quickly along the corridor and into another zone. Moira was shivering. She was having trouble feeling him now. Just find Ian, she was thinking. Just bring back our son.

At the end of the corridor, Paul approached another door. The door opened for him and he moved through. Then he was gone. Moira felt their connection go dead. She had not known until this moment that their connection had been as fragile as a string stretched between two cups in a child's game of telephone.

Seigle's Descent

THE MAN STOOD before his mirror and took a pair of scissors to his beard. Wads of coarse hair fell into the basin. He took a paper towel and wiped the first round of hair from the sink. Then he lathered and scraped down to his pasty skin. Splashed warm water on his face and wrapped it in a hot towel afterwards. His white face emerged like a cavefish from the depths of darkness. Randy Seigle rummaged in the back of the bathroom cabinet under the sink and found a little aftershave left in a bottle—so old the cap was rusty. Had to run to the toolbox for the pliers to open the lid. He used to cull out his beard some, trim it neatly around his cheeks and mouth and splash on a little scent. He let the genie out of the bottle, patted both sides of his face. This time, the aftershave stung. He yipped when it hit his vulnerable skin.

He'd almost forgotten the reason he'd grown the beard in the first place, forgotten the old acne scars that had embarrassed him into hiding. The scars looked better; they had faded over time. His skin was smoother than he remembered.

A knock came on the kitchen door. Then someone stepped into the house without an invitation.

"Hey, buddy," Jeff called. "You ready to go?"

"Ready," Seigle said.

"Let's hit it, then. My engine's running."

"Sure you want to take yours? We could take mine."

Seigle stepped into the kitchen with the towel slung over his shoulder.

"God," Jeff said, when he looked at Seigle's face. "What'd you do to yourself?"

PAST LATE SPRING's yellow-throated irises, blue-hooded, like flashes of indigo buntings in summer leaves; beyond May apples, wild and shy beneath their green cabanas; past redbuds glazing wooded hillsides with blood; past faded daffodils, grape hyacinths, trillium, and the pink and white Catawba blooms, Jeff and Seigle started out before dawn with their gear. They dragged across the fields and up the shale ridge, to the spot marked by Turner's X. Jeff and Seigle, no one else. After Seigle had dug out the first slivers of shale fossil between the giant pricky pears, he had called Jeff in to help him. For several months they had widened the opening by pickax and shovel, increased it to a four-foot channel, so that a man could crawl through on his belly.

In the middle of his kitchen table, Seigle had left a photocopy of the relevant part of Turner's map. No note, just the 8x10 map detail, weighted down with a white pottery mug that Jessy had given him before writing him off. It was the only thing he owned that was decorated with a flower. The potter had penned "Iris" in tiny script below the flower. Every morning Seigle drank out of that mug, some days kicking himself about letting Jessy go, some days resigned, even angry at her and filled with self-justification. But he had never screwed up his courage to call her. He felt like a book with a missing page. He could skip over it and read on, but the hole in the story stayed. Every day he thought about her, in spite of himself.

Jeff and Seigle stood at the opening, pausing a moment before going through with their plan.

"This land still belongs to the old farmer," Seigle said. "Everything above and below. We're here by permission only."

"Doesn't have to stay that way. How old do you think he is anyway?" Jeff asked.

"Maybe ninety. That may be underestimating it." Seigle shrugged and smiled.

Jeff was taking in the information, rubbing his chin. "Your face looks like shit."

"Thank you," Seigle said.

"You're welcome. Let's get going. Pin my tail on."

Seigle hooked the rope end to the emergency, first aid pack. "Donkey's got its tail," he said.

Jeff squatted and started worming his way through.

As he waited his turn, Seigle couldn't help but think of Floyd Collins, who died in the 1920's, wedged in a narrow shaft, blood rushing to his head at the bottom of a ten-foot chute, with a steady drip of water falling onto his scalp. And the last time anyone talked to him, Floyd raved about angels and chicken sandwiches, liver and onions. He tried to con his rescuers into risking their lives to free him by lying that he'd gotten his pinned legs and arms free. His brother fed him sandwiches until part of the shaft caved in and no one could get down far enough again to reach him. By the time rescue shaft had been dug down the other side where the soil was more stable, Floyd was dead. *Great omen.* Seigle had a mind that worked toward disasters—he reviewed Floyd's fate, and then he started working his way along the horizontal shaft he and Jeff had dug, pulling his sack of gear behind him: water, high-energy food, waterproof container of matches and candles, flashlight, batteries, gloves, space blanket, meters for measuring angles and depths, as well as compasses and the usual assortment of carabiners, ascenders, and rappel racks. A shitload of nylon rope, divided into tidy bundles. Each man wore coveralls, seat and chest harnesses. Jeff had a carbide lamp on his hard hat, Seigle the despised LED lamp on his helmet. They shared a first aid kit and one steel ladder. Seigle had the ladder.

Seigle's last glimpse of sky told him there was yet another storm brewing. For a solid week the rain had brought with it high wind and lightning. One night they had stayed out so late they'd not made it back into Blacksburg and slept instead near the hole they were digging. Awakened in the middle of the night by whipping wind and sheets of rain, they had found shelter in a low dip of ground. Seigle could smell it before it hit. It made the hairs stand up all over his body. A tree took a direct lightning strike that split it top to bottom not fifty feet away.

"Goddamn," Jeff had shouted. The only human noise.

The tree had continued to flame like a signal flare through the heavy rain.

A week earlier they had unexpectedly completed the passageway. Jeff had taken a torch and worked what turned out to be the last few inches, passing the dirt out cupful by cupful. Seigle had heard a whoop and then Jeff had backed out again, smudged and excited.

"We're going to need some rope, padre. I think we've found the shaft. We're at a drop."

"How much?"

"More than we've got, but give me what we brought."

Jeff had tied the rope together and dragged it into the hole, disappearing. Once he'd crawled to the end of the shaft again, he dropped the rope down without plumbing bottom.

"Gonna need more, like I thought," Jeff had said, emerging.

Now Seigle started his descent, slowly feeding the rappel rack and walking his way down the rough walls of the shaft. A strong draft of dank air, like smoke finding its way out a chimney, rushed around him as he lowered his weight on the line. Seigle rested on an outcrop for a minute or two, sending down a light spray of pebbles.

"Hey, man, watch it," Jeff called.

"Sorry."

"It's okay. You're almost home."

Seigle finished his descent, dangling in air as the walls widened steadily away from him. The farther he descended the more the shaft widened, until fifteen minutes had passed and he'd played out over four hundred feet of rope. His altimeter confirmed the distance. Not by any means a record, but a record for Seigle, and a perfect occasion for testing rappel racks, revamped back in the sixties by Appalachian cavers to replace cumbersome and balky winches. All of their gear was improvised from either miners or mountaineers.

Seigle touched down beside Jeff and they set about surveying the first, narrow chamber, trusting that it led someplace finer. Not much of a find itself, it stretched twenty feet and diminished at the end to twelve inches in height. And that was the only passage, the only funnel out.

They wormed through the opening, leaving their packs behind in the first chamber. Down a steeply angled bank, they scrambled over loosely strewn rock to a shallow pool marked by rimstone where water was low, and a new lip was forming. A steady dripping down the wall from the ceiling fed the pool. Seigle reached into the water and lifted a cave pearl. The polished deposit seemed to emit an inner light in his hand. He raised it for Jeff's inspection.

"I seen those before," Jeff said, turning back to the chamber wall, casting his carbide lamp over soda straws and mushroom stalagmites without stopping to inspect or admire any of the formations.

"Do you hear water?" Jeff asked.

"The dripping into the pool," Seigle said. The sound he heard best was his own pumping heartbeat.

"No—it's something else."

Jeff wandered on, and Seigle started after him, toward what he thought would be the far side of the second chamber. He didn't yet imagine its real dimensions.

The fourteen-foot roof over the pool was only a ledge, as Seigle discovered when he popped from beneath its overhang and the vaulting roof expanded beyond his flashlight's power. They began charting and mistook stands of story-high boulders for walls, backtracked around and then climbed over them. Jeff continued to mention the sound of running water he was hearing, and after a while Seigle thought that maybe he heard it, too. A firecracker had taken out some of his decibel range so long ago that he forgot what he was missing. Sometimes Seigle thought he heard the rushing inside his own skin, the liquid and static tone of the body's tide rising and falling. He had never known Jeff to show such sensitivity before. He couldn't be sure they were hearing the same sound.

All the same, Seigle was listening intently. To something inside or outside, high on the wall, or perhaps beneath the limestone, when Jeff's steps just ahead of him dislodged some rubble and the floor dropped out from beneath a narrow rim they had been blithely crossing. It was like spring ice cracking. And beneath them a wide mouth opened. No telling how deep it went. They inched backward, pressing their knees to the edges until the floor rose to meet the wall again. Seigle was breathing hard and felt a little squeeze shoot through his chest that told him he needed to rest. Leaving Jeff, he crawled back into the first chamber, opened his pack and ate a sandwich. In a few minutes Jeff followed.

"Where'd you go, padre?"

"Hungry," Seigle said, thinking about the fact that all of the food in a cave, unless animals cannibalize each other, must come from outside. Seigle was thinking about this as Jeff reached into his own pack and pulled out a sandwich and a jug.

The Land Between

"Thought we might have been getting too close to the Murder Hole for your comfort," Jeff said and bit off half of his sandwich. He was a greedy eater, fast and efficient, like an alpha dog after a choice bitch.

Seigle watched as Jeff licked his fingers even though they'd been clawing rock half a day and the nails were black with dirt. Probably started that way. Seigle's hands were clean and soft. He had worn his gloves. Only removed them to eat.

"We're all cave creatures," Seigle said.

Jeff gulped some water.

"As above—so below, " Seigle continued. "The only difference being that in a cave the effects of a closed ecosystem can be felt more quickly."

"Whatever," Jeff said. "I knew you were going to get religion some day. I have a nose for kooks."

"You think I'm cracked, then."

"As I sit here, you're crazier than anyone I know."

"How do you mean that?"

"Tell me what you're thinking, padre."

"Stop calling me that. What I'm sitting here wondering is whether or not the sun can be considered to be outside or inside our system, whether the sun is an outside force for this tired planet, a power to stave off inertia."

"See what I mean, padre. You want to know what I'm thinking about?"

"I don't know."

"Pussy. Licking off the salt." Jeff grinned. "Well, I'm going back in. You coming?"

"In a few." Seigle rubbed his stomach. "I'll catch up."

The food had set his stomach on fire instead of resting him. Now he had a horrible case of indigestion on top of being tired. Seigle watched Jeff wriggle through the opening into the second chamber, thinking he probably shouldn't let the shitbird go alone.

On the Other Side of the Door

PAUL WALKED THROUGH the underground corridor banded with intermittent lights, iridescent like firefly bellies. The greenish flashes gave an eerie tint to his skin as he passed from light to darkness to light again. Moira felt that the darkness would swallow Paul whole. She felt fear rising from her feet to her throat. The symbiosis was severed, but she found that she could still see Paul, watch him as if he were in a silent movie. She followed him through the corridor and though the door at its end, which was standing open.

The room appeared empty except for a row of working computer screens. Each computer was sorting through a number sequence, calculating whatever equations it had been given to solve.

Paul moved closer to the screens and then no farther; he turned his head as if to listen, and all at once a white cat, like a plump Buddha, bounded onto the long computer table and settled in to wash its paws. Paul made a relieved step toward the computers, and the cat sat up attentively. When Paul made another step the cat opened its mouth, pulled back its lips from sharp teeth and hissed. Another motion caught Paul's attention, and he glanced back just in time to see the door to the corridor swing closed on its own. When he looked back to the cat it was casually washing itself and appeared, with fur fluffed, twice its already impressive size. The Buddha cat seemed to forget Paul unless he moved toward the computers. In which case the cat arched its back, hissed, and sent a warning look directly into his eyes.

The cat relaxed and continued its grooming, but Paul could not budge from the spot he occupied without reactivating its motion sensor.

All at once Paul decided to make his move. He leapt the five quick steps remaining between himself and the row of lighted computer screens, all the while waving his arms. The cat sprang from the table just as Paul arrived. When Paul let out a yelp of pain, Moira could hear as well as see him again. The Buddha cat had sunk its teeth into the meat of Paul's leg as if it were a pork chop. Trying to dislodge the cat's fangs from his calf, Paul fell to the floor. Moira felt the sting and pull of the cat's bite as it held on fast.

"So I see you've met Quark." It was Andrew Polaski. His wiry frame towered over Paul. "Quark! There now, enough!" The cat only responded when Polaski kicked him in the ribs, skirting away then with the taste of Paul's blood in its mouth.

"I see you've responded to my invitation," Andrew said and paused. "What happened to you anyway, did you get in a fight?"

"An earthquake." Paul rubbed his leg and sat on the floor at Andrew Polaski's feet. Then he pulled himself up with the aid of a desk. When offered a metal chair, to which Polaski motioned, Paul plopped into it.

"Our Quark can be vicious. Simply cannot be charmed." Andrew took a chair near Paul's. The computer screens worked away on their mathematical tasks.

"Where is Ian?" Paul demanded.

"And after all of your trouble, I'm afraid you'll have to be going," Martin said, coming toward them. "But what do you think of the operation, now that you're here?"

"I think something smells," Paul said. "What have you played me for?"

"You've been an excellent salesman, Paul. We couldn't

have done it without you," Martin said, eyeing Paul's recent stitches and bandages.

"I'm a scientist, not a salesman," Paul said.

"That's exactly why you've been so convincing," Martin said. "You've expanded our clientele enormously and I'm very grateful for your hard work. There could be rewards—"

"What absolute unqualified shit," Paul said, without raising his voice.

"Product development? Is that more what you had in mind? That's the next phase. You and Andrew could work together."

"And what if I'm not interested?"

Martin glanced toward the locked door, Paul's only way out. "When we explain it to you, I think you'll be interested. What are you going to do, go back to the woods of West Virginia?"

"It's Virginia, the woods of southwest Virginia," Paul said.

"You shouldn't be out here," Martin said.

"I think I was issued an invitation." Paul glanced toward Andrew but said nothing more.

"I think you stole my keys," Martin said.

"He had to know at some point," Andrew interjected.

"I disagree," Martin said.

"Where is my son?" Paul asked again.

"What does he mean?" Martin turned to Andrew.

"I don't know." Andrew scooped up Quark the cat into his lap and stroked it from head to tail.

"Like hell. So what happened to you at Goldstone?" Paul asked.

"He didn't go through the chain of command," Martin said.

"Yes. I skipped to the top man, and the department didn't much care for it." Andrew stroked the cat gently.

"What department?" Paul asked.

"Energy," Martin answered. "Andrew received a message from our distant neighbors, and instead of passing it up the usual chain, he started at the top of the loop."

"Where was the signal coming from?" Paul asked.

Andrew massaged Quark as he answered. "Pisces. I was fired for being in communication, not for breaking the chain of command."

"But the whole Goldstone project is a listening station. Wasn't that your job?"

Andrew laughed. "I hate to burst your bubble, but they know what's out there already. They've seen it as well as heard it. Currently they're spending their efforts, and our taxes, to communicate with it and convince it to—go away and leave our little earth alone. But there's no alone—there never was. We're an important species as it turns out. Important and dangerous. We're what the rest of the universe used to be."

Paul rubbed at the bite on his leg. The bleeding had stopped. "That's a little far-fetched, don't you think?"

"I told you Andrew, he's not ready for the truth. And now what do we do with him? Golden parachute time? Drop him out of the plane over a desert because nobody's going to believe him anyway?"

Andrew released Quark and he came tumbling toward Martin.

"Collar your damn cat before I skin it," Martin said.

"There's something you should know," Paul said.

"What's that?"

"If I don't show up back at home soon, Moira is going to mail an envelope addressed to the local police. There's a note inside with all of my suspicions scribbled on it. And there are a couple of kids hidden here somewhere."

"What crap," Andrew said. "Don't believe it."

Martin moved to a computer keyboard, and soon afterward the door to the tunnel swung open. In the tunnel beyond the door stood Ian and Broder.

"What the hell?" Martin said, turning to Andrew.

"Come here, son," Andrew said.

"I promise I'll drive straight home, Dad," Broder said.

"Not in my convertible, you won't."

"I'll take him," Paul said. "He can ride with us."

THE THREE OF THEM walked out of the tunnel together.

"Mr. Robbins," Broder began, once they had climbed out of the tunnel and the sky was stretched over them, with innumerable blinking stars.

"Save it for Ian's mother." Paul was limping on both ankle and calf. Not one good leg left to stand on. "I'm not in the mood. And you, Ian, I can't believe you did this, deceived us this way."

"It was my fault," Broder said.

"You bet it was," Paul said.

"I wanted to," Ian said. "I got Broder to bring me out here."

"You've been here before?" Paul asked, incredulous.

"I followed my dad."

"You followed your dad—you're not supposed to be driving."

"I got my learner's permit."

"Great," Paul said. "Fat lot of good it did."

When they got back to the gate it was standing open, and Moira was waiting there for them.

Inside Time

Seigle wormed back through the passage and into the large chamber. It was more difficult with a full stomach, and he had a little pain shooting up his arm, but nothing appealed to him more than to finish mapping this room. The food and rest had revived his interest.

"Jeff," he called.

Hearing no answer, Seigle called Jeff's name again. This was not something he was prepared to hear, this silence.

He raised his voice a third time. "Jeff!" he called, with more urgency. Where could he have gone so quickly? Where could he be that his ear could avoid picking up Seigle's voice? Even the sound of Seigle's own breathing now seemed to echo out, swallowed by the chamber like a drop of water down a well.

The long ragged ripple of Seigle's voice reinforced the size of the darkness, the immensity of this chamber. Not one sound returned to him. It was as though the emptiness began and ended with Seigle, a harsh commentary. Something like loneliness was springing up, black ice inside him, but it was worse; it felt like betrayal. Jeff was playing with him, playing him for a fool. He wouldn't give him the satisfaction. Seigle became the cave itself. He felt his chest walls and the chamber walls expand and contract with each of his breaths. The fibrillation within his ribcage increased. His breaths turned shallow. He shouted again for good measure and the sound just bounced around like a stray bullet.

Inching around the wall's perimeter, on the path he had traversed with Jeff, Seigle began to take deep, conscious breaths, to work through the anger he felt. He was wise to the ledge this time, the drop off into nothingness, and started in the opposite direction. Seigle meticulously pounded pitons, laying guide ropes. The work steadied his hands and calmed the racing, shallow rhythm of his heart. If he were to lose himself he knew it would be over. He would instead be the captain who lashed himself to the wheel of the ship. Wherever it sailed in this gale, he would ride it.

The LED lamp on his helmet did not reach far enough ahead. As he inched around the wall, navigating boulders and reclaiming what he thought to be the periphery, he was running out of rope. The wall doubled back, looping toward a center vortex, to form a twin bubble of a room. With his attention divided between curiosity and fear, the rope in his hand told him, without question, that he could retrace his steps and find the wormhole back to the world he had left. He kept pounding in pitons and stringing himself along. He removed his gloves. This work was by feel not by force.

He became so lost in his purpose that he nearly missed a pattern etched into the wall. His hand ran over the ridges of chiseled lines, stopping him. Turning toward the wall, Seigle then stepped back from it to study the design. There, revealed by his light, he saw a solitary figure surrounded by vertical jags of rain or falling sunlight. From the figure's head grew two horns. But beneath the horns was the unmistakable shape of a man. A closer look at the wall yielded more images, some faint, geometrical signs, recognizable quadrupeds, wolves, deer, lizards, and then more anthropomorphs, human figures linked together in a chain. Each bore the horns. Seigle stood before the wall, reading it without any notion of what it was telling him beyond the fact that others had been here. Long before. Other lives had passed here.

Every five minutes or so, Seigle glanced at his watch, one of those enormous kinetic wristwatches that was designed to withstand a nuclear explosion. With each glance he mentally noted the time. Nevertheless, he was losing track of it, or it was losing its meaning. It was as if the hands literally stopped, while he studied the wall of images, then leapt ahead, spinning wildly as he tried to peg the true time by relating present to past. It no longer gelled. He had stopped pounding pitons when he found the petroglyphs and pictographs.

As more and more images rose out of the rock—faces, floating hands of ocher and blue, mountains, lakes, rivers, maps, stories of the hunt, children falling headfirst into the world—he did not know whether he was beside himself, above, or inside for the last or first time. Forgetting anything of use, as the fabric of daily meaning frayed and the web of eternity opened, he finished his slide outside of time, beyond, further than any time or place, outside all of his frames of reference.

With only the quick beating of his heart, Seigle crouched in the darkness, all of his rope played out. With no words in his mind or consciousness to call his own, his identity—what was that in dark dampness, in cold crouching silence with nowhere left to roam, with only a decisive step away from the rope left to make?

Seigle did not know how long he crouched, waiting at the end of his rope. His world had become the room, the room he couldn't scope, the step he couldn't take. Nothing left or entered this room; he began and ended here, and all he heard was his own breath, as if he were inside a seashell rushing without relief. His circulation pushed against an underground stream. How long had he been hearing that water, the rushing water that Jeff had first mentioned? He had no idea.

His breathing labored, his damaged heart complaining, clutching the last inch of rope, Seigle said a name into the darkness once more. A name with a question mark. "Jeff?"

One more step, still clinging to the rope, using his arm as the last linkage. He wouldn't let go, but then he did, somehow the rope trickled out of his grip. He had to know what was just beyond. Moving into the dark space with his headlamp shining ahead, he saw the floor level and turn softly, dissolving into sand, a signature confirming the chamber's history. Seigle's flashlight caught brief fire in the sand, flushing out the iridescence of thousands upon thousands of abalone shells ground to glistening powder, like maize on a grinding stone. Seigle's footprints slurred the sand's surface, over what was once covered by sea.

There are moments in this life that shine briefly but define everything of importance before and afterward. This is what it means to fill to capacity and beyond, he thought, to burst into a sphere of pure consciousness beyond a man's usual boundaries. Seigle moved toward a sound so faint he could not have heard it. A beckoning sound. Blindly, he walked forward, with a crazed confidence unfolding in his chest like a bright bloom. Blackness split open before him, just before squeezing shut. He pushed through it, feeling the enfolding terror that comes only out of emptiness, out of fear of nothingness and an encounter with it that teaches you it is really, really there. Not just a theory, but a certainty.

When the terror rises to its full height and stands over Seigle, cloaking him with its shadow, he feels it grip his throat. Struggling, in hand to hand combat against the fear, he throws himself forward and flails into the fight. Pure fear, and pure hate. And his arms swim wildly while his opponent tries to tear out his throat. This is when the message of contact reaches his mind—contact with flesh. Seigle is opening wounds and drawing blood. His eyes have been closed, clenched tight, and he opens them, seeing only vaguely at first, as if through a film. Seigle squints against the darkness, against the truth.

"Jeff?"

"Yes."

"Jeff, for Christ's sake."

"Randy, you ass, I should have killed you like I dropped that deer right under your friggin' nose." Jeff clings to Seigle, even as Seigle punches him again, sliding his fist across the blood mask of his friend's face. The two men hold each other tightly in the center ring of darkness. Head to head, they tumble to the silt and the cave wall pulses with light from their thrashing.

"Why did you shoot that deer?" Seigle demands. He wants to kill Jeff for taking that life.

"Because you're so full of shit," Jeff says.

"Why didn't you answer me when I called?"

"I lost myself," Jeff whispers. "I lost it, man. I heard you out there, and I couldn't answer."

"You were jerking my chain," Seigle says. "You're too mean to die." Seigle pulls Jeff toward his chest, and the emptiness fills with the sound of Jeff's crying. And all at once Seigle softens. For different kinds of men this might have been a tender moment. "It's just the darkness," Seigle says into Jeff's ear. "It's only empty space. Where's your cap lamp, buddy?"

"I don't know. Lost, I guess."

It had happened to the best cavers, Seigle knew. The immensity spreads out and out, filled only by human frailty, insignificance, brief blundering years, reduced to minutes, to breaths in and out. Agoraphobia underground is the fear not of being seen but of vanishing. Though these might seem contradictory, they are the same.

"It can happen to anyone," Seigle says.

Jeff is still crying.

"Try to get a grip," Seigle says.

But another voice answers too suddenly and bears down on them. A fist of water pounds out of nowhere, sprays Seigle's helmet loose, pulls the horn of light from him in one blast, engulfs and swallows both men, sending them tumbling in its swift, pulsing chute. Seigle tries to hold on to Jeff, as his body stretches out and out, into pure strings of energy. He sees the bright cord issuing from his solar plexus and ending in a tangled knot. Careening through dark, cold water in a frenetic dance that pulls the partners apart, Seigle feels this last connection snap, and a last kernel of pain pop inside the veins webbing his heart.

Neither hate nor fear nor purpose—neither past nor present nor future. Nothing can save him and nothing is necessary. Seigle's will vanishes into the rushing water, as he shoots into God's eye, letting go of everything that has already let go of him. All he can know is this iris, this sharded flower, this disappearing. Apart from any one or any love, and way past time, Seigle vanishes into the dark truth of water.

Turtle Dreams

"Mom!"

The alarm in Ian's voice pierced the distance and pulled Moira to him though the dark, sleeping house.

"I'll go," Paul said.

But she touched him and rolled out of bed. "I'm already up. I'll go."

Moira eased into bed beside Ian, letting him fold into her arms and nestle. She felt his weight against her full belly and knew she would grow even larger in the next weeks. "You're safe," she told him. "It's just a bad dream."

"No, this was real," Ian said.

"It's okay." Moira hugged him. She felt Ian relaxing, falling back asleep in her arms. Before he left her there holding him he said, "I saw them diving off a high rock. They had lights on their heads, the way they did when Broder took me to see them."

Moira felt herself stiffen; it was if her heart stopped while she remembered what she already knew, from a long time ago. She was dropping back into herself from a height, like a gold ball entering the top of her head and settling through her chest in a straight line until it dropped through her and out, finding the red, molten center of the earth, finding her center and balancing her there. She heard a high, fierce cry like a gull's bleat or a karate master's shriek. Then she remembered something more: the series of dreams she had dreamed about the man and the door, all of those dreams she had forgotten upon waking. Until now. Now she knew they were real dreams. *They were real.*

When she closed her eyes she saw the man she had seen before the door turn toward her. "When you say coincidence, we say turtle dreams," he said. "The way things work together. Turtle dreams are glimpses of the whole design."

"You believe in a plan?" Moira asked.

"You would say that we do."

"Who are you?" Moira asked. Moira could hear everything around her—Ian's steady breathing, the clock ticking forward, and yet she was unable to break free. She wanted to be dreaming again, to cry out, as Ian had. She wanted to turn back all of this knowledge. Instead, she surrendered.

"Space is the house of consciousness. I am here to help you. Unless you had admitted me I couldn't be here. Life doesn't stop with these borders. In what you see as emptiness, energy is dancing."

Moira fell silent in the face of too many questions.

"Before freed particles can change form or decay they are stored by photodissociation, split into their color dimensions. This dissociation is reversible by application of infrared radiation, requiring far less energy than chemical reactions require on earth. And the fuel is 100 percent efficient. No waste products. The top quark functions like a free electron in a photovoltaic conversion. The fifth is free to carry electricity."

"Why are you telling me this? I didn't even take high school chemistry, let alone physics."

"Because you are a doorway, a receiver. You will lead Paul into this knowledge, and he will know what to do with it."

"You got that wrong—Paul's not going to have anything to do with this."

"This is Paul's purpose and soon he will remember everything that he knows."

The sun was streaming in through the window. Moira looked at the clock hands and saw that they had stopped in the night, near four o'clock. Ian stirred against her, and she felt as if she, too, were just waking up. But this time she remembered everything.

"Mom, what are you doing here?"

"You had a bad dream."

"I don't remember."

"Well, you called me." Moira combed her fingers through his hair.

Carlos skidded across the room on the scatter rug, lumping it up in the process.

"No!" Moira said, and rolled to her feet.

The dog bounded toward the bed and placed his paws on the edge, ready to ease the rest of his body onto the bed if he received the slightest invitation.

"Good morning, boy." Ian rubbed his head and Moira watched as Carlos inched first one front foot and then the other onto the bed.

Just as the dog leapt, Moira said, "Don't!" Carlos landed on the blanket beside Ian.

"Tell him to get down."

The phone was ringing and Moira headed out to answer. There was no transition. Life kept unfolding without a seam.

Moira placed the receiver to her ear and said hello.

"Hey, it's Jessy."

"Jessy, how are you?"

There was a silence at the other end of the line that turned into a series of sounds that could only mean tears.

"What's going on?" Moira asked, gently.

"He's gone," Jessy said. She took a deep breath and continued. "He seems to have found that cavern. He went down."

"Alone?"

"With his partner, Jeff Stacey."

"The entrance they found, where they went in, it's caved in on itself. A sink hole that's collapsing. It's filling with underground water. Every day it gets bigger." Jessy stopped and drew a breath.

"I'm sorry," Moira said.

"Have you ever been really wrong about someone?" Jessy asked.

"Whatever happened, it's not your fault."

"I think I could have been in love with him." There was a long pause and an audible intake of breath. "I hung up on him." Jessy cried in earnest then.

Moira cradled the receiver against her ear as if she could lend physical comfort. "Why don't you come out here?"

"I've got to be here when they find him."

It had been Randy Seigle Moira had seen when she collapsed in Mitchell Cavern. He was the man washed out onto the rocks. Neither he nor Jeff Stacey would be found alive.

"After they do—you come out here," was all Moira could say.

Climbing the Mountain

MOIRA FELT a burst of energy as she cleaned house that morning. Paul walked through the rooms wearing a walkman, vacuuming in his shorts. The weeks off had been good for him. He was tan and fit with only a tracery of scars on his face. The glass shards had been working their way out.

Andrew Polaski had been indicted on intellectual property theft, in connection with his former Goldstone position. Martin had been charged with conspiracy. Their motion for preliminary injunction against the Department of Energy had been denied on grounds of sovereign immunity. The government's prerogative. Martin's company was headed into bankruptcy and the government's case was going forward. Paul had been granted immunity in exchange for his testimony against Martin.

Moira dusted and straightened, doing the light work. She opened the closets and lined up the jackets. On the floor she spied something and carefully bent to pick it up. She wound Seigle's red scarf about her hands, then set it aside for Jessy.

"I'm going for a walk," she mouthed to Paul as he went by.

The air felt nourishing, almost like food. All of the colors of the day shone more brightly and strongly. She didn't stop walking until she reached the "No Trespassing" sign hung on the fence that ran the periphery of Owl Mountain. Trisha had found out that the site was covered under

NAGPRA, the Native American Graves Protection and Repatriation Act. The mountain was a sacred burial ground.

Moira's swollen body housed more water than muscle, but she willed herself over the fence. She scraped her upper arm over the barbed wire and was left with a stinging, dotted line of blood. But it was only a scratch, not deep.

From dream or memory, she recognized the path and started walking along it, up Owl Mountain, past dark boulders etched with petroglyphs. She walked and walked, steadily ascending, until she stood, sweating and aching with a little cramping in the gut, at the pinnacle of Owl Mountain. A cracked shape of stone—the owl's eyes that looked more like those of a fierce, dark angel—towered over her. The shape of rock was what she had known it would be and embodied everything she feared. On its face it resembled the boulders she had already passed, but instead of one or two petroglyphs it bore a prolific burden of signs, ranging from abstracts to animals, stick figures, and perspective renderings of men on horseback. The horses only came in with the Spanish, so these panels were much more recent. Moira's cramps were light, lighter than she remembered her menstrual cramps ever having been. The sun was hot on her head and she was thirsty. She had run out on impulse, without bringing a water bottle.

As Moira lost herself in the etched images, a birthing scene materialized from what had seemed to be only chaotic lines. The round shape falling feet first out of the woman was as large as her torso. Moira remembered that ecstasy—the joy of releasing the burden. She touched the image, a segment of recorded time. It wasn't much to go on and yet it was everything. It meant continuity.

Through the middle of the rock a vertical crack was weathering its way through, opening the rock to the heart. By wind and scant rain, by shafts of sunlight, the opening had broken through a petroglyph of a turtle shell and was slowly working its way down to the earth itself. Moira pushed her hand into the cool gap and felt it narrow, shutting down to a tight iris of rock that would admit her no further. She tried to look within the rock where she had pushed her hand, but of course her hand filled the space, blocking her view.

The rock spoke with a clear voice. From below and above issued the many-layered stories in a cacophony of tones. The stories loosed themselves suddenly and tumbled through Moira. It was as if she caught and held each human soul's journey, irrespective of time and place, and for an instant released it from the earth. All of these stories were speaking at once, falling like an avalanche from the summit of Owl Mountain. Moira could close her eyes and look out over the earth to see all of its sacred places spilling forth light. From a long panel Moira saw the figures floating free of the rock. These were the shamans, the go-between race. From their heads sprouted horns of light connecting above and below—these were the givers of visions. The cornucopia of insight. On the surface of the earth were places where water surged, transforming darkness into light. These were dangerous vortexes. She saw the sinkhole that had opened around the mouth Seigle had entered. She saw a river rising out of vast caverns below the surface to fill everything between that cavern and what had been known as The Murder Hole.

In the rushing current was the body of a broken man. And near the mouth of a resurgence that had once been a mere trickle through a crack in a rock—was the body of another man. She knew that Seigle had drowned before the waters had a chance to spit him out. But his essence was spilling light. She was looking across the whole human tribe and all she could see were versions of this light scattered in all directions, each star necessary. She saw her mother and her father, one dead and one living. Her father was on the side of the living, still on this side.

She felt a cramping sensation and warm water spreading over her legs. The clear fluid ran down the slopes of Owl Mountain. How would she drag herself back home? Her nose and teeth were numb, as if she had drunk too much wine. She tried to recall her labor with Ian; she hoped she had time. She started down the slope, watching each step. Each time the cramp came she was stopped by it and fell into a squat, living only inside that sensation, until it passed. Then she would drop back into this world, struggling onto her feet and keep walking. She knew that the contractions were really the opposite, the cervix's expansion. After another sharp spell sent her squatting through the pain, she rolled onto her side to rest. When she felt the next cramp, like a belt tightening across her lower back, her heart began to flutter, beating fast. She breathed deeply and told herself to open into the pain. With Ian's birth this stage of the journey had gone on for hours, even before the water broke.

As she rested she focused on a line of four human figures, like linked paper dolls carved into the rock. A breeze moved like velvet over her skin. She checked her watch and saw nothing there of meaning. She unlinked the watch from her wrist and threw it on the ground, thinking, *This is my time. Now.*

MOIRA RISES TO HER FEET and walks until the next contraction stops her. The pain winds around her body, and without thinking she pushes through the contraction. With the next wave she strips herself naked. Now nothing but sunlight covers her. She pants through the squeeze and sees her baby's head between her legs. She reaches to stroke the black hair matted on the crown. The baby slowly turns, and one after the other her shoulders slip free. Her waxy, wrinkled body swims out into her mother's hands, still dangling by a pulsing cord.

    Moira rolls onto her back and pulls her new daughter onto her stomach, up to her heart. Together they rest, still bound, both crying with joy.

The End of the Turtles Foretold

It was said that when the last Turtle swam into the rock the sun would stop turning darkness into light on the earth. But the Turtle tribe is gone, no one knows where, yet the days still brighten and sleep. It seems that the prophesies of old were wrong, or maybe the Turtles are still waiting to be born. No one can measure how much time commands the truth. If truth commands the time, then the Turtles are still living and always were. Some say they only live in legend.

It is said that when the last Turtle swims into the rock the sun will darken and burst. It is said that when the last Turtle swims into the rock the earth will be as an ice crystal where nothing can thrive.

It is said that when the last Turtle awakens from the burrow and spring sings to her to arise it will be as in the Turtle tales of old: the tribe lived beneath the earth in underground seas that mirror the seas on the surface. But the salty water down below was darkness itself, and the Turtles swam on feeling alone.

It is said that when the last Turtle grips the earth with its claws, it will be as it was for the tribe after the water receded, when the earth cracked once, draining the underworld seas. The slick, blind Turtles awoke in a dusty cave. They had always breathed through gills, like fish, but in the cave they found their lungs for air, their gravity, and they learned to breathe and plod. Water had washed their colorless shells to a shine, but then dust pooled in the heavy green and brown and orange cracks.

When the last Turtle remembers the second cracking of the earth, when Transcendent One stumbled up as if from death in the Far Chamber to lead others to light on the surface of the earth, the time will be near for all to forget.

Forget the upper world where steep hewn footholds formed ladders scaling rock faces to a civilization of caves in which each family dwelt.

Forget the discovery of other tribes, and the trading of precious gifts, the clattering of exchange in shells.

Forget the envy of other tribes that erupted like boils and scattered the Turtles into smaller and smaller camps.

Forget the Turtles who swam through the sky.

Forget the Turtles who danced through the waves.

Forget the Turtles who spoke truth from their hearts.

Forget the Turtles whose oil burned steady and bright.

Forget the Turtles who witnessed wars but never took a life.

When the last Turtle swims into the rock, the water inside the crusty creature will breathe out like a last, drowning breath, leaving only dust to meet dust. On the surface of the rock the Turtles will be encircled and dancing, like ghosts that rise into form only to float into the sun's eye. The figures etched on the rock face will blend together with the surface of the rock itself, and no one knows how long the pigment of the pictographs will last, how long before the chiseled petroglyphs crumble. No one can trace their lineage, just as no one can trace the passage of the last Turtle, pinpoint it in time.

When the last Turtle swims into the rock it will be as it was in the beginning, when everything was written. Now it's time to begin the last story. Close the book.